TH

Roisin Meaney was born in Listowel, Co. Kerry, and now lives in Limerick, where she teaches at a primary school. She has also taught in Dublin and Zimbabwe. She has had a varied career, working as a freelance copywriter, a secretary for a Japanese trading company and a painter of cartoons in children's bedrooms. She is currently working on her second novel, in between doing cryptic crosswords and watching *Coronation Street*.

ROISIN MEANEY

THE DAISY PICKER

TiVOLi

Tivoli
an imprint of Gill & Macmillan Ltd
Hume Avenue
Park West
Dublin 12
with associated companies throughout the world

www.gillmacmillan.ie

0 7171 3673 6

Print origination by
Carrigboy Typesetting Services, Co. Cork
Printed and bound by Nørhaven Paperback A/S, Denmark

*The paper used in this book is made from the wood pulp of
managed forests. For every tree felled, at least one is planted,
thereby renewing natural resources.*

A catalogue record is available for this book
from the British Library.

1 3 5 4 2

Dedication

Thanks a Bunch

To Mam and Dad, for being a rock of support,
in this as in everything.

To Ciars, for generously sharing his San Francisco
home with me and my laptop.

To Treas, Tomás, Colm and Aonghus, just for being there.

To David Rice, for giving me the gentle nudge I
needed to set off on this thrilling journey.

To Alison, Deirdre and Tana, for licking me into shape.

To Cliona, Chris and all at Tivoli, for guiding me
safely through the process.

To Faith, my far from secret agent, for looking after me.

To Charlie Varon, a valuable mentor and a very nice man.

To John Regan, for kindly sharing his knowledge
of woodcarving with me.

To Orla, Mags and all my great friends, for being
nearly as delighted as I am.

To Judi, a fellow writer-in-progress and a valuable
sounding-board.

To Liz, for whipping out the camera and doing the needful.

To Annaghmakerrig, for allowing me to live like a
writer for a summery month.

To Lizzie O'Grady, for coming when I called her.

Chapter One

'That you, Lizzie?' Mammy, from the kitchen.

No, Mother, it's the Queen of England. I got a key cut for her at lunchtime. Tell Daddy to put on a clean shirt.

Wisely, Lizzie O'Grady does not say this out loud. Peace at all costs, as Pope John XXIII always said. At least, Mammy says he always said it. Listening to her talking about him, you'd swear they met every Friday for tea and scones at the Vatican café. 'Peace at all costs, Mrs O'Grady,' he'd say, passing Mammy the pot of raspberry jam. 'Amen, Your Holiness,' Mammy would answer, lowering her eyes in reverence and nearly getting a dollop of jam on the crisp linen tablecloth; that would take some penance.

'Did you get the white pudding?' Mammy again.

God almighty, I haven't my key out of the door and the woman is looking for her white pudding. Lizzie

1

feels like telling her they were out of it at Tesco, but there was a special offer on hamsters, so meet Bill and Bob. She grins at the thought of Mammy's jaw dropping in horror.

Then she thinks of the Pope and pulls her key out of the door and turns her head towards the kitchen. 'Yes, Mam, got it.' *Because the world would definitely screech to a halt if the O'Gradys had to do without their white pudding on a Thursday night.*

She hangs her jacket and scarf on the hallstand, beside Daddy's second-best grey check and on top of Mammy's powder-blue padded. Then she drops her Tesco bag-for-life and has a closer look at the face in the hallstand mirror. Straight brown hair to her shoulders, with a fringe that wanders down to her eyebrows; unremarkable grey eyes. Long, dark lashes, though – easily the best thing about the face. For the laugh she tried fluttering them at Tony once, when they first started going out, but he just looked alarmed and asked her if she needed Optrex.

Clear skin, thank goodness – she's never really been spotty – with a sprinkling of freckles across her nose, as if some careless painter had shaken his coffee-coloured brush too near her. In an idle moment last summer she took an eye pencil and joined them up. Italy, if France had stuck out a toe and knocked it sideways a bit.

She used to be full of freckles, practically covering her nose and tumbling across her cheeks. *Thank God they're nearly gone – but gone where? Off in search of adventure, I suppose. Off to find a more exciting face.* She bares her teeth. Not exactly Hollywood-white, but straight enough; and most of her fillings are tucked away in the back. Lips could be poutier, skin could be dewier; and who told those crow's-feet they could park themselves there? Just because she's forty-one, they needn't think they have the right.

She supposes her face is normal enough – nothing that would make children run screaming from her in the streets, but nothing that would make anyone do a double-take either. In fact, no one except Tony has looked twice at Lizzie for quite some time now; and he's so used to looking at her that he probably doesn't really see her any more, not properly.

Forty-one and still living at home with Mammy and Daddy. Big fat baby. Well, not literally fat – although the tummy could be flatter, and the thighs could not in all honesty be described as firm; when she clenches her bottom the backs of them crinkle up horribly. She supposes it's cellulite, and has decided to ignore it in the hope that it'll go the way of the freckles.

She hasn't worn a bikini in over ten years, and she gave up sleeveless tops after the night she caught sight of a flabby arm in a mirror behind a bar and looked around to see who was wearing the same top as her. She goes from a loose 14 to a tight 10, depending on her willpower and the season. Her appetite is depressingly healthy, and she walks only when the weather's

3

not too terrible. She's tried gyms over the years, and callanetics, and once she signed up for kick-boxing classes, but nothing's grabbed her for long enough to make a difference.

One of these days she'll tone up, definitely. Any day now.

She feels something bump against her leg and bends down. 'Hello, fatty.' She strokes the soft ginger coat, and Jones purrs and butts his head against her hand. She hefts him into her arms and shows him the cat in the mirror.

'Look at the state of you – you're obese. I'm like Twiggy next to you. Aren't you mortified?'

Jones nuzzles against her neck, not in the least mortified. Lizzie went to Limerick for a day's shopping about six years ago and came back with a tiny Bustopher Jones mewing in a cardboard box on the back seat of the car. She'd walked past a pet shop and there he'd been, standing up against the window, mouthing out at her. Lizzie had taken one look at the little pink pads against the glass and fallen in love forever.

When she arrived home with him, Mammy ranted about fleas and ticks and dead birds and said Lizzie needn't think *she* was going to look after him, God knew she had enough to do, and she presumed Lizzie would be taking him with her when she got married – but he won her over in a week with his kittenish charm. Lizzie came downstairs one morning to find her standing over him as he lapped up a saucer of sardine juice with his tiny pink tongue, managing a surprisingly loud purr at the same time. Mammy looked at Lizzie, arms folded across her dressing-gowned chest, and dared her to comment. Lizzie had enough sense not to.

After a fortnight they stopped calling him Bustopher Jones and switched to Jones – he didn't seem to mind. He was greedy and lazy and alarmingly stubborn, and Lizzie adored him. His appetite was huge; on top of the three meals they fed him, Jones begged what he could from the neighbours, who were well used to his mournful mewing at their patio doors.

'Lizzie? Are you there?' Mammy is still waiting for her white pudding.

'Coming.' Lizzie puts down her giant cat and heads off to help Mammy with the Thursday-night dinner: rashers and sausages and soft fried eggs and white pudding, and Mammy's bran-laden brown bread, to keep everyone regular.

As she opens the kitchen door, the savoury smell of frying meat hits her nostrils, and her stomach rumbles in anticipation.

Mammy looks up from the spattering pan. 'There you are. Any sign of Tony?'

Lizzie shakes her head, glancing at the clock on the wall. 'It's only twenty to.'

In all the Thursday nights he's been coming to dinner at the O'Gradys', Tony has never arrived before ten to six, or after five to. You could set your watch by him – him and his Iced Caramels.

She puts her bag on the table, takes out the white pudding, peels away the plastic and begins to slice it thickly, the way Daddy likes it.

'Any news in town?' Mammy turns the rashers on the grill.

Not really – unless you count the earthquake, just before the volcano. And of course the flood didn't help.

Passing her the sliced pudding, Lizzie racks her brain. 'The traffic was heavy at the roundabout; it took ages to cross.' Well, it was better than nothing. 'And there was a big queue at the cash machine by the library; I was sorry I hadn't used the one on the square – I was frozen standing there. I suppose I shouldn't be surprised, two weeks before Christmas.' She goes to the bread bin and takes out a quarter of Mammy's bread. Tony will eat two slices exactly.

Mammy pokes at the sausages to make room for the pudding, and just as she fits them all onto the pan the bell rings. She puts down the fork and starts patting her hair. 'That'll be Tony now. Will you let him in, Lizzie?'

No, I'll shove a rope ladder out the landing window. Lizzie opens the front door and Tony steps inside, rubbing his woolly hands together. He still isn't wearing the sheepskin gloves she got him for his birthday in October; probably saving them for the heavy-duty cold in January.

'Hello, love. Isn't it perishing?' He brushes her cheek with frozen lips. 'Nice and warm in here.'

In the kitchen, Lizzie watches as he goes to Mammy, who's just pulled off her apron – 'There she is' – and pecks her cheek before presenting her with the bag of Iced Caramels from his pocket. Mammy always takes them with the same mixture of surprise and delight, as if he's never brought them before. As if he's the only one who ever brings her anything. As if she likes Iced Caramels.

When he first started coming to dinner, Tony asked Lizzie what sweets her mother liked. She told him, 'The pink and white ones'; and when he arrived the next night with his bag of iced caramels, she hadn't the heart to tell him it was marshmallows she meant. Every Thursday Mammy takes the bag from him, and every Friday she passes them on to old Mrs Sweeny a few doors down, who loves them.

'Lizzie, take Tony's coat, and call Daddy.' Mammy is pouring a generous dollop of whiskey into a glass. 'Desperate out, isn't it, Tony?' Lizzie hears Tony agreeing about the desperate state of the weather as she hangs his coat and scarf in the hall. She wonders what would happen if he ever disagreed with Mammy, about anything. Or had three slices of bread instead of two. Or turned up for dinner on a Wednesday night, just for a change.

She gives herself a shake and puts her head round the sitting-room door. Daddy is reading the paper, as she knew he would be. 'Dinner's ready, Daddy.'

He puts down the paper and smiles over at her. 'Right, love.'

Lizzie's stomach rumbles again as she walks back into the kitchen; you'd swear she hadn't eaten for a week, instead of just over four hours ago. Right now she could eat a horse if someone served it up on a big dinner plate with carrots, peas and a baked spud dripping with butter. Maybe a dollop of Ballymaloe relish on the side.

She's never been in hospital except as a visitor, and never stayed in bed for longer than two days. She's never broken a bone, never even cracked anything. Every three months she donates a pint of brimming-with-goodness blood to her local clinic, and she never feels faint afterwards. (Of course she always has the bottle of Guinness they provide, just to be on the safe side.) She hasn't seen the family doctor in so long, she'd probably walk past him in the street. She's the healthiest person she knows, and she knows quite a lot of people after forty-one years of living in the same biggish Irish town.

Healthy, engaged, steady job, everything mapped out for her. There is no earthly reason for her to feel unhappy and frustrated and desperately lonely; to be convinced, as she takes her seat at the table and smiles across at Tony, that if something doesn't change very soon she'll curl up and die. That she's been slowly dying for a very long time.

How has she come to this? When she was growing up she had lots of friends, and even a few boyfriends. She had her share of Valentine cards and oh-my-God-there-he-is crushes, and bags of vinegary chips after the pictures and goodnight kisses a few doors down in case Mammy was looking out.

But one by one the friends drifted, most into marriage, one into a convent, one to Australia, two to London. The boyfriends drifted too – they never seemed to last longer than a few weeks; and except for one, whom she secretly mourned for a while, Lizzie waved them all off happily. They left no space in her life; her heart was still annoyingly intact.

She longed for a bit of real, honest-to-God heart-break; something that would have her polishing off a whole pound of Milk Tray and bawling her way through a box of tissues, the ones with aloe vera so her nose wouldn't go too red and raw. Or maybe she'd go off her food and take to the drink; yes, that might be more tragic. Sometimes she imagined a mild breakdown – nothing too scary, just a few weeks in bed with a pack of Prozac and Mammy running upstairs with trays of steamed fish and Complan. But it never happened. No one was ever interested enough in her to break her heart.

And then she went to work at Julia O'Gorman's restaurant, and five years after she started, Tony O'Gorman came home from Scotland to work in the family business and they started going out. And six years later they got engaged.

And they've been engaged for eleven years. As the Americans say, do the math.

They made plans. Of course they made plans. Like any engaged couple, they settled on a date and booked the church and the hotel and pored over travel brochures for the honeymoon. And then, two weeks before the wedding, as Lizzie was struggling into the dress for the final alterations, Tony's father dropped dead in the kitchen one morning, so of course they cancelled.

They rescheduled for a year later. This time, a burst pipe flooded the restaurant, forcing it to close down for a couple of months while the refurbishments were done. They couldn't leave Julia on her own at a time like that – of course not.

The third time, six years into the engagement, they got as far as three days before the wedding. The bridesmaid was dressed, the holiday in Wales was booked, the flowers were ordered, the presents were piling up in the sitting room, Lizzie's weight loss was coming along nicely. Then, in the middle of *The Late Late Show*, the phone rang. When Daddy answered, a distraught Julia O'Gorman told him that Tony had been rushed to hospital with appendicitis. Lizzie wanted to go ahead and get married in the hospital, but Mammy wouldn't hear of it. After all those lovely presents, she'd never be able to hold her head up in Kilmorris again if they didn't give everyone a good day out.

The time after that, it was Daddy's hernia. And then came the Big Row: Lizzie in tears, insisting they set a new date, and Tony refusing to plan anything under duress – couldn't Lizzie see this was the busiest time in the restaurant, his mother wasn't up to it, hadn't they all the time in the world? They made up, of course they did; but for a long time after that neither of them mentioned the W-word. They went out every Sunday night as usual (the only night the restaurant was closed, and both of them were off), and Tony came to dinner every Thursday evening, just before Lizzie went on duty at half seven; but the subject didn't come up between them again for at least a year after the Row.

And then, every now and again one or other of them would say, 'We should really set a date,' and the other would agree that they really should, and somehow it never got beyond that. One day they'll probably just elope, and Mammy will have to lump it, and that'll be that.

And Lizzie is dying. Healthy, employed, engaged Lizzie O'Grady is dying of boredom and frustration and impatience, and with the effort of trying to hide it all and pretend that everything is fine, just great, and that she'll be married any day now to the love of her life.

'Pass the bread to Tony, Lizzie.' Mammy points towards the plate of sliced bread that's positioned exactly halfway between Tony and Lizzie. She thinks of the Pope and picks it up and holds it out to Tony.

He pats his stomach like he always does. 'I shouldn't, but I will; can't resist your bread, Maura.' He smiles over at Mammy, and Mammy smiles back at him like it's the first time she's heard it. Sometimes Lizzie

11

wonders if Mammy loves Tony more than she does; he's the son-in-law she prayed to St Jude for, years ago, when all of Lizzie's friends were settling down.

But Lizzie loves him too – of course she does. She'd hardly have stayed engaged to him for eleven years if she didn't, for goodness' sake. Isn't he decent and reliable, and doesn't he always remember her birthday, and aren't vouchers much better than something she mightn't like and might have to bring back on the sly or wear to please him? And isn't he good to his mother, insisting that she always comes first? That's what sons are supposed to do, aren't they? That's what she'd want *her* son to do.

Not that she's likely to have any now.

But she can't blame Tony for that; it's hardly his fault that they've left it too late for children – she had a say in it too, didn't she? So why on earth does she feel trapped and suffocated and locked away in a tower with no door, sitting at her little high-up window looking out at the world? Rapunzel with shoulder-length brown hair; fat lot of good that'd be when the prince arrived. She'd have to jump out the window to him – probably break her leg, or land on him and squash him to death.

'What are you smiling at?' Tony pops a bit of sausage into his mouth.

Lizzie lifts her cup and shakes her head. 'Just something I saw on telly last night. How was work today?' And he begins to talk about the restaurant, and she

12

looks across at him and sees his honest face and reminds herself that this man has chosen her, out of all the single females in Kilmorris, to share the rest of his life with. Her Tony.

After dinner Mammy says, 'Lizzie, get the cake,' and she takes her lemon poppyseed cake from its tin and cuts a slice for everyone. Tony beams as she puts his slice in front of him. 'Another delicious cake, Lizzie; I'm a lucky man.'

Mammy beams back at him as if she'd baked it. 'She's great at the cakes, all right; I don't know when I had to bake one last.'

And Tony, right on cue, says immediately, 'I'm sure it would be just as good, Maura; she didn't steal it.'

Lizzie eats her slice and watches them saying exactly the right things to each other. Funny, how things work out. She left school after Leaving Cert and got a waitressing job in O'Gorman's – just for the summer, to make a bit of cash for the year she was going to spend travelling with her friend Síle. Then she was going to come home and start working as a baker.

Baking is her passion. It's all she ever wanted to do. From the time she realised that you could put together a lot of things that couldn't be eaten on their own, and add a bit of heat, and produce something delicious, she was totally hooked, happiest up to her elbows in flour and surrounded by spices and bowls of beaten eggs, and little bags of sesame seeds and caraway seeds, and books with oven-temperature charts inside their front covers. She made her first Christmas cake at eleven, nearly delirious from the smell of fruit soaking in dark rum, and from then on Mammy never baked another one. Now Lizzie makes eight cakes every October, for various relatives and neighbours.

She has a stack of books beside her bed, and every one of them is totally dedicated to the art of baking. Each night she devours them, poring over the ingredients of cottage cheese dill bread, learning the difference between *biscottentorte* and tiramisu, licking her lips over summer berry strudel. She bakes as often as she can, whenever she and the kitchen are free at the same time. As well as keeping Mammy and Daddy well stocked up, Lizzie bakes for everyone else, too. When she goes to visit friends, she brings a cake; if the friends are married with children, they get a bag of cookies or buns. When Mrs Geraghty up the road had a stroke Lizzie visited her with a plate of light lemon squares. When Louise and Derry got engaged, they asked her to make a cake in the shape of a plane for the party; they'd met on board an Aer Lingus flight to Rome. To date she's made cakes for six weddings, eleven christenings and countless birthdays.

When she started, she experimented all the time. She wanted to conquer the mysteries of baking – find the perfect temperature to rise yeast at, get the balance just right between sweet and tart in a strawberry rhubarb pie, stop those blasted cherries from sinking to the bottom of her fresh cherry cake. She had her share of disasters – every so often Jones would sniff at his bowl and wonder what on earth he was being dished up, or Daddy would be emptying the kitchen bin and discover a plastic bag that felt mushy and warm. But she learnt as she went along.

And the plan always was that one day she'd stand in her very own bakery, and people would make a special detour for a loaf of her four-cheese-and-onion bread, or a box of her triple chocolate chunk cookies, or a warmed slice of her Spanish tortilla tart. She'd have a little counter at one side where people could sit and eat, and she'd take orders for birthday cakes in the shape of racing cars, and wedding cakes with each tier a different recipe. And children would stand on the path and breathe in the aromas that wafted out, and beg their mothers for a bun. Oh, she had it all planned.

Except that, before she found a way to tell Mammy and Daddy that herself and Síle were heading off after the summer, Síle decided to go to college instead of Europe, and Lizzie couldn't face the prospect of going alone. She thought she might as well stay on at O'Gorman's while she decided what her next step should be; better to be earning a few quid than sitting at home doing nothing.

It simply didn't occur to her to go ahead with the baking plan; she still yearned to see a bit of the world – she'd never been further than Dublin – and she knew that, once she started baking for a living, that'd be the end of her travel plans. So she whiled away the hours in O'Gorman's imagining herself on a beach in Greece or picking grapes in France or climbing a mountain somewhere in Africa. She was desperate for a bit of excitement, but she couldn't bring herself to make the break on her own.

On her way home from work after telling Julia O'Gorman that she could stay on for a while, Lizzie opened a savings account. She promised herself it was just till next spring; then she'd definitely take off – on her own if she had to.

But somehow it never happened. In the spring Julia made her head waitress, Monday to Friday, eight to four – this was before they started doing evening meals – with a series of teenagers to train in and keep an eye on, and a stream of regular customers who felt safe in the unchanging world of O'Gorman's, where you had your dinner in the middle of the day and you went home to your tea. And Lizzie stayed on, because the longer she put off her round-the-world adventure, the further away from her it seemed to go.

She didn't find anyone else to go travelling with – her friends were well settled into relationships, or had already moved away, or were in the middle of their studies – and when it came down to it, she just couldn't face the notion of heading off alone. The furthest she got with her plan to become a baker was going around the three bakeries in Kilmorris and asking if they needed any help. None of them did, and she hadn't a clue where to go from there.

And so it went. Occasional visits to the cinema, on her own or with whichever of her increasingly rare boyfriends happened to be on the scene; the odd coffee with one or other of her old pals who squeezed her in between ballet runs and music lessons; and evenings at home with Mammy and Daddy and crosswords and telly and Scrabble and how was your day and have some more cabbage, it's not worth keeping this bit and I hate to throw it out and my knee was at me again last night and will you get some white pudding for the dinner.

And now here she is, engaged for the past eleven years to the son of her mother's best friend, and still dreaming about becoming a baker. As she changes into her black skirt and white blouse after dinner, Lizzie suddenly thinks: *Maybe it isn't too late.* What has she got to lose by giving it another go – finding out more about what steps she should be taking? Really, she gave up far too easily last time. She's never even talked about it with Tony; by the time he arrived on the scene, her dream was well tucked away. But she's so much more experienced now . . . Zipping up her skirt, she feels a flutter of hope. *Maybe it isn't too late.*

As Tony walks her back to the restaurant, she decides to test the waters.

'Darling, you know how much I like to bake.'

He looks indulgently at her, squeezes her shoulder. 'I do, pet – and you're great at it. Those cakes you make are really delicious.'

Lizzie smiles; so far, so good. 'I've been thinking of going into it full-time – you know, making it my career. What would you think?'

He looks puzzled. 'Full-time? But how could you do that, with your job at the restaurant? You'd never manage the two, pet.'

She shakes her head, still smiling. 'No, of course I wouldn't. I'd have to give up the restaurant – get a job in a bakery for a while, till I had enough experience to open up my own little place.'

Tony stops walking, turns her to face him. She looks up at his horrified face and feels her heart sinking. 'Lizzie, love, you're not serious. Tell me this is a joke.'

Her smile disappears. 'What would be so terrible about it? It's not as if O'Gorman's would collapse without me – you could get any number of waitresses to do what I do.' As she speaks, she feels something heavy settling around her.

He's shaking his head slowly, hands on her arms. 'Lizzie, love, that's not the point. We're getting married, or have you forgotten? You'll be part of the family, part of the business. You can't just walk out on it like that.'

She starts to speak, but he's not finished. 'Look, pet, it's one thing to be able to turn out a nice cake or a loaf of bread, but it's a whole other story to make a living out of it. What do you know about setting up your own business, hmm?'

She feels a stab of anger. 'Well, obviously I'd have to –'

He interrupts her, hands still trapping her arms. 'Look, pet, this is a crazy idea. You bake wonderful cakes; no one's denying that. But you're a waitress – an excellent one – and you're marrying into a restaurant business. I think you need to get your priorities right here, Lizzie.'

Again she has to fight down a spurt of anger. 'Tony, please don't lecture me about where my priorities lie. I don't see why my having a different career should in any way be seen as disloyal –'

He cuts in again, speaking slowly, in a way that makes her want to slap his face. 'Look, love, all I'm saying is that we'll be in charge whenever my mother retires, and it would be a bit silly if you were off baking cakes when we were trying to keep the restaurant going.' He drops her arms and puts his hands in his pockets. 'Where would the money to open up your own place come from, anyway? Have you thought of that?'

It's the one thing Lizzie was hoping he wouldn't bring up. They've been putting money into a joint account for years, but that's earmarked for the two of them; it's 'ours' rather than hers. She couldn't expect him to hand it over – and it would be petty to take out her half.

'I could see about getting a loan . . .' But she knows she's on shaky ground now. Why should she expect

19

any bank manager to hand over the kind of money she'd need? It's not as if Tony would offer the restaurant as collateral.

He sees her uncertainty and puts an arm around her shoulders. 'Lizzie, love, it just wouldn't work, with two businesses to manage – you'd be dead out.' *You*, not *we*. 'I'll tell you what – I'll speak to my mother about letting you do some baking for the restaurant, instead of ordering it all in. I'm sure she'd be delighted to have some home baking to serve up.' He takes her arm again and begins to steer her gently in the direction of O'Gorman's. Subject closed.

And Lizzie imagines baking apple tarts and chocolate sponges and fruitcakes for O'Gorman's until Julia retires – and then baking exactly the same tarts and sponges and cakes after that; because why on earth would Tony want to change anything when he's in charge? His life is exactly the same now as it was when they got together. He still lives at home with Julia, and even after he and Lizzie are married, that isn't going to change: Lizzie will just move in. Julia will need minding as she gets older – they couldn't possibly desert her.

Tony still has his golf, and his Toastmasters, and his fortnight in Bundoran every September with Julia. He and Lizzie go away for a week in May – well, he wouldn't feel happy leaving Julia on her own for any longer; surely Lizzie can understand that.

And for the past twenty years Lizzie has been saying *Yes, of course*, and *Yes, I understand*, and *No, I don't mind*, and now, as she walks arm in arm with the man who's just crumpled up her dream and tossed it into the gutter, she wonders how long she can go without telling someone she's dying.

Chapter Two

It's time for Lizzie's check-up.

She goes every six months without fail; she figures her teeth need all the help they can get. As well as the fillings in the back she has two crowns in front, cleverly disguised as real teeth, and most of the time, unless she opens her mouth really wide, she gets away with them. Otherwise she has no major mouth problems. Joe, her dentist, is cheerful and talkative.

'Well, Lizzie, looks like the rain is here to stay. Open a bit wider if you can there; that's great . . . Ah yeah, bit of shadow there – nothing serious . . . Sorry, that's a bit sensitive there, is it? . . . How are your parents keeping?'

Lizzie spends so much time wondering how to give the shortest possible answers with her mouth full of his hand doing something vaguely uncomfortable that the visit is usually over before she knows it. She suspects Joe's chat is a cunning ploy to distract her, and she has to admit that it usually works. She never really minds her visits, except when she needs an injection. Her toes curl as Joe approaches with a mini road-drill and plunges it into her jaw for what seems like forever, chatting away happily as he fills her with pain.

When she arrives for her check-up, Dorothy shows her into the empty waiting room – 'Won't be long, Lizzie' – and disappears. Lizzie knows from experience that it'll be at least half an hour – Joe needs his chat. She glances around the familiar room.

Posters on the wall that she knows off by heart: one telling her to floss, another showing her how to recognise the first signs of gum disease – presumably for the benefit of those who ignored the first poster – and a third explaining how to brush properly. Out the window she can see Joe's little garden, covered with piles of brown leaves from the tree in the corner. An almost-bald Virginia creeper hangs on grimly to the end wall. A few frozen-looking shrubs huddle along one side.

She looks down at the magazines in front of her. Sixty-four-year-old Dorothy seems to be Joe's main supplier of magazines; apart from a few car and fishing ones – presumably donated by him – most of them are either religious or aimed at the housewife, and all of them are well past their sell-by date. Lizzie skims the front covers and sees 'Bread to Butter Him Up' on an ancient *Woman's Friend*. She flicks the pages and finds the bread recipes; nothing she hasn't already tried to butter up Daddy and Tony with.

Her eye is caught by the headline on the opposite page: 'If I Had My Life To Live Over'. She begins to read about an eighty-five-year-old woman from the hill country of Kentucky, who made a list of all the things she'd do differently if she were given the chance to start again:

I'd ride more merry-go-rounds,

I'd take more chances,

I'd pick more daisies,

I'd eat more ice-cream and fewer beans,

I'd climb more mountains, swim more rivers, watch more sunsets,

I'd start barefoot in the spring and stay that way later in the fall . . .

When Dorothy puts her head around the door, forty minutes later, Lizzie is sitting quite still. A magazine lies open on her lap, but she's not looking at it; she's gazing straight ahead, in the direction of the window and the garden beyond. Dorothy thinks, *But she doesn't see it*, and then wonders where that thought came from.

'Right, Lizzie, he's ready for you now.'

Lizzie turns her head and astonishes Dorothy with a dazzling smile. 'Thanks, Dorothy.' She stands up slowly and puts the magazine on the table, then walks out the door and up the stairs to Joe's surgery. Something about the way she moves reminds Dorothy of her son, who went through a bout of sleepwalking when he was five or six, giving her the shivers whenever he appeared on the landing in his pyjamas, eyes open but completely unseeing. Luckily he grew out of it after a few weeks.

Dorothy closes the door and goes back to her desk, wondering, but completely unaware – how could she know? – that Lizzie's world has just shifted on its axis. Dorothy, mother of three and grandmother of four, one with diabetes, has no idea that the words of an old American woman have somehow poked their way through the shell that has surrounded Lizzie for so long.

And, sitting in Joe's chair and trying to tell him in one syllable how Daddy's leg is doing, Lizzie wonders how he can't hear the beating of her heart. Among the jumble of feelings racing through her, one thought is sitting quietly in her head.

It's not too late. I'm only forty-one and it's not too late.

Walking home half an hour later with a mouth full of plaque-free teeth, Lizzie takes deep breaths and tries to think straight. What has happened to her? Why is she full of this energy, this force that's propelling her feet quickly towards home, as if there's something that she can't wait to do when she gets there?

There is. When she reaches the house she goes straight upstairs. Mammy calls, 'That you, Lizzie?' from the kitchen, and she calls back, 'Yeah,' and keeps on going. She hardly knows what she's doing; it's as if something stronger has taken over, as if on some level she's not in control any more. And, instead of scaring her witless, this strange new phenomenon is filling her

25

with an excitement she doesn't remember ever feeling before. It's as if she's being shaken awake, and she can't wait to jump out of bed.

When she gets to her room she takes out her writing pad with unsteady hands and writes, 'Dear Julia, I wish to inform you that I intend to –' and tears it out and starts again: 'Dear Julia, It is with sadness and –' and tears it out and starts again: 'Dear Julia, I find myself in a unique –' and tears it out and starts again.

> *Dear Julia,*
> *I'd like to hand in my notice. I will be leaving O'Gorman's in two weeks, on Friday January the third. I hope this does not inconvenience you too much.*
> *Yours sincerely,*
> *Lizzie*

She pulls the page out carefully and folds it up and puts it into an envelope. Then she goes downstairs and eats her dinner.

Steamed fish and soft cauliflower and mashed carrot and parsnip – Friday-night dinner. Lizzie can't understand how Mammy and Daddy are chatting away as if nothing has changed; can they not see that nothing is the same, that nothing will ever be the same again? For the first time she can remember, she has to force herself to eat. Her stomach is so full of butterflies, she's afraid there won't be room for the fish.

That evening, work flies by; she can't believe it when she looks at the clock and sees it's a quarter past eleven. She tries to remember one order she took and can't. She knows she's spoken to Tony – he's on duty tonight too – but she hasn't a clue what either of them said. She seems to be moving faster than usual, rushing past tables, flying into the kitchen, collecting plates of food from the chef, scribbling down orders. She wonders why no one comments.

When the last customers leave at ten past twelve – what did they eat? – she goes to where Julia is bagging the takings.

'Julia, I need to have a word.'

Julia glances up, then back down at the bundles of notes in front of her. 'What is it, dear?'

Lizzie takes a deep breath. 'Julia, I'm handing in my resignation.' Julia's head snaps back up, and Lizzie says, 'I'm leaving,' and holds out the envelope.

Julia looks at the envelope, and back up at Lizzie, and says, 'Leaving?' in a voice that really means, *Kindly explain yourself.*

Lizzie forces herself to look straight back at her. 'Julia, I know this will come as something of a shock' – Julia's mouth is a thin line, the eyes that meet Lizzie's are narrowed – 'but I have to get away; I . . . I need to sort things out. I hope you'll understand – and of course I'll work out my notice. It's all in there.' She holds the envelope out further and waits.

Julia looks down again at Lizzie's hand but makes no move to take the envelope, so Lizzie puts it down on the table between them. Then she gestures towards

27

the back of the restaurant. 'Excuse me, Julia, I have to find Tony.' She walks over to the kitchen door, well aware that Julia is watching her. Her legs feel shaky.

Tony is cleaning off the worktops in the kitchen; he doesn't trust the job to anyone else. He glances up and smiles as Lizzie walks in – 'Not gone yet, love?' – and Lizzie leans against one of the giant cookers because she's not sure her legs will hold her up.

'Tony, I have something to tell you.' Her mouth feels dry; she longs for water.

Something in her voice makes him look at her more closely. 'What is it?' He holds a yellow sponge in his hand. She keeps looking at the sponge, watching the suds drip from it onto the worktop.

'Tony, I can't marry you. Something has happened – something that has made me feel differently, about everything . . . I'm sorry, but I can't go ahead with . . . We can't get married.'

As she trails off, knowing she sounds ridiculous but not having a clue what else to say, he puts down the sponge and peels off his rubber gloves. He doesn't look too worried – he probably thinks she's bluffing, trying to make him name a date by putting pressure on him. 'Look, Lizzie, why don't we go and sit –'

She takes off her ring and places it carefully on the worktop, out of the way of the suds. The rubber gloves sit, palms together; they look like they're praying. 'Tony, I'm sorry. I'm going to be finishing up here in two weeks, and then I'm leaving Kilmorris.' God, where has that come from? She had no idea she was going to say that; but, even as she says it, she realises that of course she'll be leaving Kilmorris. How could she stay now?

Tony takes her by the arms and puts a now-let's-be-reasonable smile on his face. 'Lizzie, what are you talking about? We're getting married. We can book a church tomorrow if you –'

'I don't love you.' And there it is. The words hit the walls of the kitchen and bounce off the steel surfaces and squelch through the suds he hasn't wiped away. His face goes blank and he drops his hands.

'I'm sorry, Tony. I'm really sorry.' She pushes herself away from the cooker and walks out of the kitchen.

Julia, who must have heard, stops her – 'Lizzie, wait a minute' – and hands her a brown envelope. 'I think it's probably best if you don't come back, under the circumstances. This is what you're owed, and I'll send on your P45.'

Lizzie can't make out whether she's mad at her or not; there's no sign on Julia's face to tell her. She takes the envelope and says, 'Thank you, Julia,' and walks out the front door. On the way home she wonders what Julia will tell her regulars.

She wonders what Julia and Tony are saying about her now.

Then she wonders how on earth she's going to tell Mammy and Daddy.

Chapter Three

Mammy nearly dies.

Lizzie sits them both down the next morning and tells them she's going away for a while. They look at her blankly; then Mammy says, 'A little holiday, is it? Not before Christmas, surely? You'll wait till the New Year.'

Lizzie takes a deep breath. 'Not just a holiday, Mammy. A . . . I don't know; a change of scene, I suppose. I've never lived anywhere else only here; I'd like to see a bit of the country, settle somewhere new for a while, see how it goes.'

Mammy looks bewildered. 'But what about Tony? What about your job? You can't just head off like that; you have responsibilities.'

'Actually' – Lizzie crosses her fingers under the table – 'the engagement is off. And I've resigned from work.'
Here it comes.

Mammy's hands fly to her face. 'Oh my God, Lizzie, what are you telling us?' Lizzie doesn't know whether she's more shocked about the engagement or the job. Daddy just sits there; he's used to letting Mammy do the talking. He doesn't look too surprised, though. Lizzie wishes she knew what he was thinking.

She takes another deep breath. 'Look, this is something I have to do. I was feeling – I don't know – smothered; I wasn't happy . . .' She breaks off; how on earth can she make them understand? She tries again, reaching for Mammy's hands across the table. 'I have to go away for a while, think things out – be on my own for a bit . . .'

Mammy pulls her hands away, takes them off the table altogether. 'So this is how you repay us – by making us the laughing-stock of Kilmorris. And I can't imagine how poor Julia must be feeling – deserting her just before Christmas.'

Lizzie feels her temper rising. 'For your information, I offered to serve out my notice, work over Christmas, and poor Julia refused.' She makes her voice soften. 'Look, Mammy, this is not about you or Julia; it's about me, and my happiness. Don't I matter more than what the neighbours will say?'

It's no use. She might as well talk to the wall.

Mammy goes round to see Julia that afternoon, and comes back looking grim. 'That poor woman is broken; I hope you're happy with yourself, Madam.' And Lizzie – who can't imagine the carefully groomed

31

Julia O'Gorman even slightly cracked, let alone broken – doesn't bother trying to reason with her any more. What's the point?

On Christmas Day, after a glass of Harvey's Bristol Cream, Mammy tries a new tack. 'Why don't you take a little break, Lizzie? Go walking in the Burren for a few days – or what about somewhere nice and sunny, Lanzarote maybe? The Curtins went there last spring and loved it. You could stay in a little hotel for yourself, somewhere central – you don't want to take any chances in those places. You'd have the beach for your swim, and you could go to a few museums if they have any there. Treat yourself to a good dinner at night; Patsy Curtin said it was very cheap to eat out.'

Mammy pauses, pours another inch of sherry into their glasses. 'And I'm sure Julia would be delighted to take you back after, and forget all about this little – upset.'

And Lizzie explains gently that she isn't going to book into a B&B in Connemara, or head off to Lanzarote where the Curtins were. This is something she has to do, and it's going to last longer than two weeks, and she's leaving on Monday week, and there's nothing more to say, except that she hopes she'll go with Mammy's blessing.

Mammy stands up and goes over to the cooker to check on the turkey. She turns around after closing the oven door, and Lizzie's heart nearly cracks at the hurt look in Mammy's eyes, and she almost changes her mind. But then she thinks of the old American woman, and twenty years of pretending, and she closes her mouth and says nothing. And Mammy lifts the lid on the saucepan of Brussels sprouts – almost pulpy enough for consumption – and that's the end of that.

That afternoon, Daddy gets Lizzie on her own. He comes into the sitting room, where she's making a list of all she has to do before she goes, and he stands by the couch and says, 'Lizzie, about this plan of yours –'

Lizzie puts down her notebook and looks up at him. 'It's no good trying to stop me, Daddy – I've made my decision.'

He smiles and shakes his head. 'I've no intention of stopping you. You do what you have to do, and good luck to you.' And he takes a folded piece of paper out of the pocket of the cardigan Mammy got him for Christmas and hands it to her. 'That'll help you make a start.'

Lizzie looks down at the cheque and her eyes fill. She blinks. 'Daddy, I don't need –'

'I know you don't, but I do.' He hesitates. 'And, Lizzie –' She looks up at him. 'I think it might be best if we kept this to ourselves.' She wants to hug him, but it's not something they do, so she just nods and thanks him and tucks the cheque into the pocket of her linen trousers as he leaves the room.

On New Year's Eve, Lizzie sits at home with Mammy and Daddy, watching someone from RTÉ counting down the seconds – she was supposed to be going out to dinner with Tony – and when it's next year they shake hands and Daddy says, '*Go mbeirimid beo ag an am seo arís*,' and Mammy and Lizzie say, 'Amen.' They finish their drinks – one each, whiskey and 7-Up for Daddy, gin and tonic with lemon and no ice for Mammy, red wine for Lizzie – and then Daddy locks up for the night and they all go to bed. And Lizzie hugs her plan to herself, and counts the days, and waits. Not long now.

On Monday the sixth of January, she's going to haul her stuffed rucksack downstairs and fling it into the back of her blue Fiesta, with her baking books and her portable telly and her CD player and her cryptic-crossword book and her travel Scrabble and Jones. She's going to say goodbye to Mammy and Daddy, and she's going to drive away to the rest of her life. She's not planning to travel the world – she has Jones now; and anyway, it's not how far she goes that matters any more.

She hasn't a clue where she'll end up, or what she'll do when she gets there – apart from finding a way to bake for a living – and she's as excited as a child on Christmas Eve. She wants to open up and reach out and grab hold of whatever is flying past, and just hang on tight.

She goes into the bank one day and transfers half the joint-account money into a new current account in her name. It'll keep her going while she finds the bakery job. She notices that Tony hasn't touched a cent.

After dinner on Friday the third of January, she helps Daddy with the washing up. She always washes, he always wipes – she doubts that he knows where the Fairy Liquid is kept – while Mammy adds a half-bucket of coal to the fire in the sitting room and then puts on her slippers. When every piece of evidence that dinner took place has been destroyed, Lizzie heads upstairs to have another go at her rucksack. It's been packed for over a week, but she loves taking it apart and starting all over again. Every time she does this, something else gets left out or put in.

She decides the hairdryer can come out. She's going to cultivate a new look – tousled hair and long floaty dresses. The only problem with this is that she doesn't have any floaty dresses, long or short. She doesn't have any dresses, full stop, except a black velvet knee-length one with lacy sleeves that she bought on impulse after Síle got engaged, years ago, and they went shopping after a couple of glasses of sparkling wine. She let herself be talked into the dress, and now she only takes it out on the rare occasions when she needs something a bit posher than faded jeans. She wore it to her school twenty-year reunion and spent the night trying to remember names, and looking at photos of babies, and trying to sound convincing when she explained why she'd been engaged for eight years and why it didn't bother her a bit.

But her calves are a bit hefty and she feels better when they're well hidden from public view. And she loves her jeans. They probably do nothing for her (Mammy says they do nothing for her; Mammy loves her black velvet dress), but when she climbs in they wrap themselves tenderly around her and hug her curves. *Hello, Lizzie, here we are again; just snuggle in and get comfy.* Thank God for denim, in all its glorious blue shades.

Right, she'll have tousled hair and jeans and no make-up. She takes out her two lipsticks and her eye pencil (the same one that she used to join up her freckles) and the ancient tube of foundation that she never uses anyway, and leaves in a tube of even more ancient hair gel so she can scrunch her wet hair and make it look all tossed and dead sexy.

After a minute, she puts back the eye pencil and the hairdryer. Maybe she'll have sleek, shiny hair instead, and dramatic eyes. Then she puts back the lipsticks; sleek hair and dramatic eyes would look funny without a bit of colour on the lips. But that's it; she puts her foundation and a half-full pot of powder blusher in the bin, and before she can change her mind she lifts the plastic bag out of her wastepaper basket and brings it down to the big black bin in the garage.

She goes back upstairs and has another rummage. After a minute she goes downstairs to get the foundation and blusher out of the bin. You never know when you might need perfect skin and a rosy glow. It's not as if they're heavy; and she can always dump them later if she finds she's not using them.

As she goes back up to her room again, Lizzie wonders for the millionth time if she's a little insane – heading off without an idea where she's going to end up. Maybe Mammy is right – maybe she *should* just go to someplace like Lanzarote, or somewhere more exotic like Barbados, for a week. On the other hand, the fact that she hasn't a clue where she's going means that she can go wherever the hell she likes. And she knows well that a week of lying on warm sand in the sun might be pure bliss, but it isn't going to fix what's wrong. She needs to make a complete change, whatever that takes. A fresh start. She likes the way that sounds – like something just out of the oven, fragrant and steaming.

She passes Tony in the street the day before she's due to leave, and she says hello. He looks through her.

The following morning, on Monday the sixth of January, Lizzie stands by the open car door in her old navy winter coat, rubbing her gloved hands together and freezing quietly. In the boot of the Fiesta are her rucksack, her telly, her CD player, Jones's litter tray, her bag of baking books and a couple of jackets. On the passenger seat, safely belted in, is Jones in his carrier. She debated leaving him until she got settled somewhere, made sure he'd be welcome; but the thought of taking this giant leap without him was just too scary – she needs his furry, lazy bulk beside her to go through with it. She'll just have to find a cat-friendly place to live in.

She looks at him sitting in his carrier, looking faintly bored. *He's* not scared of a giant leap – well, in theory, anyway; she doubts that he'd manage a baby leap, let alone a giant one, in real life.

Beside the car are her parents, standing close together on the frozen path. Lizzie stamps on the ground to get some feeling back into her toes.

'Well, I'd better get going, I suppose.' *Before we all solidify.*

'Did you take the holy water?' Mammy is still dead against the move, but she's concerned about her daughter's immortal soul.

'I did, yeah.' It's sitting on the shelf under the dashboard, a little plastic bottle that Mammy filled at the church the other day.

'Let us know when you've a place to stay,' Daddy says.

'Course I will; I'll ring as soon as I've landed somewhere. Don't worry about me.'

That's a good one – like asking the spring clematis over the garage not to bloom till September this year because Aunty Kate is coming to visit from America with her new husband and step-kids and you want the place to look well. Mammy and Daddy have no one else to worry about; in forty-five years of marriage, Lizzie is all they managed to produce. She's lived under the same roof as them for forty-one years, apart from the weeks driving around Cork or Kerry or Galway with Tony. Now she's thrown a backpack into the boot of the car and she's disappearing God knows where for

God knows how long, and she tells them not to worry. Very funny.

Daddy came home with a book from the Tourist Office the other day. He'd paid seven euros for it – the price was written on the front cover – and he handed it to Lizzie after dinner, when Mammy had disappeared into the sitting room.

'Now, you can pick out a nice place and give them a ring.'

Lizzie took it from him and opened it with a sinking heart. It was full of self-catering houses and apartments by the sea, or in towns near golf courses, or just outside villages, all approved by Bord Fáilte; and she knew that, wherever she ended up living, it wouldn't be in one of them.

To keep the peace, she promised Daddy she'd take the book with her and be guided by it. 'It's just that I don't want to pick anyplace yet, while I haven't worked out where I want to go. I might be travelling around for a while before I find a place that appeals to me.'

He looked at her, trying to understand, and nodded.

The book is sitting in the little pocket in her door, beside her road map of Ireland. She's planning to give it to the first charity shop she passes.

Mammy puts a hand on her arm. 'Now, Lizzie, you know you can still just go for a couple of weeks and come back. It's not too late to change your mind; your bed is always here, and Julia would have you back in the morning if I had a word with her.'

And I'd last another six months and then throw myself off the tallest building in Kilmorris. Lizzie smiles and puts her arms around her and knows her bed will always be here, and knows she'll never live here again. Mammy smells of rashers and Pledge and hairspray.

'I'll remember, Mammy.'

'You make sure you find someplace nice to stay. Make sure it's not damp.'

Lizzie nods. 'I will. And you take care. I'll give you a ring this evening.'

'Do that.'

Mammy moves back as Daddy steps forward – after forty-five years together, they're perfectly synchronised. Daddy puts out his hand, but Lizzie ignores it and puts her arms around him. She can't remember when she hugged him last. He feels narrower than she expected.

'Bye, Daddy.'

'Bye now, Lizzie. Mind yourself.' He pats her back twice, then drops his arms and steps back from her.

Lizzie slides into the driver's seat, pulls the door closed and winds down the window.

'Drive carefully,' says Mammy.

'I will. Bye now. Say bye, Jones. Go in out of the cold now; ye'll freeze. Talk to ye later. Wish me luck.'

'Good luck,' they chorus, standing close together. Mammy tucks her arm into Daddy's and waves at Lizzie with her other hand. 'Make sure you wrap up well.'

Lizzie starts the engine and moves off, waving awkwardly out of the window, watching in her mirror as the couple on the path get smaller. They look old and unfamiliar, this white-haired man in his grey suit and this neat little woman in a brown tweed coat over her blue-and-white flowery apron, not going in out of the cold, just standing there together and waving. Pretending that they don't mind her going, that they'll be just fine without her. From his carrier, Jones mews once.

Wave goodbye, Lizzie. Wave goodbye to forty-one years of waiting for something to happen. Forget O'Gorman's and Tony and Tuesday-night bacon and cabbage, and rubbing Deep Heat into Daddy's bad knee and finding Mammy's tatty purple slippers that never seem to be where she left them last night. Now pull yourself out of the rut, wind up your window and say hello to the rest of your life.

Her cheek is itchy; she puts her finger up to scratch it and finds a tear. She doesn't remember feeling sad.

Chapter Four

Lizzie rubs the tear away, blinks and checks the clock on the dashboard. Ten past ten. She never understood why people called it 'tinker's time' until one day she suddenly realised you were supposed to say 'tin past tin'.

She's got the rest of the day to go – where? The absurdity of the fact that she hasn't a notion where she's going makes her smile. She pulls over and reaches for the road map. Imagine if Mammy came along with her shopping trolley; they'd have to say goodbye all over again.

She looks at the map. Kilmorris is right in the midlands, about seventy miles from the west coast. She fancies living near the sea, in a place much smaller than this one – a fairly big village, or a small market town maybe; big enough that she won't stand out, small enough that she'll get to know people fairly easily.

They spent a few holidays by the sea when she was young, staying in rented houses or caravans and having lunch in pubs where old men in tweed caps played fiddles and tin whistles and belted out rhythms on bodhráns. She remembers the salty tang of the periwinkles Daddy used to buy in little white paper bags and fish out of their shells for her with the pin that came with them, and the sticky balls of candyfloss she'd pull apart with her hands. She used to love the smell of the seaweed and the noise of the waves in the evening when they'd go walking along the prom after dinner, Lizzie full of huge yawns after the day of sea air.

Yes, she wants to live by the sea. She'll take the road going west and head for the coast, and then meander around a bit until she finds somewhere that she likes the look of. And maybe she should aim to be not too far from a fairly big town, so she can have a bit more of a social life if she feels the need. She folds up the map again and sets off. Through the next lights and left at the roundabout, and she'll be headed west.

She's just past the roundabout when she sees him. Thumb raised, sitting on a backpack twice as big as hers. Longish fair hair, hand-knit baggy jumper, jeans, sandals – *God help us, sandals in January in Ireland*. He has thick woolly socks on under them, but still. He must be insane.

Lizzie has never hitched a lift, and never given a lift to a hitchhiker, in her life. Tony didn't believe in it – 'Let them get the bus, that's what they're for' – and she's a bit wary of picking up someone when she's on her own in the car, especially if he's a man with long hair who shows definite signs of madness.

And then she remembers the old woman from the hill country of Kentucky wishing she'd taken more chances. Ah, hell – she's looking for a change, isn't she? And what can happen to her at tin past tin on a Monday morning? Jones will mind her. She pulls over, forgetting to indicate – another first – and checks that her handbag is safely under her seat while she waits for the hitchhiker. Jones will have to move into the back; he won't mind.

The lunatic hitchhiker hefts his backpack up and lopes on long legs to the car. Lizzie leans across and opens the passenger door, and he sticks his head in, smiling. He has lovely, even white teeth.

'Hi, how ya doin'? Happy New Year. Thanks for stoppin'.'

His voice is slow and drawly, and American. That may explain the sandals. And the madness. Lizzie smiles back at him, glad she stopped. *Sorry, Tony.*

'Happy New Year to you. Where're you headed?'

'I'm goin' to Rockford.'

'Fine; that's on my way.' Rockford is about fifteen miles down the road. 'Help me move Jones into the back.'

He squats down, puts a finger through the wire front of the carrier and scratches Jones's head. 'Hey, buddy, sorry 'bout that.' Jones closes his eyes and purrs loudly.

Lizzie unbuckles his seat-belt. 'He doesn't mind; he's a real sweetie.'

As she goes to lift the carrier, the hitchhiker takes it from her. 'Here, I got it.' He hefts it easily over the front seat and settles it in the back. 'There you go, Jones; all safe and sound. Let's clip you in there.'

Then he picks up his rucksack and hauls it in beside the cat-carrier. 'Hey, Jones, keep an eye on my stuff, OK?' He wags a finger at Jones, who blinks back at him.

Lizzie laughs. 'Shut up and get in before you freeze us out of it.' She wonders if he'll mind being told to shut up. Probably not – the free lift will take the sting out of it. He hops in and pulls the door shut, and she puts the car in gear and drives off. The hitchhiker turns sideways in his seat and pokes a finger in at Jones, who mews at him.

'I'm Pete, by the way.'

'I'm Lizzie – and Jones you've already met.' She glances down at his feet. 'Do you mind my asking why you're in sandals in the middle of an Irish winter?'

Pete smiles ruefully. 'Yeah, looks kinda strange, I guess. My boots are wet through from yesterday, so I had no choice.' *Good, at least he has boots. Not totally insane, then.*

'You must be frozen; hang on.' She directs the hot air towards his feet and turns it up full blast. As he begins to feel the warmth, he wriggles his toes and sighs happily.

'Hey, that feels gooood.' He manoeuvres out of the sandals and pushes them aside, then wriggles his thick-socked toes again. Lizzie smiles; he reminds her of Jones – slow, lazy, easy.

'I presume you're American.'

He cocks his head at her and puts on a mock-astonished expression. 'Hey, that's amazing. How the heck did you know?'

She laughs. 'Whereabouts in the States?'

'Tennessee, and upstate New York, but I been livin' here in Ireland for the past year.' She loves his drawl; much more attractive than the flat Kilmorris accent.

'Don't tell me – you came to find your roots.'

He grins and shakes his head. 'No, ma'am. Don't believe I've a drop of Irish blood in me, unfortunately. No, I came here to get away from all that US crap. Got tired of the whole materialism thing there – all those weapons, all that macho stuff, specially after 9-11; I wanted to take some time out and just chill.'

Hmmm – a not-so-typical American. 'So you came over to holy Catholic Ireland.' Pete raises his eyebrows at her and smiles, but says nothing. 'You must like it if you're still here.'

He nods. 'Sure do. Good people, still got some values.' He looks over at her. 'So what's your story?' He cocks his head at the cat-carrier. 'Where're you and Jones headed?'

Lizzie grins. 'We're going on an adventure.'

He raises his eyebrows in delight. 'No kiddin' – sort of a Thelma and Louise thing?'

She's thrilled at the comparison; all she needs is the scarf and the glasses. And the convertible. 'Exactly – except we don't intend to kill anyone, and we probably won't rob anyplace either.' She shoots a look over at him. 'And I should tell you that I have no intention of driving off a cliff.'

'Well, now, I'm kinda relieved to hear that.' Pete settles himself more comfortably into his seat, head turned towards her. 'So tell me more about this adventure.'

She smiles. 'God, where do I start? Until today I lived at home with my parents.'

'No kiddin'? Never left the nest?' She looks over at him again – is he laughing at her? – but he seems genuinely surprised.

'Is that unheard of in the States?'

He nods. 'Pretty much – where I come from, anyway. My buddies and me all moved out after high school. We found apartments to share.' Then he smiles, shaking his head. 'Course, some of the places we stayed in . . . even the roaches moved out. And some of the roommates I got weren't exactly house-trained.'

She laughs. 'But at least you had independence, did what you wanted. I've slept in the same bedroom since I was brought home from the nursing home. My mother cooks all the meals, same things every week: always a roast on Sunday, lamb chops on Monday, bacon and cabbage on Tuesday . . .'

He grins. 'Hey, when I lived at home, we always had my mom's blueberry pancakes for breakfast on Sundays.'

'Mmm – sounds delicious. Much more interesting than prunes and Bran Flakes.' Lizzie makes a face. 'I'm never again going to eat prunes.'

He nods. 'Good idea. How 'bout the rest of your family – do they all live at home too?'

She's amused at his assumption that she comes from a good Catholic big Irish family. 'There's just me, I'm afraid. Only child.'

'Yeah? So there's no one to take the pressure off. All the expectations are restin' on your head.'

She looks over at him, amazed. 'Exactly; that's exactly it. I never had anyone to – I don't know – dilute them with, I suppose; do you know what I mean?'

Pete nods again. 'Sure.' And he really seems to understand. 'So what made you make the break?'

She smiles as she remembers the dentist's waiting room. 'Oh, just something I read; it made me realise that I was letting my life slip by, when I could do something about it if I wanted.' As she talks, she begins to feel the same excitement bubble up in her again. She looks over at Pete. 'I was engaged, too, for years. And I worked with my fiancé, in his family business.'

'No kiddin'?' He shakes his head. 'So you finished with him?'

She nods. 'Broke off the engagement, packed in the job.' She can't believe she's telling so much to a perfect stranger. Is it because she knows she'll be waving goodbye to him in about ten minutes? 'So here I am, car packed with all my worldly goods, heading off to God knows where. I have no idea where I'm going to end up, don't even know where I'm going to sleep tonight.' She darts a look at him. 'What do you think – am I daft?'

He smiles widely at her, showing his perfect American teeth again. 'I think that's a heck of a move you're makin' there. I think you're gonna have a blast. Sounds wonderful.'

She laughs; that's exactly what she wanted to hear. 'I'm going to head for the coast; I've decided I want to live by the sea.'

He nods slowly. 'Yeah, good start, I guess. The ocean is a special place – and you've got some pretty cool coastline here.' He puts his hands behind his head and stretches his long legs out as much as the little car will allow. Then he closes his eyes with a deep sigh.

Lizzie sneaks a proper look. He's a bit younger than her; she guesses he's somewhere in his mid-thirties. Sallow skin, slightly tanned; whatever work he does – if he does any – is probably out of doors. Nice cheekbones, dark-blond stubble around his chin. No coat, in the middle of winter – mind you, that jumper looks like a blanket, and he's probably got loads of layers on under it. Hair in need of a good cut, but thick and clean-looking. Fingernails not too bad. A gold claddagh ring, and a battered leather wrist-strap with what she thinks is 'Leo' stamped on it. No wedding ring. She gets a faint smell of damp wool, and something sweet and vaguely familiar.

Suddenly he sits up. 'Hey, mind if I smoke?'

'Em . . . OK.'

Lizzie has never let anyone smoke in her car. But she can't say no outright to a stranger. Well, she could – it *is* her car, after all, and she *is* doing him a favour, but still . . . Anyway, this is the new Lizzie, the easygoing, chance-taking one. She can put up with a bit of smoke – it won't kill her. She hopes.

She inches down her window. *Sorry, Jones.*

Pete reaches behind and pulls a pouch from a pocket in his backpack. He takes out a packet of cigarette papers, then starts to roll a cigarette. He winds his window down a few inches before taking a lighter from the pouch and lighting up; he drags deeply, holds the smoke for a long moment, then turns his head towards the window and exhales slowly.

A thick, sweet scent wafts towards Lizzie. She recognises it instantly from occasional dinner parties in the past, when some of the more daring couples would produce a few joints after the meal. Lizzie was never tempted to try it – she'd felt sick for ages after trying to smoke regular cigarettes in her teens, and of course Tony never touched it – but she secretly liked the musky smell that clung to her clothes for a day or two afterwards.

She smiles to herself. *No wonder he's so mellow. Probably high as a kite half the time. The cheek of him, using illegal substances in my car.* She bets the old woman from Kentucky would have enjoyed a joint if she'd got the chance.

She looks over at Pete the pothead, and he holds out the joint to her.

'No, thanks.' *One major life change a day is quite enough.* 'So what brings you to Rockford?'

'Got buddies there, potters. They're from the States too, but they been livin' here a few years.'

'And where have *you* been living since you came to Ireland?'

He shrugs. 'Oh, I been wanderin'. Here, there . . . wherever I can find some work. I'm comin' from Tipperary today.'

Lizzie is fascinated – his life is so different from hers. She imagines what it must be like to wander round a whole new country, live in a place for a few weeks, maybe, and then just up and move. Pack your rucksack and go wherever the fancy takes you. And he thinks *she's* being adventurous.

'What kind of work d'you do?'

He shrugs again. 'Anythin' that needs doin' – farmin' mostly, or construction, that sorta stuff.'

'So now you're going to visit Rockford for a while.'

He nods. 'Yeah. They tell me there's good music there, so I brought along my tin whistle.'

She's intrigued. 'You play the tin whistle?' Definitely not a typical American.

He grins back at her. 'Sure do. Just picked it up from hearin' guys in the bars here.' He jerks his thumb towards the back seat. 'Fancy a tune?' He pronounces it 'toon'.

'Love one.' *And if he's no good, Rockford is only five minutes away.*

Pete pinches the end of the joint into the ashtray and puts the rest of it back in his pouch before turning to rummage in the backpack. His jeans are frayed at the seams. He pulls out a tin whistle and settles himself again, and then he puts it to his lips and starts to play.

He plays a tune Lizzie doesn't recognise, and it's sweet and slow and sad. She is amazed that a tin whistle can produce music like this, with every note so clear and pure. Then he goes straight into 'Ode to Joy', and behind the dancing notes she can hear the orchestra. After that he plays a lively traditional Irish air whose name she can't remember. She's back in the holiday pubs of her childhood, tapping along to the rhythms as she munches Taytos and sucks Fanta through her straw.

When he stops she turns to him. 'That was wonderful; really.' She smiles. 'You must spend a fair bit of your time in pubs to have learnt so well.'

He grins back. 'Hey, it's no big deal; tin whistle's easy. I taught myself guitar too – that was a little harder.' He turns to put the tin whistle away.

'Wow.' Lizzie is impressed. She remembers Mammy sending her off to learn the piano when she was eight. She hated every minute of it, stamping off to the sitting room and banging the door behind her whenever she was sent in to practise. She lasted eight weeks, never getting past a stumbling 'Blue Danube'. Eventually

Mammy gave in and stopped the lessons. Now Lizzie would give anything to be able to play the piano. Or to play anything at all.

She sees the sign announcing Rockford, and feels disappointed; Pete's been good company. 'Here we are. You'll have to direct me to your friends' house.'

He turns back from his rucksack and shakes his head. 'Hey, no way. The main street'll be fine. You've done enough by bringin' me here, honest.'

She looks sternly at him. 'You're not exactly dragging me across New York. It'll take about thirty seconds to bring you wherever it is.' Rockford straggles along half a main street and meanders down two little lanes off it. 'Tell me which way to go – I insist.'

He grins. 'OK, thanks a lot. I gotta look out for a store on a corner and go right.'

They find it and turn; after a hundred yards or so, Pete says, 'Guess this is it; they said the one with the pump.'

Lizzie stops and looks at the abandoned cottage he's pointing at, with the rusty pump at the side.

'No, it can't be this one.' He's got the directions mixed up, or his pals must have moved. Waist-high weeds tumble over themselves in what was probably the front garden fifty years ago. The roof was once thatched – now it's more holes than roof. The front door, blue paint peeling away, hangs half off its hinges, leaning outwards. The flaking whitewashed walls look pretty solid, but that's about it. A condemned building –

no doubt about it. Lizzie pulls in, thinking that they'll have to go back to the bit of a main street and enquire.

But suddenly, incredibly, she notices a wisp of smoke coming from the remains of the chimney – and Pete has already stepped out and is hauling out his backpack. 'I'm pretty sure this is it.'

She sits speechless; how can someone live like this? Then, from behind the house, a man about Pete's age comes sauntering; one of the potters, presumably. He's equally skinny and hairy, with identical jeans and a green army jacket, striding towards the car in big, solid-looking boots – sandals are obviously not the thing in falling-down houses.

'Hey, man, you made it.'

Pete lets his rucksack drop and they bear-hug, slapping each other's back. Then they separate and Pete gestures towards Lizzie, still sitting dumbstruck in the car.

'Sure did, thanks to Lizzie, my chauffeur. Lizzie, this is Brett.'

His pal gives her a 'Hey' and lifts his hand. Lizzie says, 'Hi there,' and waves back as she starts the engine.

Pete leans in the car window. 'Hey, you've got no place you gotta be – why don't you take a few days here in Rockford?' He turns to Brett. 'OK if Lizzie stays a while?'

Brett smiles the same slow, lazy smile as Pete. 'No problem.' He'd probably take in the Irish soccer team if they turned up looking for a few beds for the night.

Lizzie can imagine the inside of Brett the potter's house: blankets on the floor, everyone grouped round the fire, looking up at the stars through the hole in the roof. A six-month supply of pot somewhere handy. Probably all the mice Jones could catch, if he were in any state to run after them.

For a second she hesitates – Pete strumming his guitar in the firelight *is* pretty tempting – but then forty-one years of four walls and a bed at night kick in. Too much; and much too soon.

She smiles at them. 'Thanks for the offer, but I think I'll keep going.'

Pete leans in and hauls Jones back into the front seat. 'Hey, big guy, you'd like to stay, wouldn't you?' Jones blinks out at him from behind his wire. Pete looks back at Lizzie.

'You sure we can't tempt you?'

No. Not a bit sure. Not at all convinced that I'm doing the right thing. One thing I am sure of, though – that old Kentucky woman would stay in a minute. She'd be out of this car before you could say 'thermal vest'. She wonders if Pete ever came across that woman in the States. How far is Kentucky from Tennessee?

She puts the car in gear – she's really not ready. 'I'm sure, Pete, but thanks again. Look me up when you get to the ocean.'

Pete stretches over and takes her hand; his is surprisingly warm for the day that's in it. 'I'll keep my eyes peeled. Thanks a lot, hon. Have a good adventure.' He rubs Jones's head. 'Bye, buddy.'

A smile, a wave, and he's gone, striding with his friend towards the ruined house. No glass in most of the crumbling window-frames, roof open to the skies, front door practically collapsed, but a fire in the fireplace. Unbelievable.

She'd love to see where they sleep. Or maybe she wouldn't.

She liked the way Pete called her 'hon', even if it meant nothing. Tony called her 'love' or 'pet'. Somehow 'hon', in an American drawl, sounds a lot more romantic.

As Lizzie turns the car around and drives back into Rockford, a thought hits her. Through all the years she was living her standing-still life in the house where she grew up, through all the nights she spent doing cross-words with Mammy and Daddy, or having a glass of wine in the local with Tony, or poring over her bakery books, other lives were whirling by, full of doings and happenings and experiences. Hearts were breaking, mountains were being conquered, barriers were being torn down, love and hate and everything in between were being flung around willy-nilly. People were tightroping between laughter and tears, without a safety net in sight. Pete and his friends were smoking pot in ruins of houses, with nothing between them and the stars.

She's reminded of something – what? Then it comes to her: Dorothy in *The Wizard of Oz*. The bit where she's sitting on her bed, looking at the hurdy-gurdy madness outside her window – cows and wicked women on bicycles and rocking chairs, all spinning crazily past. She's been like Dorothy, looking on all these years while life hurtled by outside.

She shakes her head – it's useless to dwell on the time that's gone by; from now on, she's thinking of the future. *I'm only forty-one, for God's sake – if I'm lucky, maybe just halfway through life. Who knows what's around all the corners I haven't turned yet?*

Plenty of daisies left to be picked.

Suddenly she feels a surge of exhilaration, and she beeps the horn twice in Rockford's bit of a main street. A woman talking on a mobile phone looks over at her; Lizzie smiles and waves cheerily as she passes, and the woman smiles vaguely back at her, turning to look after the car. Probably wondering who the heck that was.

As she leaves Rockford, Lizzie O'Grady wonders how long it'll take her to find the perfect place. She'll know it when she comes to it; she's sure of that.

And when she gets there, she'll walk out of the house and into the tornado.

Chapter Five

A few minutes after six o'clock, Lizzie pulls up outside a whitewashed restaurant. The sign over the door says 'The Kitchen'. She's been wandering around all day; the perfect destination hasn't shown up the way it was supposed to, and now it's really too dark to go on looking. She'll have to put off the search until tomorrow.

She's lost count of the villages and towns she's driven through, keeping close to the coast all the time. She stopped the car in a few of them, to walk around and smell the sea and get a feel for the place. Once she thought she might have found what she was looking for, but after an hour of exploring and pottering around the shops she decided against it; nothing jumped out and grabbed her.

She stopped at lay-bys a couple of times and fed Jones, and let him wander round sniffing at the grass for a few minutes while she sat half-in and half-out of the car and looked at the map and wondered if she'd ever find what she wanted. Once, an old man out walking came over to see if she needed directions. When Lizzie explained that she was just exploring the coast, and asked about the most scenic route to the next village, he warned her not to keep to the coast road – 'It's a fierce rigmarole of a road altogether' – and advised her to stay inland for a few miles. She thanked him, waited until he'd rounded the next bend, counted to a hundred in case he turned back, and then spent the next ten miles trying to strike a happy medium between admiring the stunning views of the Atlantic and keeping herself and Jones and all her belongings from careening off one of the hairpin bends.

Now she wonders what she was expecting – what exactly *is* she looking for, anyway? Maybe she's been a bit naïve – flinging a few things into the back of the car and assuming that everything will fall into place and that she'll live happily ever after in the land of her dreams. Maybe Mammy and Daddy were right, and this was a cock-eyed idea.

She looks in the mirror; her grey eyes look black in the streetlight. She puts out a hand and strokes Jones's head through his wire, and he stirs sleepily and snuffles. The day cooped up in his carrier doesn't seem to have bothered him.

She's in a smallish town, or a biggish village, called Merway, about eighty miles from home – although, with all her meandering, she must have driven well over two hundred miles altogether. The street she's on runs more or less parallel with the coast, opening out into a little dinky square in the middle. There's the usual assortment of shops and businesses, and a scattering of private houses here and there; nothing special, nothing to make it stand out from all the other places she's been through today. Of course, it's dark now – it probably looks very different in daylight.

Her stomach rumbles; she's eaten nothing but an apple and a banana since her porridge-and-prunes-and-brown-bread breakfast at nine. Porridge and prunes and brown bread in the winter, Bran Flakes and prunes and brown bread in the summer . . . Lizzie is as regular as clockwork.

She's also starting to freeze as the car cools. Time to eat – and find a place for the night. She wonders if she'll have to smuggle Jones in. He'll be getting hungry again too; it's a while since she fed him. She'd better not delay.

As she opens the door she gets a whiff of garlic. *God, I'm ravenous.* 'Mind the car, Jones; won't be too long.' *Will he be warm enough with the heat off?* She takes her coat from the back seat and wraps it around the bottom of his cat-carrier. He's got his tatty brown cushion under him, too – he should be fine. She grabs her scarf and her bag, then steps out and breathes in the sharp evening air. It smells fresh, and salty.

The whitewashed restaurant is on the coast side of the road. The window-frames are painted red, and there are glass lanterns with fat cream candles sitting in the windows on either side of the front door. Peering through one of them, Lizzie can make out a blazing fire in the far corner; great. She opens the door and a bell tinkles, like in the sweet shops she remembers from childhood. *Two gobstoppers and a pack of sherbet, please.*

The room is small and cosy, with uneven-looking white walls, old floorboards and half a dozen tables covered in red cloths and scattered higgledy-piggledy around the room. There's a red candle in a wine bottle on every table, and they're all lit, even on the unoccupied ones. Apart from the lanterns in the windows, the only other light in the room comes from a pair of wall-lamps on either side of the fireplace, and from the fire itself. There are a couple of seascapes hanging on the white walls.

Behind the front door is an old hallstand, nearly identical to the one at home – she almost expects to see Daddy's old tweed hanging lopsidedly near the top. A giant basket of logs and briquettes and a coal-scuttle sit beside the fireplace. Louis Armstrong is singing about someone who goes to his head, under the bits of conversation floating gently about. There's a door at the far corner, near the fireplace, that Lizzie assumes leads to the kitchen.

She could hardly have chosen somewhere more different from O'Gorman's formica-topped tables and flowery carpet and local radio. Good start.

Three of the six tables are occupied. A man with a grey beard sits alone at a small one, six people – probably three couples – who don't look Irish at another, and two women with a small child in a high chair at the third.

Lizzie closes the door behind her and stands uncertainly – should she sit down, or wait to be seated? It's a long time since she's eaten out; Tony wasn't keen on helping to keep his competition in business. And Mammy and Daddy had to be dragged out whenever the occasion called for any kind of a celebration – they were really more comfortable with the tried and trusted O'Grady mealtime routine. Lizzie can't remember the last time she had a restaurant meal – Mammy and Daddy's fortieth anniversary? – and she's never eaten out alone, ever. This is certainly turning out to be a day of firsts. Mrs Kentucky would be proud of her.

She nods at the few diners who turned at the sound of the bell, and starts to unwind her scarf, to give her something to do while she thinks about grabbing a table. The little child – not much more than a baby – has stopped mashing his dinner against his face to stare open-mouthed at her, a dribble of something mushy on his chin. Then he drops his spoon with a clang, and one of the women – his mother? – bends to pick it up, and the slight tension is broken.

Lizzie has just decided to go and sit somewhere when a smiling young girl of fourteen or fifteen comes out from the back, holding a menu.

'Hello. Are you on your own?'

No, my husband and six children are on the way; just give me a minute to conjure them up. She smiles back at the girl. 'Yes, just me.'

'Come over near the fire.' The girl leads Lizzie towards an empty table to the left of the fireplace. On the way Lizzie catches the eye of the elderly bearded man, who smiles up at her. There's a little pottery eggcup, with a sprig of holly perched in it, beside the candle on her table.

'I'll hang up your scarf if you like.' *She's probably wondering why I don't have a coat. Better not tell her it's wrapped around the cat.* The girl holds the scarf while Lizzie gets settled. 'Can I get you something to drink?'

You certainly can; a big dollop of Dutch courage, please. 'Yes, I'd love a glass of red wine.' Lizzie feels a twinge of rebellion – they never have wine with meals at home, except on Christmas Day.

The girl points to the wine list on the back page. 'The house wine is the only one we sell by the glass; would that do?'

It's French, and not a name Lizzie has come across, but she wouldn't exactly describe herself as a con-noisseur. O'Gorman's only got the wine licence a couple of years ago, and Tony or Julia looked after all that; Lizzie was only the head waitress, after all. She nods – 'That sounds great, thanks' – and the girl takes her scarf and walks away.

She looks into the fire, rubbing her hands together, feeling her toes come slowly to life. There's something on the mantelpiece – she leans over to make it out. It's a little wooden clown, sitting with his legs dangling over the edge. There are real yellow laces, tied in giant bows, in his long shoes; they're the only part of him not made from wood. He's leaning back on his hands, grinning hugely, with his head cocked to one side. The detail is amazing – Lizzie can see the pores in his tongue and the ridges in his big, slightly sticking-out teeth. A comically oversized hat perches crookedly on his head. He's utterly charming, and she wonders who was talented enough to carve him. Probably he was brought back from some holiday somewhere.

Louis Armstrong is telling her what a wonderful world it is, and she has to agree. Look at her: free as a bird, with enough money in the bank to keep her going for quite a while if she's careful – not that she intends to twiddle her thumbs for too long.

Pity she hasn't got someone to share all this freedom with, though.

She thinks of Tony, setting the tables in O'Gorman's for the night. Just over two weeks ago she was setting them too – imagine . . . and then she went to the dentist.

She hopes Tony doesn't hate her for escaping.

She pushes him out of her head and turns to the menu. *Food, before I die of hunger*.

It's a folded cardboard page, handwritten. No starters, just three main courses – lamb shepherd's pie, chicken-and-bacon hotpot and vegetarian lasagne. Good home cooking, hopefully. Two desserts, apple tart and fruity bread pudding, both served with custard or ice-cream. A real comfort-food menu – perfect for the middle of an Irish winter.

Lizzie's mouth waters as she reads. She'd eat an elephant this minute if one appeared. Her waitress comes back with her glass of wine and a jug of iced water, and Lizzie tells her she'd love the shepherd's pie, please. Monday dinner at home is lamb chops; she thinks of Mammy putting two less under the grill tonight.

She picks up the glass and takes a sip, rolling it around on her tongue. The taste is woody and velvety and blackcurranty. She swallows and feels the wine meandering slowly down into her empty stomach, leaving a tiny warm explosion after it; lovely. She takes another sip and swirls it around in her mouth, tilting the glass slightly and watching the little trails the wine leaves behind when it falls away from the sides – didn't she read somewhere that that's the sign of a good wine?

She swallows again, and a pleasant buzz starts up somewhere in her head. God, her empty stomach – she'd better watch it, just in case she has to drive any further this evening. Surely, though, she'll find a bed and breakfast here, even if she has to go the length and breadth of Merway; that should take her about five minutes.

She glances around the room. Nobody is looking at her except the child, who says, 'Gah,' and bangs his spoon against his tray. Lizzie beams back and waggles her fingers at him, catching the eye of one of the women, who smiles over at her. People seem friendly here.

She picks up her glass again and settles more comfortably into her chair. The fire is warm, the music is mellow, the wine is going down very well indeed. This was really a lucky stop – as long as the food is good; and, if the smell is anything to go by, it will be.

She's not disappointed. A generous helping of what is clearly freshly made shepherd's pie sits on a blue plate. It smells wonderful. Lizzie picks up her fork and dives in. It tastes as good as it looks – succulent, herby, with lots of onions and carrots mixed in, topped with a mountain of buttery mash, browned and just crispy enough. A bonus of golden roasted parsnips – Lizzie's very favourite way to cook them – sits on the side. Divine.

She tucks in happily, stopping only to take the odd sip of wine or water until her plate has been completely cleared. She comes from a family of plate-clearers; Mammy takes it personally if anything is left, pressing the last spoon of mashed turnip on you, looking martyred as she clears away any remains. And Lizzie needs no coaxing to finish every bit of the tastiest meal she's had in a long time. Of course, it helped that she was ravenous to begin with, but still.

As she finishes, wishing she had a hunk of bread to mop up the last of the sauce – it's the only thing that's missing – the same young girl appears with the menu.

'Would you like dessert?'

Lizzie imagines a slice of cinnamony apple tart, smothered in thick, creamy homemade custard, baked by the same competent pair of hands that produced the shepherd's pie. She knows it would be delicious, and it takes a huge effort to shake her head. She's giving up desserts – one of her fresh starts. But does the waitress know where she'd find a B&B?

'Actually, we have one here. Hang on a minute and I'll call my mother.'

They have one here. Lizzie's first night away from home is turning out just fine. She sits back again and imagines waking to – what? A glass of just-squeezed juice, freshly baked crusty brown bread, a perfectly poached egg sitting on buttery toast, or a couple of fat meaty sausages – or maybe a feathery, herby omelette dripping with cheese . . . Bliss.

Everyone else has left except for the elderly man, who's reading a paper over his coffee, tilting it in the direction of the wall-lights. And walking towards Lizzie is a woman her own age or thereabouts, with short blonde hair and perfect skin and a striped apron and an anxious smile.

'Hello. Dee tells me you're looking for a bed for the night.'

'Yes, she said you do B&B here.'

The woman pulls out a chair and sits opposite Lizzie. 'We do, yes, and normally you'd have no bother at this time of the year; but, would you believe, just this afternoon I got a call – I didn't get a chance to mention it to Dee. A group of Americans – they were in here a while ago; you probably saw them.' *The three couples.* 'They've taken all my rooms; I'm really sorry.'

'Oh, right.' Lizzie feels a jolt of disappointment – so much for her lucky break. But at least she can get directions to another B&B. 'Is there anywhere else I could try around here?'

The other woman shakes her head. 'I'm afraid we're the only ones in Merway, apart from the hotel, that are open all –' Then she stops and looks thoughtfully at Lizzie. She says, more slowly, 'Now, the only thing is, I have a – ah, no, you probably wouldn't be bothered; it'd be cold – but I could put the gas fire on . . . It's just that I don't like to see you stuck . . .' She trails off, looking uncertain.

What is Lizzie being offered? The roof garden? The shed out the back? A tent on the beach? Whatever it is, she knows she'll take it. The last thing she wants to do right now is get back into the cold car and head off in search of a bed. And Jones needs to come in; he's been sitting out in that car for nearly an hour.

She smiles at the woman sitting across from her. 'I'm really not that fussy; whatever you've got will be fine.' *As long as it's not a blanket on the floor under the stars – I've turned that one down already today.*

'I'll probably be moving on tomorrow, anyway.' *And I have a rather large cat waiting for a roof over his head.*

The woman smiles back apologetically. 'Sorry – you must be wondering what on earth I'm talking about. It's actually a little caravan, out the back.' She screws up her face in embarrassment. 'We don't use it much, but it's quite sound and easy to heat – I just thought, if you didn't feel like driving all the way to Seapoint . . .'

Lizzie is intrigued – the last time she slept in a caravan was years ago, on one of the family summer holidays. They only did it a few times; the beds didn't suit Daddy's back. Could be a laugh; and she'll more than likely be moving on first thing in the morning, anyway. She nods at the other woman gratefully. 'I'm sure it'll be fine for the one night – thanks a lot. And my shepherd's pie was wonderful, by the way. I presume you're the cook.'

The woman relaxes and smiles back at her. 'Yes; cook, bottle-washer, landlady and caravan owner. Glad you enjoyed it; it's one of the favourites around here. The secret's in the garlic – I put it in everything.' She puts out her hand. 'My name's Angela, by the way.'

'Lizzie. Nice to meet you.'

Angela stands up. 'Give me about half an hour and I'll have the caravan lovely and warm for you.' She looks at the empty wine glass. 'Sit there by the fire, and I'll get Dee to bring you another glass of wine while you're waiting. Did she offer you dessert?'

'She did, and I turned her down; my New Year's resolution.' Lizzie grins. 'But I won't say no to another wine, thanks – it's lovely. Take your time, I'm in no hurry.'

No hurry at all. I've got all the time in the world; and Jones will survive another while – he's probably fast asleep. She sits back and smiles into the fire, and winks at the little wooden clown.

Forty minutes later she's standing in the middle of Angela's caravan, looking around. The gas fire is lit, and so are two green ceramic table-lamps with white shades. They throw a soft light on the little seating area with its rickety coffee table, the tiny kitchen with its doll-sized fridge and cooker and dinky sink, the built-in bookshelves – perfect for, say, a collection of cookbooks.

Angela leads her into the one bedroom, with its double bed and enormous duvet taking up most of the space. She lifts the duvet to reveal two hot-water bottles. 'You might want to wrap your nightie around them as soon as you unpack.' Then she opens the bathroom door and Lizzie sees – wonder of wonders – a tiny shower in the corner. She doubts that anyone would be able to turn around in there, but what the heck; showers are for getting clean in, not doing gymnastics.

As they walk back into the living-room area, Lizzie knows that it feels right; she can't for the life of her explain why. It's a tiny caravan, barely big enough for one, that just totally appeals to her. She has to stay here – at least for a few nights.

She turns to her new landlady. 'It's fine.' She pauses. 'Actually, I might want it for a little longer than just the one night – would that be OK? Two or three nights, maybe?'

Angela nods. 'Of course; but I'm only full inside for the next two nights – the Americans are moving on then, and I can move you into the house if you decide to stay longer.'

No; it's the quirkiness of the caravan that Lizzie wants. She thinks quickly. Could she be working on a novel? Getting over a divorce? She needs some good reason for wanting to be out here on her own – something that will have Angela nodding understandingly and saying, 'Of course, you just stay here as long as you like.'

And then she decides to just leave things alone. For all she knows, she might hate Merway when she goes exploring in the morning. It might be rough and dingy-looking and totally not what she's looking for. In the meantime, she has two nights to feel her way around the place; and if she loves it and still wants to stay, she can have another word with Angela. Surely they'll be able to come to some arrangement; it's not as if people will be queuing up for the caravan.

So she smiles and nods. 'It's a deal – I'll take it for two nights. Thanks so much.'

Angela waves her thanks away. 'The hot water comes on as you need it – you're hooked up to the house supply. Same with electricity, if you've anything you want to plug in.' She gestures towards the gas fire. 'Now, did I show you how to work this?'

Lizzie shakes her head. 'You didn't, but we have one at home exactly the same.' *And there, Angela, is where the similarity between this delightful little dwelling and the O'Grady homestead ends.*

Angela nods. 'Right, I'd better get back. See you in the morning for breakfast – just come on up to the house when you wake. Hope you sleep well.' And she's gone, pulling the door closed behind her.

Lizzie drops her bag onto the little coffee table and suddenly remembers Jones, out in the car. God, she forgot to mention him. She'll just have to hope Angela doesn't have a conniption in the morning. She finds her keys and heads for the car.

Jones is asleep in his carrier; he stirs when she hauls him out. 'Shhh – not a sound, now.' She's glad of the darkness as she crunches back over the gravel with her load. After depositing him on the floor of the living area, she heads back to the car to get the rest of her luggage.

When she's moved everything in and given Jones a saucer of cat food to settle him in, Lizzie walks back to the main street to find a callbox. If by any chance she does end up living in a caravan – her face breaks into a wide smile at the thought – she'll probably have to invest in her first ever mobile phone.

Pressing the familiar numbers, she can see Mammy and Daddy in the sitting room. The couch is directly facing the fire, but she can't remember them ever sitting anywhere except on the two armchairs on either side of it – Daddy on the left, Mammy on the right. Daddy will be reading the paper, or maybe watching a match or the news on telly. Mammy will be dipping into her little dish of pink and white marshmallows and doing a crossword, or reading her book, glasses slipping down her nose. Lizzie offered more than once to have them tightened for her. 'Ah, no, Lizzie, they're fine the way they are.' And that was that. Things were fine just the way they were. Life was fine the way it was. Why would you want to go packing in a good job and leaving a perfectly nice fiancé and heading off to the middle of nowhere? Where was the sense in that, Lizzie? Weren't you fine the way you were?

No, Mammy, I wasn't.

The phone rings four times.

'Hello?' *Good – it's Daddy.*

'Hi, Daddy, it's me.'

'Oh, that's good, Lizzie. We were a bit worried; it's getting late.'

It's twenty-five past eight, Daddy – hardly the middle of the night. 'Well, I've just landed now. It took me a while to get somewhere to stay, but I found a lovely place in the end – I'm delighted.'

'Whereabouts are you?'

I'm in Africa, Daddy. I just took the notion that I'd like a bit of sun, so I hopped on a plane. Hope you can hear me over the chimpanzees outside the window.

'I'm in Merway – you know, a few miles from Seapoint. I found a lovely B&B.' She leaves out the fact that it's a caravan; what they don't know won't keep them tossing and turning all night under the blankets. If Mammy knew Lizzie was seriously thinking of spending the foreseeable future in a tiny caravan in someone else's back garden, she'd be on Valium in the morning. 'I'll probably stay a little while here; it seems nice.'

'Ah yes, I know Merway – I've passed through it a few times; nice little place.' Before he retired, Daddy's job in insurance involved a fair bit of driving, drumming up business and investigating claims. 'Will I call your mother for a word?'

If you must. 'Do; thanks, Daddy.' She hopes to God she isn't going to get more of the why-won't-you-see-sense routine.

'Right so, love. Keep in touch. I'll get her now.' He puts down the receiver, and Lizzie looks out at the deserted street and waits. In a few seconds she hears the phone being picked up.

'That you, Lizzie?'

No, Mother; didn't Daddy tell you? It's the President of America. He wants to visit Ireland and he heard you've a spare room. Get the Mr Sheen out, quick, and don't forget to charge him well – he's loaded.

'Yes, Mammy. I'm fine. I was telling Daddy I got a lovely place to stay.'

'I heard him saying Merway; I can't say I know it.' Her voice is guarded.

Lizzie puts as much enthusiasm as she can into hers. 'It's lovely – quite small, right on the coast, near Seapoint.'

The geography of Merway doesn't seem to interest Mammy. 'I hope your bed is aired. Did you have dinner? Make sure you feed yourself right.'

As if there was the slightest danger of Lizzie ever going hungry. 'I had a gorgeous dinner – shepherd's pie. Nearly as nice as yours.' *Actually, twice as nice as yours, if the truth be told; I must tell you about garlic sometime. I also had two glasses of wine, and that I'll keep to myself. And I'm not sure about the bed being aired, but I might just keep that one quiet too.* 'Jones says hello – he was as good as gold in the car.'

Mammy isn't diverted. 'Make sure you keep warm, now; it's bitter tonight. Did you bring your woolly dressing-gown?'

'I did, yeah.' *But I clean forgot the thermal long johns, dammit.* 'Is everything OK there?' *Since I left ten hours ago.*

'We're fine. Daddy's knee is at him a bit tonight; I'd say it's the cold. We've a big fire lit.' She pauses. 'By the way, I met Tony in the street today.' *Here we go.* 'He was asking after you.'

I'm sure he was – after ignoring me the last time I met him. 'Look, Mammy, I have to go – there's someone waiting to make a call.' Mammy won't argue with good manners. 'I'll phone again in a few days. Look after yourselves. Bye, now; say bye to Daddy.'

Lizzie hangs up before Mammy can remember that they've no number for her, and walks quickly back up the street. Her forehead feels tight; she rubs it with her fingers, trying to stretch it out. She breathes deeply, drawing in the cold, salty air, and forces her pace to slow to a stroll.

That short phone call, just a few minutes, has brought it all back to her – the feeling of being suffocated, frustrated, with no way out. But there *was* a way out – thank God she finally found it.

When she arrives back at the restaurant, a Bord Fáilte sign that she missed earlier catches her eye. She smiles – Daddy would approve. As she turns in by the side of the building, she feels a surge of the same exhilaration that propelled her out of Rockford earlier. She's free; anything can happen.

And she's going to make sure that it does.

Chapter Six

After a Bran-Flake-free breakfast the next morning, Lizzie walks around her new surroundings and takes everything in: the rows of brightly coloured cottages on the outskirts, giving way to the parade of little shops and pubs – Dignam's looks interesting – on either side of the winding main street; the square, with its two banks and its ivy-covered library and Burke's, Merway's two-star hotel; the little triangular park behind the square, with its shrubbery and trees and wrought-iron benches and a bronze statue of a waltzing couple that, according to the plaque underneath it, was donated by a long-dead local sculptor.

The houses on the side streets are painted in more dramatic colours – deep pink, turquoise, egg-yolk yellow; the odd one is thatched, and some have hens clucking around the grounds. A creeper-covered stone wall hides the parish priest's dormer bungalow from the one-storey primary school, with its tarmacadam yard and basketball hoop in front. Merway's only supermarket stands between the tiny cinema that only opens at weekends and a yellow-painted chip shop.

Back on the main street, there's a fruit-and-veg shop called Ripe. The name over the door has been carved into a piece of wood and surrounded with beautifully fashioned strawberries, lemons and pineapples. The carving reminds Lizzie of the little clown on the mantelpiece in the restaurant – could they both be the work of the same person? She'll have to ask Angela.

In the stone church across the road, autumn-coloured stained-glass windows throw a mellow glow over the wooden seats. The post office is beside the church, and beyond that are the estate agent and the doctor and the hairdresser, and a whitewashed restaurant called The Kitchen, with a caravan round the back where Lizzie O'Grady, future master baker, now lives; then a final scattering of more red-roofed houses, the gardens getting bigger as they gradually peter out into the countryside.

Walking around this charming little place, Lizzie feels, more and more, that she could settle in Merway. She wanders into Dignam's pub around lunchtime and orders a glass of Guinness – *What would Mammy say?* – which she takes to a table at the bay window, not too far from the blazing fire.

The pub is quiet; there's just one other customer – a scruffy-looking young man sitting at the bar reading a paper, a half-finished pint in front of him. He glances over at her as she orders, then goes back to his paper.

There's a holiday air about the place – or is that just Lizzie remembering the childhood weeks by the sea? Maybe – but life does seem to move a little more slowly here. A man unloading boxes from a van outside the chemist's stops to chat to a passerby. Three women amble past the pub window, one holding an open bag of wine gums, looking as if they have all the time in the world. Even the businesspeople don't seem in a rush. Two men in suits are deep in conversation outside the library, which she can just make out from where she sits, and it doesn't look like they're talking shop – every so often they break into laughter. The butcher walks out of his shop and into the off-licence next door, still in his apron. Maybe he's getting *vin* for the *coq*. A man comes out of a bookshop carrying a large, flat, rectangular package; is it the elderly man from the restaurant last night – the one who was last to leave? Most of his face is hidden under a thick scarf, so Lizzie's not sure if it's him. He carries the package – a sketch pad? a picture? – a little way down the street and then turns left, towards the beach.

After the Guinness – she's decided to skip lunch and save her appetite for dinner – Lizzie wanders down the street, peering in windows. When she comes to the library she goes in, finds the cookery section and leafs through a couple of fairly new-looking books, wondering whether she'd get yeast to rise in the caravan. The library is deserted, except for a teenage boy with two rings in his left ear behind the desk, who gives her a brief smile as she walks in, then goes back to his computer.

She checks out the noticeboard, which looks like it hasn't been changed in quite a while. Some theatre group put on *Dancing at Lughnasa* in Seapoint's community hall last August. There was a table quiz in Doherty's pub in November, to raise money for cancer research. Irish dancing classes for 7–12 year olds, phone Carmel for details – no date on that one, but Lizzie is willing to bet that Carmel's pupils have well and truly mastered the hornpipe by now. A missing kitten called Doobie, friendly, black with white paws, reward offered; the notice looks like it was written by a child, or an adult who wasn't great at spelling. She hopes Doobie turned up.

She stands outside Furlong's Bakery and Delicatessen, sniffing. There's a faint baking smell, but nothing like the heady fragrance of just-baked bread and cakes that she wants to come wafting out of *her* bakery. She walks in; time for a bit of market research.

There are salads and cooked meats behind glass on one side, breads and cakes on the other; jars and tins and bottles stacked on shelves around the room; a couple of dishes of olives on top of the counter. No tables for people to sit at.

A dark-haired woman, fiftyish, stands behind the counter. She smiles at Lizzie. 'Hello. Can I help you?'

Lizzie looks at the meats and salads behind the glass. 'Yes – could I get some cooked ham, please? Three or four slices.' She needs something to keep the woman busy for a couple of minutes – and, between Jones and herself, the ham won't go to waste.

While it's being sliced, she glances over at the bakery section. The usual assortment of bread and cakes: pan loaves, cottages, brown sliced; éclairs, doughnuts, cream sponges. Nothing out of the ordinary. No cheese-and-onion bread, or pumpkin-oatmeal-nut loaf. No chocolate-and-poppyseed plait. No lime coconut layer cake.

Looking good so far.

The ham is sliced and wrapped in greaseproof paper. As Lizzie takes it, she nods towards the bakery section. 'Can I ask if you make the bread and cakes yourself?'

The woman looks surprised. 'God, no; we've no facilities here. We get them delivered from Fleming's – it's a big company just outside Seapoint.'

'Oh, right.' *So you might just be interested in taking a few locally produced loaves and cakes – if the local supplier ever gets her act together*. She smiles at the woman. 'Well, thanks a lot.'

Four slices of ham, and plenty of food for thought.

Chapter Seven

As Lizzie stands outside the caravan door in the cold morning air, a little black-and-white dog trots towards her, tail wagging. He's about the same size as Jones, a mix of sheepdog and something smaller.

'Hi there, Dumbledore; I'm still here. Have you come to tell me breakfast is ready?' She bends down and pats his head, and his tongue darts up to her fingers. 'I've got a pal for you to meet later.' Two nights in the caravan, and she still hasn't come clean about Jones. She'll have to confess this morning, and hope to God he'll be allowed to stay – and that he'll get on with Dumbledore.

Lizzie straightens up and looks towards the house. Whitewashed walls, like in front, and red windowsills; three windows on the first floor and one long one underneath, looking into the big kitchen where Angela serves breakfast.

She breathes in the salty air and glances around the garden. It could do with a bit of attention. Half a dozen overgrown shrubs down one side, a tangle of weeds pushing up in the narrow flowerbed, some bedraggled plants that she can't identify near the house . . . *Daddy would have a field day here.* The wooden tubs of snowdrops outside the back door are nice, though.

Her stomach rumbles. She imagines the breakfast Angela is about to dish up and starts towards the house. Dumbledore races past her and waits at the back door, tail wagging. 'I'm coming, I'm coming.'

The door opens just as she reaches it. Angela is holding a tea towel and wearing an apron that says 'Kiss the Cook'. Lizzie can smell bacon and coffee.

'Good morning, Lizzie. Down, Dumbledore.' She bends and scratches his head. 'He's spoilt rotten, aren't you?' Then she straightens up. 'I hope you slept OK – it was real cold again last night, wasn't it?'

Lizzie follows her in. 'I slept like a log; must be the sea air. And that duvet is fantastic – I was really cosy.' Mammy doesn't believe in duvets; far too light to have any heat in them. 'And I love that I can hear the sea from my bed.' When she woke, she pushed open the little window above her head and lay listening to the rattle of the waves on the pebbles till hunger forced her up.

Angela's kitchen has sunny deep-yellow walls, units painted in washed-out blue, a cream-coloured giant cooker and washing machine and dishwasher. It has a bare wooden floor, like the restaurant's; a big oval table sits on a yellow rug in the middle of the room, surrounded by mismatched kitchen chairs with cushions on them. Against the far wall is a dark-blue couch, turned slightly towards a worktop with a little portable TV sitting on it. The room is full of light from the big window looking out beyond the garden to the sea.

Something on the windowsill catches Lizzie's eye; she didn't spot it yesterday. 'Hey, that's like the clown in the restaurant.' It's a little wooden woman in a cook's hat and apron, holding a ladle in one hand and a saucepan in the other, and beaming.

Angela is nodding. 'Yeah, both made by Joe – our very talented woodcarver. If you hang around Merway a while you'll meet him; he has a shop down the street.' She gestures to the table. 'Grab a chair. No cereal, right?'

'Right.' No more bowls of anything in the morning for Lizzie. The table is set for just one. 'Have the Americans left already?' They'd all eaten together the morning before.

Angela puts a glass of juice in front of her, and Lizzie can see the remains of the grapefruit and orange halves on the worktop. 'Yeah, they're gone about half an hour – heading up to Donegal. We can move you in later, if you've decided to stay on.' Lizzie nods; she still hasn't asked if she can stay in the caravan. 'Here we go; mind the plate – it's hot.'

Two fat sausages, a rasher, a soft poached egg sitting on a chunky slice of toast, half a grilled tomato, and – Lizzie smiles – not a white pudding in sight. Yesterday the egg was scrambled, but otherwise it's the same.

'That looks gorgeous. Thanks, Angela.' She takes a sip of the juice; the tart, fruity taste fills her mouth. 'Don't mind me, if you've anything to do.'

Angela places a basket of thick brown toast on the table beside a plate of what look like freshly baked scones. 'Ah no, you're fine. Dee's still in bed, making the most of the holidays, so you're not last up.' She brings over a jug of coffee and fills Lizzie's cup. 'Shout if I've forgotten anything.' A bowl of brown sugar sits in front of Lizzie, and little dishes of blackcurrant jam and chunky marmalade.

Angela goes to the dishwasher and starts unloading it. 'Mornings are fairly quiet here, especially at this time of year. I just tip around for the day, really, till it's time to start the evening meals.'

Lizzie spears a chunk of sausage. 'You don't open for lunch?'

Angela shakes her head. 'Not in winter – just the evening meal, from about half five onwards. In summer I open for a couple of hours in the middle of the day for salads and sandwiches. Merway's on the tourist trail, so we can get quite busy at the height of the season.' She takes a stack of plates over to a press.

Lizzie pours milk into her coffee. 'You seem to have it well organised. It's still a lot of work for yourself and Dee, though – I presume she's still at school.'

Angela goes back to the dishwasher and starts taking out cups. 'Yeah, she's doing her Junior Cert this year; she gets the bus to the Comprehensive in Seapoint every morning. We manage between us in the winter, when it's just the dinners, but I take on a local woman in the summer. Dee – she's really Deirdre, I call her Dee – is fifteen next week; she needs a bit of freedom in the holidays, to be off with her pals.' She looks over at Lizzie. 'Are you all right for everything there?'

Lizzie nods. 'Fine, thanks.' She splits a scone and spreads it with butter, pushing away the guilt; she'll skip lunch again. 'Have you had the business long?' It's the first time she's been able to chat to Angela properly.

Angela pauses, hands full of cups. 'Let's see now, it'll be two years in March – I started it when my husband left me.'

She says it so bluntly, Lizzie immediately feels as if she's been prying. She puts down her fork. 'Sorry, I didn't mean –'

Angela starts to stack the cups in the press. 'Don't worry; there's no secret about it. He walked out one day, after telling me he'd been having an affair with a lassie down the road for six months and now they wanted to move away together. I let him go – what else could I do? – and a couple of months later I was serving up my first meal.'

She turns and faces Lizzie, and her expression is perfectly calm. 'We had this place already – we'd been running it together as a video shop, but it was always his baby, really.'

She comes over to the table, fills a cup from the coffee jug and sits across from Lizzie. 'So when he upped and moved, I sold the stock to the video shop in Seapoint and went back to doing what I knew best – cooking. I trained as a chef before we got married; I always loved rustling up a meal for a crowd. And there was no restaurant here – except in the hotel, and that one's not great. People had to go to Seapoint for a decent meal out.'

Lizzie is struck by her openness – no pussyfooting around. She's willing to bet that Angela doesn't set too much store by what other people think. Remembering Mammy's dread of upsetting the neighbours, Lizzie smiles.

Angela adds milk to her coffee and stirs it. 'My pals were great – I got loads of help with the decorating; everyone just pitched in. I went into a fair bit of debt for the new appliances' – she gestures round the kitchen, and then grins – 'but the bank manager is married to a cousin of mine, so he gave me a year before I had to start repaying. After I opened, everyone around here came in droves – they're good like that.'

Lizzie is looking across at her in wonder. 'Your marriage broke up, and you turned around, with a teenage daughter to look after, and started a business from scratch.' She tries not to compare their achievements – or lack of them, in her case; tries not to think about how little she's got to show.

Angela shrugs, looking down into her coffee. 'Yeah, I suppose it was some achievement, all right. We had the mother of all hooleys on the opening night – dinner on the house for all the helpers, and my parents arrived with a few bottles of champagne. Dee was roped in as my kitchen skivvy – but she didn't mind; she's great. My mother moved in here for the first month, as well, to get things up and running. Poor old Dad was left to his own devices.'

She picks up her cup and sips. 'Mind you, it was bloody hard work; I might be making it sound easy now, but let me tell you, I cried myself to sleep many a night – I was sure that I was taking on too much, that I hadn't a hope in hell of making it work . . .'

She puts her head to one side. 'You know, I'm not sure what kept me going, really. Maybe I felt I had something to prove – I know I was determined that I wouldn't let John ruin me. And, of course, I had to keep going for Dee.'

She smiles again, looking off into the distance. 'I know I could have found a dozen easier ways to make ends meet; but my mother always told me I was a stubborn little thing, and she was right. I got it into my head that I'd open a restaurant, and by God I was determined. Nothing was going to stop me.'

Lizzie opens her mouth to speak, then closes it again, not sure what she wants to say. Then she opens it again: she'll say what's on her mind. It's high time she started doing that.

'I wish I had your determination. I've been dreaming about a career in baking since I left school over twenty years ago.'

Angela looks back at her, intrigued. 'Have you really? Did you ever try and get a job in a bakery?'

Lizzie shrugs, beginning to be sorry she brought it up. 'I made a half-hearted attempt, and when that got me nowhere, I gave up. I got a summer job in a restaurant the year I left school, and . . . I just stayed on there.'

Angela is silent for a second. Then she says slowly, 'You had a summer job for twenty years?'

Lizzie nods. 'And for eleven of them I was engaged to someone I didn't love.' The words pop out of nowhere. As she hears them, she feels something bubbling up inside her; a giggle escapes.

She looks over at Angela and sees her trying desperately to control a twitch in one corner of her mouth. Their eyes meet and they both burst out laughing. As the full absurdity of Lizzie's confession sinks in, they roar and guffaw and slap the table in merriment.

After a minute, Angela gasps, 'Dear God – you'd get into the – Guinness Book of Records – no problem; I must see if – they're in the phone book.'

Lizzie is off again, holding her sides and trying to breathe. 'Stop – I'm going to rupture something . . .' She tries to control the laughter, but it keeps bubbling up and flowing out of her – and, with it, all the loneliness and frustration of the past. She feels like she's sliding out of something heavy and clammy and skipping away, lighter and happier.

Finally Angela wipes her eyes with her sleeve. 'God, I needed that. I haven't had a good laugh in ages.' She looks over at Lizzie, who's still giggling quietly. 'Did your poor fiancé have any idea you wanted to be a baker?'

Lizzie nods, feeling the laughter ebb out of her as she hears Tony telling her that it was one thing being able to bake, and quite another knowing how to run a business. Angela would have shoved his patronising opinions down his throat; why the heck hadn't *she*?

She picks up her coffee cup. 'He wasn't very supportive. Wanted to keep me as a waitress – it was his family restaurant I worked in.'

'Ah, it's all becoming clear.' Angela nods. 'So you're making a fresh start now, like I did.'

'God, yeah . . . I suppose I am doing the same thing you did.' It hadn't occurred to Lizzie how similar their situations were. Each of them had come to a point in her life where radical change was called for – even if they'd come to that point from very different positions. And if Angela could turn *her* life around, with a young daughter to cope with too . . .

Lizzie thinks about Deirdre, having her whole life changed at a time when she'd have been pretty fragile, just starting into her teens. 'Deirdre must have found it tough, when your husband left.'

Angela nods. 'Yeah, she was very upset at the time; but I have to say that John's been pretty good about keeping in contact with her. They're always on the phone – he got her a mobile soon after he moved out, probably so he wouldn't have to talk to me when he rang her – and every few weeks he comes and takes her out to Seapoint for the day and spoils her rotten. She's coped very well with the break-up, poor old thing. And she's a great help to me – I'd never manage without her.'

She glances up at the clock on the wall and stands. 'Right, enough of all this chit-chat. I'll go up now and change those sheets, and you can get started on your packing after your breakfast.'

Lizzie takes a deep breath: now or never. 'Actually, Angela –' How to put this without sounding like a lunatic '– I know it might seem a bit strange, but – well, the caravan is the first place I've had all to myself – and I really don't find it a bit cramped; and it's not cold at all – the gas fire is brilliant – and I'm sleeping like a log out there, honest . . .' She's babbling; *Get to the point.* 'So I'd really like to stay out there instead of coming in here, if that would be OK.'

Then she stops and waits. *Please say yes. Please say yes.*

Angela turns with her hand on the doorknob and stares back at Lizzie. 'Are you telling me that you'd rather live in a teeny little caravan by yourself, in the middle of winter, than in a nice warm house with a charming woman and her equally charming daughter?'

But she's smiling. Lizzie takes heart from that and plunges on. 'Well, when you put it that way . . . But, Angela, honest to God, I love the little caravan. It's like my very first flat, where I can come and go as I please, and not be answerable to anyone, and not have to be in at six for dinner every evening, and not have to explain why I'll be gone all afternoon tomorrow . . .' Babbling again; *Shut up, Lizzie*.

'Well, I suppose if you'd really like to try it . . .' Angela looks highly amused, and with a surge of relief Lizzie realises that she's going to agree.

She beams. 'Oh, great – thanks a million. You can work out a weekly rate – whatever you think is fair; and if you'd prefer me to eat in the restaurant, rather than in the caravan, that's fine.' She had the vegetarian lasagne yesterday evening, and wasn't disappointed – but it might be nice to do her own thing sometimes, too.

Angela shakes her head, still amused. 'Actually, I don't mind a bit where you eat – good luck trying to produce anything fancy on that teensy cooker, though. No, you suit yourself – we can make it totally self-catering, if that's what you want. It might have to be a casual arrangement, though, if you know what I mean; I'm not sure the Bord Fáilte people would understand.'

'Fine.' Lizzie nods, delighted. If Angela told her she'd have to have her breakfast up a tree with Jones, she'd agree.

Jones. Oh, God, she'd better come clean about Jones.

She stands and picks up her empty plate and cup. 'There's one other thing.' *God, I hope this doesn't scupper all my plans.*

'Stop.' Angela grins and puts her hands over her ears. 'I don't think I can take any more surprises this morning.'

Lizzie smiles apologetically. 'It's just that I have a cat. He's in the caravan right now. I meant to tell you the first night, but I forgot . . . He's house-trained, though, and no trouble really; I have a litter tray . . .' She trails off, waiting nervously.

To her dismay, a horrified expression appears on Angela's face. 'A cat? Oh, no – sorry, Lizzie.' She shakes her head firmly. 'Absolutely no way; I'm highly allergic. You'll have to get rid of it, or leave, straight-away. Sorry, out of the question.'

Lizzie can't believe it. Just when she thought she'd found a home she could be happy in, it's about to be snatched away. Serve her right for not confessing the first night. Her heart sinks, but she nods. 'Right – sorry . . . I'll go and –'

'Lizzie.'

She looks back.

'Just kidding.' Angela's grinning widely. 'Actually, Dee loves cats; she'll be thrilled. I'll send her down to

93

you when she gets up, to check him out. Mind you, I'm not so sure how Dumbledore feels about them, but we'll get around him.'

Lizzie feels a surge of relief. She smiles back at Angela. 'Phew – thanks again. And I promise I've nothing else hidden up my sleeve; that's it.' She puts her crockery into the dishwasher.

Angela opens the door into the hall. 'Right, then; see you later. You can decide yourself whether you want to eat in the restaurant, or' – she smirks – 'in your caravan. And we'll sort out the money side later, too; I'll do a few sums.'

She goes out the door, leaving Lizzie standing in the kitchen pinching herself.

Two days since she left Kilmorris, and already she's found a place for herself and Jones to live. What's more, she's by the sea, just like she wanted. And Angela seems lovely.

Not bad for a start. She crunches happily over the gravel back to her caravan.

Chapter Eight

The days pass; Lizzie fills them with wrapped-up walks along the beach, and her book and her crosswords, and dipping into the shops, and driving into Seapoint to the pictures, and planning her meals, and writing the odd letter home, and being hauled into the kitchen now and again for coffee and a chat with Angela.

She's starting to meet people. The elderly man who was eating alone in the restaurant on her first night turns out to be an artist; she sees him every time she walks along the beach. He stands before a rickety-looking easel on the lawn of a house just up from the pebbles, and he waves whenever Lizzie passes. She's dying to have a look at what he's doing, but she's shy about approaching him. Maybe she'll meet him in the supermarket and get chatting. She wonders if he ever paints anything but the sea.

She asks Angela about him. 'Oh, that's Dominic – wasn't he here the night you arrived? He's a regular, comes in for his dinner about once a week. Lives by himself – I don't think he was ever married – in that gorgeous little stone house that's practically on the beach. You must have passed it in your wanderings – it's on the road down from the square, on its own, dark-blue door. I've got two of his paintings in the restaurant, actually; you might have noticed them. He always paints the sea – says it's different every time he looks at it.'

Angela says that Dominic's work is on display in a few galleries and craft shops around the county, and until a few years ago he sold mainly to tourists over the summer months. 'Then one day – I suppose it'd be about five or six years ago now – he got a call from some gallery owner in the States, whose sister or wife or something had bought one of Dominic's paintings when she was over here on holidays. They made some deal together, and now a lot of Dominic's stuff goes straight over there. I'd say he's not short of a few bob, and I'm very glad we bought our two when we did – they'd probably cost a bomb now.'

Lizzie goes into the restaurant the next day to look at the paintings. She's struck by the way he's captured the power of the Atlantic – looking at the turquoises and greens and blue-whites and greys colliding on the canvas, she can almost feel the spray. She can understand how someone from a desert-y place like Arizona might be drawn to paintings like these. They'd hang them on white walls in hot dry rooms, and look at them and hear the rush of the waves and smell the salt.

She looks at the little clown on the mantelpiece again. There seem to be quite a few talented folk in Merway. Maybe it's catching – she might be composing symphonies before the year is out.

When Lizzie drops into Merway's only laundrette with her bundle of washing, she gets to know Rory and Aisling, the owners. Aisling tells Lizzie one day that, given the choice, Rory would much rather be out fishing than handing out change at the laundrette or looking after their two small children. 'I suppose I'm what's known as a fishing widow – he's never here when I want him. Although he does bring home the dinner most times, so I forgive him.'

Rory grins and confesses that it's all true. 'Any time you fancy getting up at half past four and joining me, Lizzie, you're welcome. I'll make sure you bring Angela home a few mackerel.' Lizzie laughs and tells him not to hold his breath.

She's tasted some of Rory's catches. Angela buys anything he doesn't keep for himself, and adds it to that evening's menu as a special. Her fisherman's pie is in big demand when it appears, brimming with chunks of fish and vegetables and hard-boiled eggs, and smothered in a rich creamy sauce topped with bubbling melted cheese. Mammy rarely cooks fish – Daddy isn't gone on it – and when she does, it's steamed and served with soft cauliflower, or mashed carrots and parsnips, and no sauce. No wonder Daddy isn't too keen. Lizzie is willing to bet that he'd go mad for a big helping of fisherman's pie.

She's started to experiment with food Mammy never heard of – bean sprouts, pine nuts, fresh ginger, water chestnuts. She tosses them all with strips of beef or chicken in a wok she picked up in Seapoint, and adds a few chunks of pineapple to liven things up. (She tries to imagine Mammy putting pineapple into anything except a bowl of custard, and fails.) When she's sick of stir-fries she bakes a spud in the teeny oven and fills it with whatever takes her fancy – sour cream with a few of Angela's chives, fried onions and grated cheddar, a spoonful of prawns, a dollop of baked beans. Or she beats up a couple of eggs, adds a bit of chopped ham and onion and tomato and mushrooms, and fries it. She loves the haphazardness of it all; there's no routine, no set time to eat, no special dishes for certain days. Mammy would have a canary.

She can't believe all the foods she's never tasted before – avocados, salsa, mangetout, feta cheese, sun-dried tomatoes, mango chutney and black bean sauce, capers and pilchards and monkfish. And whenever she uses herbs, they're fresh; Angela is adamant about that. 'Don't let me catch you with any of that dried rubbish.' She gives Lizzie two little pots, one of basil, one of mint. 'To get you going; you can start your own off later.'

And every night, in a small act of rebellion, Lizzie has a glass or two of wine with her dinner.

Another local she's come across on her travels is Maggie Delaney, the middle-aged widow who owns Blooming Miracles, Merway's small but well-stocked garden centre. Maggie is barely five feet tall but for some reason everyone around Merway calls her Big Maggie.

Angela has told Lizzie that Tom Delaney, eight years older than Maggie, dropped dead of a massive heart attack three years to the day after walking her down the aisle. 'They were having dinner in the hotel to celebrate their anniversary, and Tom was dead before they got to the main course; just dropped like a stone into his soup, the creature.' He was thirty-nine; Maggie never remarried.

Lizzie often goes into Blooming Miracles; she loves fresh flowers, and keeps the caravan well stocked. She adores the moist, scented air that rushes to meet her as soon as she opens the door and steps down into the shop, past the pot plants and seed-packets and buckets of whatever flowers are on sale. She watches Maggie's hands wrapping her selection in pale-blue tissue paper.

'You must love being in this atmosphere, Maggie, surrounded by gorgeous scents all day.'

Big Maggie looks up from the flowers. 'Oh, indeed I do, Lizzie; I couldn't live without my greenery. I'd just curl up and die if I was hemmed in by brick walls and nothing growing.'

Angela has warned Lizzie not to be too chatty in Blooming Miracles. 'If you think I'm a gossip, you ain't heard nothing yet. Anything you say to Maggie will be all over Merway in the morning, you can be sure. Just watch what you tell her.'

So Lizzie answers all Maggie's questions cautiously – she's not sure how long she'll be around, really; no, it was nothing major that made her move here, just looking for a change; no, she didn't know anyone here before she came; yes, the B&B is very cosy altogether, lovely. Yes, she'll probably look around for a job if she decides to stay.

She doesn't mention the caravan to Big Maggie, although she doesn't imagine that it'll stay a secret for long in Merway. Someone is bound to see her coming and going from it at some stage.

She meets Nuala and Ríodhna, the farming sisters who deliver their organic produce to Angela and to Ripe, the fruit-and-veg shop with the gorgeous carving over the door. They always have time for a few words as they unload their deliveries.

'Where did you get that lovely scarf, Lizzie? . . . Ah no, don't tell me that came from a charity shop, I can't believe it; you have such an eye for these things . . . Ríodhna, look at Lizzie's scarf – isn't it just like the one you were raving about in that place in Seapoint the other day? You won't believe what Lizzie paid for it. Go on, guess – you won't believe it. You'll be sick when you hear.'

On the Tuesday of her second week in Merway, Lizzie opens the door of Ripe. A man comes out from the back and smiles at her. 'Hello.'

'Hi – I'm looking for lemons.' She's decided to go for it and try making a lemon tart in the caravan. Might as well see what that oven is capable of. Mind you, if she's planning to bake for a living she'll need one a lot bigger. She might have to have a little word with Angela about using her kitchen when it's free. It's either that or move somewhere else; and the longer she lives in the caravan, the more she loves it. Surely they'll be able to come to some arrangement – Angela is so easy-going about everything else.

'Lemons – just over there.' His eyes are very blue; vivid, you'd call them. Nice smile, too. There's no one else in the shop, and Lizzie feels she should say something as she puts a few lemons into a bag.

She thinks of the name over the door; that'll do. 'I love the sign outside, by the way – the carving is fantastic.'

He looks over at her, eyebrows raised. 'You have good taste. That was made by a very skilled craftsman. Lives near here, in fact.'

She nods. 'Yes, I've seen more of his work – a little clown, and a cook; at least, I'm assuming they were all done by the same person.'

He looks thoughtfully at her. 'A clown and a cook – now where would they be?' Then his face clears. 'Ah, you mean the ones in Angela's house.'

101

'Yes.' She's surprised; how could he have known about the cook? The clown, maybe – it's in the restaurant for all to see; but the other one is in the kitchen, where no one goes except the overnight guests. And, presumably, friends of Angela's.

She glances at him again. He's a good-looking man, a bit older than her; early fifties, she'd say. Dark hair, almost black, cut very short; jeans and a faded green shirt. No wedding ring. Maybe he has breakfast in Angela's kitchen now and again . . .

Lizzie remembers something. 'He has a shop around here, hasn't he? The woodcarver, I mean.'

He pauses, her change in his hand. 'Well, yes and no . . . Tell you what, keep an eye out as you walk around the shops – you'll find a few surprises in the windows.' Then he hands her her change. 'Thanks; see you again. You're staying at Angela's, I believe.'

She looks at him in surprise again, and he grins. 'Maggie was talking.'

She walks out, bemused. So this is what living in a village is like. And what did he mean, 'Yes and no,' when she asked him about the woodworker having a shop? Either he has or he hasn't. And what was all that about surprises in the shop windows?

As she leaves Ripe, she comes face to face with the scruffy young man who was in the pub at lunchtime the other day. She holds the door open for him and he walks through without thanks, leaving a smell of stale cigarettes behind him. Charming.

102

It doesn't take her long to find the surprises. In the corner of practically every shop window is a little carving: a Cinderella slipper in the shoe shop, a chubby piglet in the butcher's, a pair of scissors in the hairdresser's, a bunch of grapes in the off-licence. They're small enough to miss unless you're looking for them, but each one is carved with the same delicacy and talent as the clown and the cook.

Lizzie feels curious about this woodcarver leaving his mark all over the place. She wonders when she'll finally get to see him, and where his shop is hiding.

Not everyone in Merway is friendly. Occasionally Lizzie comes across a bored shop assistant who barely looks at her – and Angela has told her to watch out for Gráinne in the newsagent's. 'Odd as two left feet – a cousin or something of Brian, who owns it. But she'd pick a fight with Nelson Mandela if he had the misfortune to wander in – give out to him for divorcing Winnie or something. My advice: grab your paper and don't hang around, or she'll find something to moan about.'

On the whole, though, Lizzie decides that she's made a good choice in Merway. It isn't really too small, even if word does travel fast. She likes the idea of being a stone's throw from everything. The pebbly beach at the bottom of the garden – fourteen paces from the caravan door – is a huge bonus. And she's only seven or eight miles from Seapoint, which is almost as big as Kilmorris.

After just a couple of weeks here, she's getting to know people and settling in. The caravan is just grand, plenty big enough for her and Jones, and cosy with the gas fire on. The picture on her telly is a bit snowy – Angela says it's probably because she's so near the sea – but she doesn't watch it half as much as she did at home, anyway. Angela and Deirdre are lovely to have around. And, after a shaky start, Dumbledore and Jones are slowly learning to tolerate each other.

On Sunday evening, the end of her second week in Merway, Lizzie decides that she's settled in enough to move on with her plan. She knocks on the kitchen door; the restaurant is closed on Sundays, so hopefully Angela won't be busy. She needs someone to run her ideas by.

'Come in.' Angela is sitting at the table, a cookbook propped open in front of her. She's wearing glasses that Lizzie hasn't seen before. 'Hi there; plug in the kettle, would you? I'm just planning the dinners for next week.'

Angela is a comfort-food fanatic. She's told Lizzie that she tries to create meals that make people happy. 'I don't mean eating as a substitute for love, or any nonsense like that; but when you have a meal that you really enjoy, it should leave a sort of glow behind. That's always my aim when I cook, especially with this winter menu – all creamy and slobbery.'

Now Lizzie looks over her shoulder, and Angela points at a recipe for a mushroom stroganoff. 'This'll be my veggie one, I think. It's so creamy and yummy, and it's served with rice, which means that one of my other dishes will probably be a curry.'

'Mmm.' Lizzie's mouth waters at the thought of a spicy beef curry; Mammy was deeply suspicious of anything foreign. 'I'll have to come up and sample those.' She goes over to the singing kettle and scalds the teapot. 'Angela, I want your advice.'

'Hmmm?' Angela is thumbing through another book, flicking the pages rapidly. 'Curry, curry . . . What's on your mind?'

Lizzie fills the pot and brings it over to the table, then gets two cups and the milk. She sits opposite Angela and puts her hands in front of her on the table. 'I'm going to start looking for a job.'

Angela looks up from her book and peers over her glasses at Lizzie. 'Good. What kind of a job?'

'Well, remember I said I'd love to be a baker? I thought I'd start with – Furlong's, is it? the bakery here in Merway – and ask them if they need any help; and if they don't, which they probably won't, I could go into Seapoint. What do you think?'

Angela takes off her glasses and closes the book. 'Hold on a minute. You're serious about baking for a living?'

Lizzie looks at her in surprise; she thought she made that clear the other day. 'Yes, dead serious. It's what I've always wanted.'

'And you're going to look for a job here in Merway.'

'Well, I thought I'd start here, yeah.' Is Angela giving her a funny look?

'In Furlong's.'

'Yes . . .' Something is definitely up. Angela is staring across the table at her so intently that Lizzie feels uncomfortable.

Then Angela picks up the teapot and pours. 'Tell me this. Are you any good at baking? Honestly now.'

It's so unexpected that Lizzie nearly laughs. She turns her palms up and makes an embarrassed face. 'Well, I think I'm quite good . . . Everyone seems to like what I bake, and I've been at it for years, since I was eight or nine. I've made Christmas cakes forever, and I've tried loads of different breads, and umpteen kinds of pastry –'

Angela picks up the milk and adds a drop to her tea. 'Well, you can forget about going to Furlong's.'

Lizzie nods; at least Angela is starting to make sense. 'Right; I didn't really think they'd have work, in such a small place –'

'No; I mean, forget about trying to get a baking job anywhere around here, Lizzie.' Angela looks calmly across the table at her.

Lizzie feels her heart plummet to her boots. 'What are you saying? You don't think there's anywhere around here that could take me on?' She doesn't think she can bear to see her dream disappear for the second time. 'Not even in Seapoint? The woman in Furlong's told me –'

'Oh, no, I'm not saying that at all.' A tiny smile is starting at the corner of Angela's mouth. 'In fact, I know exactly where you can get a job – starting tomorrow, if you like.'

'What?' Lizzie's jaw drops a mile; her heart does another lurch. 'Angela, you're not making sense. Tell me quickly what you mean; you've me totally addled.'

The smile blooms on Angela's face. 'Right here, you goose. In this very restaurant. You've just been inter-viewed, and you've passed – subject to your stuff being edible, of course.'

'What?' Still Lizzie is bewildered. 'But you're a great baker – your scones in the morning, and all those desserts you serve up –'

Angela sighs. 'Time to come clean.' She looks over at Lizzie. 'I can't bake to save my life. Honest to God.'

Lizzie shakes her head, smiling. 'Angela, that's so not true, and you know it – don't you feed half of Merway every night?'

'I do, yes.' Angela nods in agreement. 'I give them a good home-cooked dinner, not too dear. And then I offer them apple tart that's made with frozen pastry, or lemon meringue pie that comes out of a packet. I buy the meringue cases for the baked Alaska. Lucy Furlong supplies any cakes I need. And look – you may as well know the whole awful truth . . .' She gets up and goes to one of the presses. 'Those lovely breakfast scones?' She holds up a packet of scone mix. 'Mr Odlum helps me out there.'

She comes back to the table and sits down. 'Think, Lizzie – have you seen me produce a cake out of that oven since you arrived? Or have you eaten a slice of bread in this kitchen that wasn't wrapped in waxed paper?' She shrugs. 'No matter what I do, my bread weighs a ton. My madeira cake takes one look at me and sinks. I have never in my life got dough to rise.' She grins across at Lizzie. 'I'm a disaster when it comes to baking – it was the one thing I failed miserably at when I was training to be a chef.'

Lizzie remembers wishing for a hunk of bread to mop up the shepherd's-pie sauce on her first night in Merway. And she'd given up desserts, so she couldn't judge them. 'Well, now that you mention it –'

Angela spreads her hands out, palms up. 'See? And then you come along, and you can bake, and you want to feck off to Furlong's. There's gratitude to me for putting a roof over your head.'

Lizzie smiles. 'And do you mean it about me working here with you?'

'Do I what? I can cook, and you can bake.' She lifts her cup. 'Are we a match made in heaven, or what?'

Lizzie can't believe it. A baking job, right under her nose. Working with Angela. Here in this kitchen, two seconds from where she lives.

'Well – what do you say?' Angela is waiting.

Lizzie picks up her cup and clinks it against Angela's. 'I say you've got yourself a baker.'

Chapter Nine

And so it begins.

Lizzie joins Angela in the kitchen every afternoon and chooses three different loaves of bread from her many recipes – cheese and black pepper, garlic and herb, sun-dried tomato, lemon poppyseed, pumpkin, rye, potato. Sometimes she makes rolls for a change – sesame seed, olive, five grain, ciabatta – or breadsticks, or savoury scones.

While the yeast is rising she makes three desserts, which she changes every week. She and Angela sit down every Sunday night and choose the three for the following week. It can take quite a while.

'Ooh, sticky toffee pudding – yes, please.'

'That's very heavy with your main courses; aren't you doing a carbonara next week? And the goulash is very rich too. What about this one, razzleberry crisp? It's full of fruit, and really light. Or a mousse – I've a lovely brandy-and-ginger recipe.'

'OK – but I want the sticky toffee pudding next week, or you're evicted. And that orange-and-carrot cake, too, or I start charging Jones rent.'

'Yes, boss.' There's no doubt about it: Lizzie has died and gone to heaven.

She can't believe that two restaurants can be so different. The cosiness of The Kitchen, with its roaring fire and candles and mellow wooden floor; the simple, delicious meals that Angela changes every week; the friendliness of the customers, who often chat away to one another across the room and who don't mind waiting twenty minutes for their herby chicken with fragrant rice; the soft jazz of Ella Fitzgerald or Nina Simone in the background . . . It's all light years away from the dreariness of O'Gorman's, with its patterned carpet and people who sit silently at tables with plastic flowers in china vases while they chew the same old food, day in, day out, listening to someone they know playing a request for Aunty Pauline who's just had a hysterectomy.

At night Lizzie lies in her big double bed under her feathery duvet and listens to the sea fourteen steps away, and tells God that she's very, very grateful. And she wonders if there's any chance that Tony could meet some nice girl who loves being engaged, and who isn't too pushed about getting married. And she knows she's asking a lot, but maybe Daddy's bad leg could be sorted out too – it's been at him for ages.

And if there's the smallest possibility of her meeting someone nice who likes fresh-baked bread and fat ginger cats, she'd be even more grateful.

'Lizzie, if you had to think up a business name, what would it be?' She and Angela are in the kitchen one afternoon, just starting on the preparations for that evening's meal.

Lizzie considers. 'For my baking, you mean? If I had my own range of products?'

'Yeah.'

'Well, let's see . . . what about Daily Bread?'

'God, no – too religious; it would put all the atheists off.' Angela looks at the ceiling. 'Sorry, God, but I have to be honest; you can understand that.'

Lizzie grins at her. 'OK, then, what about Pat-a-Cakes?'

'Absolutely not – too babyish. They'd think all you made was fairy cakes and Rice Krispie cookies.'

'Right then . . . Mrs Bun the Baker?'

'Nah, sounds a bit housewifey. And you're not, anyway, are you? You're Ms Bun; and that just doesn't have the same ring.'

Lizzie laughs. 'God, you're hard to please – and I'm running out of ideas . . . What about Bun in the Oven?'

Angela doesn't even bother to look up from the chopping board. 'I'll pretend I didn't hear that.' Then she stops and points half a carrot at Lizzie. 'Maybe you could go into partnership with Big Maggie and be Baking Miracles.'

Lizzie giggles. 'Or Blooming Bakery.'

'Or what about Lizzie's Loaves? Hey, that's not bad.' Angela chops carrots thoughtfully.

Lizzie grins as she kneads the dough for that evening's caraway-and-rye bread. 'But that sounds as if I only do bread, when we all know that I can bake just about anything – apart from the lemon tart I attempted in the caravan a while back. I told you about that, didn't I?'

It turned out flat and soggy – clearly the miniscule cooker hadn't been designed with a delicate touch. Such a waste of those lovely lemons. 'Hey, that reminds me – the guy who owns the fruit-and-veg shop down the street . . .'

'Joe? What about him?'

'What's he like?' She remembers the gorgeous blue eyes, and the very pleasant smile. And the fact that he knew exactly where Angela's wood carvings were. *Let's see if she gets embarrassed.*

Angela picks up a potato and starts to peel it, not looking in the least embarrassed. 'Joe? He's a pet. He's the one who made Deirdre's clown, and my cook – very talented.'

Lizzie shakes her head. 'No, not the woodcarver, the fruit-and-veg man.'

Angela peels on, nodding. 'Yeah; they're one and the same.'

'What? *He's* the one who made them? But hang on, he sells fruit and veg – and you said the woodcarver has his own shop.' This isn't making sense.

Angela turns, amused at Lizzie's confusion. 'Yes, he has, but he doesn't sell carvings in it – he sells fruit and veg. He just carves the wood in his spare time.'

'I see.' Or does she? Lizzie brushes the hair out of her eyes with a floury hand. What did he say, when she admired the sign outside the shop? Something about it being made by a master craftsman who lived in the area . . . but that was himself he was talking about. So he was just being funny.

And of course he knew where the wooden cook was, if he made it. And Lizzie remembers asking him if the woodcarver had a shop, and he said something like 'He does and he doesn't' – and sent her around looking into the shop windows for surprises. And not a hint of a smile on his face.

He seems like a bit of a joker. She smiles down at the dough and begins to pound it again. 'So the clown belongs to Deirdre.'

Angela nods. 'Yeah, he made it for her when John left – I thought it was really sweet of him. She put it in the restaurant so everyone could see it.'

Lizzie wonders again if there's anything going on between Angela and Joe. She's as good as single now, and he . . . 'Is he married?' She remembers noticing no ring.

'No.' Angela shakes her head. 'Though not for the want of trying by half the eligible females of Merway. He's had his moments, like the rest of us, but no one's managed to drag him up the aisle yet. As far as I know he's unattached at the moment.'

She puts the peeled potatoes into a saucepan and narrows her eyes at Lizzie. 'Why all the questions about our Joe, young lady? Are you keen?'

Lizzie laughs and squashes the dough into the baking tin. 'Actually, I was wondering if *you* two had anything going on – you know, the cook, the clown . . .'

Angela shakes her head, smiling. 'No, we're great pals but that's as far as it goes. I didn't know him all that well growing up – he's about ten years older than me. It's only really since John left and I started my own business that we've got friendly. He was a great help at the start – sold me veg for next to nothing till I got set up with Nuala and Ríodhna. And you needn't read anything into the carvings; Joe carves for everyone – practically every shop in town has a piece in the window.'

'I know – I saw them. In fact, he was the one who told me about them – without telling me they were his. And when I admired the sign over his door he told me about the master craftsman who'd made it.'

Angela laughs. 'Typical Joe; the man has a wicked sense of humour – just comes out of nowhere and surprises you.' She looks at Lizzie, and her smile fades. 'You haven't come across Charlie, have you?'

Lizzie thinks of the men she's met in Merway; the name doesn't ring a bell. 'Don't think so. Who's he?'

'Joe's nephew from London; arrived out of the blue a few months back and just moved in.' Angela makes a face. 'He hasn't exactly endeared himself to the folk around here – spends his time in the pub, or swanning around the place in Joe's car. I don't know why Joe doesn't just tell him to get lost; he's not exactly a help to him – I've never seen him working in the shop, and he's probably eating Joe out of house and home. And I'd bet anything he's not paying a cent towards his keep.'

Lizzie remembers the young man she passed when she was leaving Ripe, the same one who'd been in Dignam's. 'Is he mid-twenties, longish brown hair, thin face?'

Angela nods. 'That's him – shifty-looking.' She covers the potatoes and glances at the clock. 'God, we'd better get a move on.'

Later that evening, on her way back to the caravan for the night, Lizzie pauses with her hand on the door handle. Then she walks on to the bottom of the garden. She stands by the rickety old wooden fence that Angela keeps threatening to replace.

On a clear, frosty night like this, she can see a million stars and one moon, or a bit of a moon. She breathes in the pure, salty air and gazes up, wrapping her arms tightly around herself. The waves rattle the pebbles, pulling them out to sea. The stars are amazing. She loves how visible the night sky is, here in Angela's back garden. The bit of a poem that she always thinks of when she looks at the stars is rattling around in her head:

Looking up at the stars,
I know quite well
That for all they care
I can go to hell.

She loves those lines – the way they turn around and surprise you at the end; she's always loved surprises. Tony was never much of a one for them, though – always so predictable, with his vouchers and chocolates . . .

And now she's living in a place that has a surprise in every shop window.

She turns back and walks towards the caravan.

Chapter Ten

Lizzie can't believe she's been three months in Merway, but there it is in black and white. Tomorrow morning she'll be tearing March off the calendar and crumpling it into the bin. April already; imagine.

She goes out to make her weekly phone call home. For once Mammy has real news for her.

'I was talking to Julia today.' Pause. Lizzie's heart sinks – Mammy is slowly coming round to the fact that Lizzie has made the break, but still . . . 'Tony has a new girlfriend: Pauline Twomey. I think you knew her sister in school – Maeve, was it?'

Pauline Twomey; three years younger than Lizzie – and about three stone lighter. Hardly anything there to put his arms around. Hasn't taken him long to get over Lizzie.

But she's happy for him – she really is.

'Lizzie, are you there?'

No, Mother, I've gone off to slit my wrists. 'Yes, I'm still here. That's good news about Tony; I hope he's happy. How's Daddy's leg?'

A sigh from Mammy's end. 'Sure, not too good, really, Lizzie. I keep telling him he should go to Dr Cronin, but I might as well talk to the wall. That old Deep Heat isn't making a blind bit of difference.' Pause. 'Hang on, he wants a word.'

'Hello, love.' He sounds the same as ever – Lizzie can see the grey Fair Isle cardigan that he's worn forever; or is he wearing the one Mammy got him at Christmas? The grey is a bit darker on the new one.

'Daddy, how are you?'

'Fine, love; can't complain.' Not a word about the knee. 'How's it going there with you? Any plans to come back and see us?'

'Yeah, I will, honest – just as soon as Angela can give me a few days off in a row; she's a bit stuck at the moment.'

She's given them to understand, without actually lying, that she's practically indispensable to Angela. 'I don't know how she managed before me; she was as good as running the B&B single-handedly; she was worn out' – *Sorry, Deirdre* – 'and now that I'm baking for her regularly too . . . it's a bit hectic, even with the two of us.' If they only knew she spends less than four hours a day working . . .

Hanging up, she feels a twinge of guilt: she really must get back home for a weekend soon. Maybe straight after Easter – The Kitchen should be fairly quiet then.

Next morning Lizzie stands outside Ripe and tries to put her finger on what's different. It seems exactly as it always is: a big wheelbarrow on either side of the door, one filled with fruit, the other with veg; windows shining, as usual – Joe keeps the place spotless . . .

And then she sees it, poking out from behind the beautiful wooden sign over the door. It couldn't be – but it is.

Grass.

Tufts of grass are sprouting from the top of the sign, all the way across. *What on earth?* She blinks hard and checks again; it's definitely there.

She goes inside. Joe looks up from behind the counter. 'Hi, Lizzie. Nice day.'

'Hi, Joe.' Should she say anything? How exactly should she put it? 'Your sign is growing grass' sounds a bit silly.

He's looking enquiringly at her. 'Have you forgotten what you wanted?' He always looks like a smile is just waiting to happen. And those blue eyes definitely grow on you.

Lizzie blinks. 'No, no, I'll just get them.' She fills her bags, still wondering if she should mention the grass. Maybe he's done it on purpose. Maybe it's a sales gimmick of some sort.

By the time she's got everything, she's decided to say something. She waits until she's paid him. 'Em, Joe . . . I want to show you something outside a minute.'

He hands her her change, eyebrows raised. 'Outside?'

'Yeah, just outside the door.' She's beginning to feel sorry she brought it up. Of course he knows about it – grass doesn't suddenly appear overnight on a wooden sign. Fruit and veg, growing stuff, all that kind of thing – it must be a marketing thing. But it's too late now; he's walking with her to the door. God, this is going to be mortifying.

Outside, she says nothing, just points up to the grass. Joe looks up, then draws in his breath. 'Good God. Where did that come out of?'

Whew – he didn't do it, then. She's not going to look like some prize eejit. They stand looking up, Joe shaking his head in bafflement.

'I don't believe it; it's back.'

'What?' Lizzie's head swivels back to him. 'You mean it's happened before?'

He nods his head, still gazing up. 'Oh, yes. It always seems to happen around this time of the year.'

'Joe, you're not serious.' Signs don't suddenly start to sprout grass – even signs advertising things that grow. 'Are you saying this happens regularly?'

'Yes. Very strange.' He's still nodding slowly, still looking up at the grass. 'Every year, always on the same date.' He looks back at her, his face serious.

'Lizzie, you don't think that it could have anything at all to do with the fact that it's . . . April Fool's Day?'

Not a flicker of a smile. How does he do it? Lizzie slaps his arm, half annoyed, half amused. 'Joe, you eejit – have you nothing better to do?'

He grins, rubbing his arm. 'Nothing at all; isn't it terrible? What kind of a place have you decided to come to, at all, at all?' He's highly amused at the success of his joke; and she's the perfect target – such a gullible ninny.

She tries to look stern and fails utterly. 'I'm beginning to wonder. Maybe I should go back home for myself – at least they leave the grass on the ground there.' Damn – she can't keep a straight face like he can.

'Ah no, stay – I'll be good.' He starts back into the shop. 'Well, I'd better get back inside and wait for my next victim – I mean customer.'

'God help them.' She heads off down the street.

'And, Lizzie –'

She turns.

'Have a nice day, now.' And he's gone.

Lizzie smiles and walks on with her bag of fruit, shaking her head. He's full of surprises, that man.

Wait till she tells Angela.

Chapter Eleven

'Turn around.' Angela looks carefully as Lizzie swivels her head. 'It's gorgeous.'

'Really?' She puts up her hands and touches her hair – it still feels very strange. 'You're not just saying that?'

'Absolutely not. It really suits you; it's much nicer than before. I love the way the wax lifts it, shows off the layers. And the highlights are great – just in time for summer, such as it is.'

That morning Lizzie had woken up and looked in the mirror and decided she needed a change – a totally new look. So she got into her car, drove to Seapoint, found the trendiest-looking salon and marched in. Three hours later and a hundred euros poorer, she came out with a brand-new blonde crop.

She loves it – and so, it seems, does Angela. 'We have to go out and show off that hair. There's a session in Doherty's on Sunday night. You'll drive Johnny

Morris wild.' Johnny Morris is a soft-spoken local man who occasionally plays the fiddle in Doherty's. He's also the wrong side of ninety.

Lizzie looks sternly at Angela. 'I'll have you know that I'll be setting my sights a lot younger than Johnny Morris.'

'Well, you never know . . .' Angela edges towards the door of the caravan. 'Joe McCarthy might be there too.' And she's gone, just before Lizzie's cushion hits the door.

Lizzie opens her wardrobe. Nothing jumps out at her; just the same old jeans and tops. She needs something new, to go with the new hair. She'll head back into Seapoint tomorrow; there are a few decent boutiques there. Maybe she'll get a pair of those low-rise trousers everyone is wearing; if she sucks in her tummy, she just might get away with them.

And she has no idea where Angela got the notion that she's interested in Joe McCarthy. For goodness' sake, she's just over a big break-up.

Not that she's lost much sleep over that. Sometimes she wonders idly how Tony and Pauline are getting on. Do they go out every Sunday night, like she and Tony did? Does he go around to the Twomeys' for his dinner every Thursday? She wouldn't be at all surprised.

It's funny: Sunday has turned out to be Lizzie's main going-out night in Merway, too. For years it was the only night when she and Tony could go out together – and now, with The Kitchen open every other night of the week, it's the only one that suits Angela. Mind you, nights out with Angela – usually in one or another of Merway's four pubs – are a lot more fun than a couple of glasses of wine in the local with Tony.

One night Lizzie tells Angela about Pauline Twomey.

'He has a new girlfriend – Mammy told me.'

Angela gives her a sympathetic look. 'I bet you were disappointed when you heard.'

Lizzie starts to protest – 'God, no' – and then realises that, oddly, she *was* a bit taken aback. 'Well, I suppose it was a bit of a surprise . . .'

'Human nature.' Angela nods. 'You don't want him, but you're damned if you want anyone else to claim him.' She pauses. 'When John left, I was devastated – completely broken-hearted. But then, I still wanted him, very badly.' She shrugs, runs her hand through her sleek blonde hair. 'He was the love of my life. We grew up together. Our first date was on Valentine's Day, when I was fifteen – just Dee's age, imagine.'

So she was with the love of her life for around twenty-five years. Lizzie can't begin to imagine how that break-up must have felt. She remembers longing for a bit of heartbreak when she was younger. Maybe she was as well off without it.

She glances sympathetically at Angela. 'Poor you; it must have been horrible.'

'Yeah, it was. Horrible.' Angela looks down at the table and rubs her eyes with the back of her hand – is she brushing away a tear? Then she smiles faintly. '*We* hadn't a long engagement at all – hardly any engagement, really. He proposed in February – Valentine's Day again; I was twenty-four – and we married in June.' She makes a face. 'Actually, it's a good job we did: Deirdre was born seven and a half months later. John's mother convinced herself, to the day she died, that Dee was premature.'

Then she looks up at Lizzie. 'He'll be here tomorrow.'

Lizzie looks back at her. 'Who'll be here?'

'John; he's due to see Deirdre. He phoned a couple of days ago and arranged it. He'll take her out for the day to Seapoint – spoil her rotten, as usual. And then she'll come back and be down in the dumps for a week.'

Lizzie wonders if she'll finally get to meet him; so far she's missed him when he's called.

Angela absently runs her finger along the side of the table. 'Dee's such a quiet little thing, it's hard to know what she's thinking. I hope she's not bottling things up; she knows she can always talk to me.'

'No sign of a boyfriend yet?' At fifteen, Deirdre must be beginning to realise that there's an opposite sex.

But Angela shakes her head firmly. 'Not a hint, thank goodness. Once she discovers boys, that'll be the end of the studying, if she's anything like her mother.'

John Byrne turns up the following morning. Lizzie is in the kitchen, trying her hand at making a sourdough starter, when Angela comes in and says, 'Lizzie, this is John. John, Lizzie is my new lodger, and my excellent baker.' There's something in her manner that

Lizzie hasn't seen before. Her smile snaps on and off; she seems ill at ease in the company of the man who shared her life for so long.

John isn't what Lizzie would call handsome – not in the way that, say, Joe McCarthy is – but he has a nice open face, and warmth in his eyes. She can see what drew Angela to him.

Deirdre looks a lot like her father. They both have the same brown hair and green eyes – Angela is blue-eyed, and much fairer – and she's inherited his height, too. At fifteen she's already an inch or so taller than Angela, who's about Lizzie's height – five four or five; John is nearly a head above that again.

'Are you planning to stay long here?' he asks Lizzie. He probably wonders what on earth brought her to Merway.

'Not sure, really; I'll just see how it goes.' Instinctively she's cautious with him, doesn't feel like going into detail.

He nods; then Deirdre comes flying down the stairs, and they're gone. Angela is quiet for the day, checking the clock often. Lizzie does most of the talking while they're getting the evening meals ready. When John and Deirdre get back, around eight, he doesn't come in with her – just drives off.

As she watches Angela admiring Deirdre's new make-up collection ('Look, Mum, it's got everything – look at all the brushes . . .') Lizzie's heart goes out to her. She clearly still has feelings for John – maybe not love any more, but strong feelings all the same.

Lizzie thinks about the woman John went off with. She seems to remember Angela saying that she was local. Is she much younger than Angela? Does Deirdre ever meet her with John? Do her parents know Angela – do they ever bump into her in the street? Lizzie can't imagine how a meeting like that would go.

Then she wonders what hope there is that any love can survive, if a relationship that sounds like the perfect one can just crumble and die like that. Maybe couples like Tony and herself, who didn't have such a big emotional investment, would actually have a better chance of making it. If she'd stayed in Kilmorris, they'd probably have trundled along together for another twenty years – not ecstatically happy, but content enough, maybe.

And then she tries to figure out why, in the face of all this doomed-relationship and heartbreak stuff, she still hopes to God she'll find someone with the power to seriously break her heart.

Chapter Twelve

Angela looks at the brown-paper package, then back up at Lizzie. 'How did you know?'

'Deirdre told me; and don't kill her – I swore her to secrecy.'

She shakes the package gingerly. 'When's yours, so I can get my own back?'

'Not till September.' It's only the last day of April. 'And don't worry, I'll leave plenty of clues lying around when it gets near. Hurry up and open that.'

Angela pulls the paper apart and peers in. 'Oh, wow.'

She takes out the framed photo and holds it up. Then she turns a beaming face to Lizzie. 'It's great. Did you take it?'

'I did.'

Lizzie thought of it a few weeks ago, when she was racking her brains for a birthday present for Angela. She was looking absently around the caravan, and her eye fell on a photo of a much smaller Jones that Daddy had got framed for her one Christmas. That was an idea: she could take a photo of Dumbledore, or maybe Deirdre – or how about the two of them? – and put it in a nice frame.

A handmade frame. Hand-carved. Now where would she get a frame like that? She'd have to find herself a master craftsman.

She went straight to Ripe the next morning.

Joe was sweeping the floor. 'You're up early.'

'I'm always up early – I'm just not usually around town till later,' Lizzie answered. 'Joe, I have a request.'

He leant on the brush. 'As long as it involves fruit or veg, I can probably help.'

She smiled. 'Well, it doesn't; it involves wood. And a bit of labour on your part.'

That smile was just waiting to happen again. 'Tell me more – this sounds interesting.'

She told him her idea of the photo. 'I need a frame for it, and I wondered . . . would you be able to make one for me?' She gave him a pleading look. 'There's a cake in it for you – baked by a master baker.' By this time everyone knew she was baking for Angela.

'Oh, we're bartering, are we now?' Joe looked thoughtfully at her, leaning on his brush. 'And what if I want more than a cake?' No hint of a smile.

Lizzie did her best to look as if gorgeous men flirted with her every day of the week. With a gigantic effort, she kept her expression neutral.

'What would you be thinking of as suitable payment?' She hoped to God she wasn't blushing.

'Oh, I don't know . . .' He looked off into the distance. 'An expertly-made wooden frame . . . would probably be worth – hmmm . . .' There was a long silence while he pretended to do sums in his head, mouthing, 'Carry the two . . . divide by four . . .' He knew well that Lizzie was desperately trying not to get embarrassed; and he was doing his level best to embarrass her. She wanted to slap him. In the nicest possible way.

Finally he looked back at her. 'At least two cakes. Big ones, with fresh cream, and maybe a bit of jam.'

She laughed at him. 'Consider it done; and thanks a million, Joe.'

He bowed his head. 'My pleasure. What size were you thinking?'

So she told him, and they talked about a design; and she stood beside him and watched the dark hair on the backs of his hands as he scribbled on a pad, and she looked at his rolled-up shirt sleeves and she thought how good olive green was against his skin, and she smelt the spice of his aftershave, and she tried to sound calm.

Lizzie and Deirdre waited for a fairly sunny day; then, as soon as Angela had driven off for Seapoint, they went into the garden and found Dumbledore, hiding from Jones under his usual bush. Deirdre sat on the ancient wrought-iron seat at the bottom of the garden, with Dumbledore on her lap. The sea was in the background – you could see it through the gaps in the fence – and the sky was pale blue. Deirdre was wearing a khaki top and cream-coloured combats and smiling her shy smile, and a little breeze lifted her long hair slightly as Lizzie took the photo. Dumbledore was looking up at her, tongue out.

When it was developed, Lizzie was delighted. She got it blown up to a bigger size, then put it carefully into the frame Joe had provided.

Now she says, 'Happy birthday to you,' and hugs Angela. 'Thanks for being the best landlady I've ever had; and the fact that you're the only one I've ever had has nothing to do with it.'

Angela hugs her back. 'Oh, Lizzie, it's great – I just love it. It'll take pride of place in the restaurant. Nearly takes the sting out of being forty.' She makes a face. 'Nearly – but not quite. My only consolation is that you're still older than me.'

She looks at the photo again. 'The frame is fabulous.' She traces over the ivy twined with flowers winding round two of the corners. 'Would I be right in guessing that young Joe McCarthy had a hand in it?'

Lizzie is blushing – she can feel it, crawling up her neck. 'Well, I wanted something really nice, and he's the only –' She stops and watches the smirk spread over Angela's face. 'Leave me alone, you bully; I've just given you a present.'

Angela holds up a palm. 'Say no more – I promise not to tell the whole of Merway that you fancy the

130

pants off the local fruit-and-veg man; although . . .'
She looks thoughtfully at Lizzie. 'I may just have to say
it to Big Maggie – that poor woman could do with a
little bit of gossip to brighten her days. I'll make her
swear not to tell anyone, honest.'

She ducks as a cushion comes flying at her. 'Steady
on, Lizzie – what would you do if Joe saw you flinging
cushions around the place? He'd be shocked – he
thinks you're a real lady.'

Lizzie giggles, picking up another cushion and hugging it to herself. 'Yes, I'm afraid I am a bit smitten.'
She looks hopefully at Angela. 'D'you think the feeling
is at all mutual?'

'Definitely. I've seen the way he looks at you when
he thinks no one sees him.' Angela gets a glint in her
eye. 'Just what we need to brighten our days – a bit of
romance around Merway.'

'Hang on, now; don't get carried away here.' Lizzie
has visions of Angela taking on the role of match-
maker; how mortifying would that be? 'There'll be no
fixing anything up, d'you hear me, Angela Byrne?'

Angela is the picture of innocence. 'I've no idea
what you mean. I wasn't thinking anything of the sort
– the very notion. But' – she turns a mischievous face
towards Lizzie – 'wouldn't it be only natural for me to
have a bit of a do for my fortieth – maybe a little
cocktail party in the restaurant on Sunday night? I
could invite a few friends around. And, naturally
enough, Joe McCarthy would be on the guest list,

being a close friend of the birthday girl. And of course there would be nothing wrong with fellow guest Lizzie O'Grady indulging in a bit of . . . mild flirtation with him. And, sure, wouldn't it be only natural for him to give back as good as he got?' She laughs at Lizzie's blushing face. 'Now what could be wrong with that?'

'You don't fool me for a second; you're a schemer to the core.' Lizzie feels the blood slowly draining from her cheeks. 'But I have to admit a cocktail party sounds good.' She points a finger across at Angela. 'As long as you swear on the future of this restaurant that you'll have no surprises up your sleeve – like everyone disappearing off into the kitchen and leaving me and Joe alone.'

Not that I wouldn't jump at the chance to have Joe to myself; especially if I thought the feeling was mutual – and Angela seems to think it might be . . .

Angela shakes her head. 'Oh, no, there'll be none of that – I have a feeling I won't have to do a thing to help this romance along.' Then she stands up. 'Now, we'll have to decide on the guest list later – I have cleaning to do, birthday or no birthday. Hand me that apron. Has the post arrived yet?'

Lizzie stands too. 'I'll go and check.'

There are four envelopes on the mat. One is for Lizzie, in Mammy's writing. Mammy writes about once a fortnight – Lizzie can hear her talking every time she reads one of her letters.

. . . There's a new butcher beside the shopping centre – you know, where the dry cleaner's was – but

he's no good. We had some of his chops last night and they were all gristle . . . I met Veronica Dooley in the library today; she was asking for you. I thought she'd put on a lot of weight . . . Jack and Catherine O'Neill are going to Canada in the summer, and they only back a few months from that coach tour of Italy. I don't know where they get the money . . . I hope you're keeping warm; it's very cold still at night, we haven't taken off any blankets yet . . . Daddy's leg was at him in bed last night, he had to get up and put on the Deep Heat . . .

She enjoys Mammy's letters; sometimes, reading them, she feels a pang of what she thinks might well be homesickness, but then she remembers Tony and O'Gorman's and the white pudding, and the pang usually disappears pretty fast. She still has to make plans for a trip home, though – she's let it slide a bit. She can't go next weekend, with the party on, and the following one is very busy . . . She'll go in the middle of May, definitely.

The other three letters are for Angela – Lizzie hopes they're birthday cards. She takes them into the kitchen; Angela has started washing up.

'One for me, three for you.' Lizzie puts Angela's post on the table.

Angela comes over, peeling off her rubber gloves. 'Goody.' She picks the envelopes up and looks at the first one. 'Mam, the pet – she never forgets.' She glances at the one underneath. 'What's that – some oul' junk.'

She turns over the third one – a big cream envelope – and looks at it for a few seconds.

Her back is to Lizzie, who has opened Mammy's letter and started to read. She giggles. 'Angela, listen. "The O'Driscolls" – they're our next-door neighbours – "have got a new cat, who insists on using our garden as his toilet. Daddy's pansies are starting to go all brown. He's put down a few of those plastic bottles, although I can't see for the life of me how they'd work . . . " It could only happen to Mammy.'

No response from Angela. Lizzie looks up; Angela's head is bent forward and something about her back looks wrong. Lizzie goes over to her. 'Angela, what is it?' *Don't let her have bad news, not on her birthday.*

Angela turns and looks at Lizzie, her face drained. She holds out a birthday card. 'It's from John.' Her mouth stretches in what Lizzie presumes is meant to be a smile. 'My husband has written to wish me a happy birthday. Isn't that thoughtful of him?' Tears appear out of nowhere and roll down her face. She puts a hand to her mouth and the tears run over it.

Lizzie can't bear to see the pain on her face. She puts her arms around her and holds her. 'Oh, Angela, you poor thing. Poor you.' She hates John Byrne, hates the power he has over her friend – with one thoughtless gesture he can squeeze the happiness out of her. Could he possibly have thought she'd like to get a birthday card from him? Or did he do it deliberately to hurt her? Surely not; she remembers his open, pleasant face.

After a while Angela pulls away and wipes her eyes with the back of her hand. 'Sorry, Lizzie.' She goes to the sink and splashes cold water on her face. 'Silly to get so upset – the eejit probably thought I'd enjoy it.' She turns around, dabbing at her face with a towel. 'He didn't send me one last year – which killed me at the time – so it was the last thing I expected today.'

What is the man playing at? Maybe he has qualms of conscience about the break-up. Maybe Deirdre reminded him, the last time they were out together, and he felt duty bound. Lizzie is willing to bet his new lady knew nothing about it.

She looks at Angela. 'Bet her cooking isn't a patch on yours.'

Angela looks back and sniffs. 'Bet she can't boil an egg.'

Lizzie considers. 'Bet she likes sweet white wine.'

A tiny smile appears at the corner of Angela's mouth. 'With cheese-and-onion crisps.'

'Bet she burns his shirts when she irons them.'

'Bet she doesn't own an iron; he has to put his shirts under the mattress at night.'

'Bet she reads magazines that are meant for teenagers, and thinks they're great.'

'Bet her custard is always lumpy.'

'Bet she loves Jerry Springer.'

'Definitely.' Angela gathers up her rubber gloves and turns back to the sink. Lizzie picks up Mammy's letter. 'Well, you've just earned yourself the mother of all birthday cakes for Sunday night – if you still want to go ahead with the party.'

Angela looks over at her for a second, then nods firmly. 'You bet I do – and I'm having lots of little nibbly posh things. And if that birthday cake has more than four candles, you'll pay.'

Lizzie smiles and puts a hand on Angela's arm. 'I won't say he's not worth it, because that's as useless as saying there are more fish in the sea. I will say that he must be crazy to have left you for anyone else.'

Angela's eyes fill up again, and she dabs at them with the towel. 'Thanks. Of course you're right.'

'I'll come a bit early for today's shift – I'm putting on a little extra dessert in honour of the day. Can you guess?'

Angela shakes her head. 'Sorry – not in the mood for guessing.'

'Well, I'll tell you, then; it's sticky toffee pudding. We'll go on our after-Easter diet tomorrow.'

'Definitely.' Her smile is watery. 'Thanks, Lizzie. See you later.' As Lizzie goes out, Angela calls after her, 'Think about who we should ask on Sunday – apart from the obvious.'

On her way back to the caravan, Lizzie sees Dumbledore under his usual bush, fast asleep. Ten feet away, under a neighbouring bush, Jones sits and watches him. Not spitting or hissing, like he used to do every time he laid eyes on the poor dog; not even waving his tail. Just watching.

She smiles. 'Come on, puss.' And she and Jones walk towards the caravan.

Chapter Thirteen

Lizzie unscrews the tub of hair wax and peers inside. It smells vaguely fruity. She looks at the side of the tub; the writing sounds loud. *Get that just-out-of-bed look! Have fun with your hair! Mess it! Play with it! Scrunch it! Do whatever feels good!* She's wary of all the exclamation marks.

She pokes a finger into the tub – it feels like putty – pulls out a little blob and spreads it between her fingers. Now what exactly did they do at the salon? She wiggles her hands into her hair, scrunching it around a bit, squeezing handfuls of hair at random. Then she checks in the mirror, turning her head this way and that. Not too radical; good. She pulls a bit of hair down in the front, and pushes another bit back. Fine.

Now for the face. She runs her eye pencil along the bottoms of her eyes, then brushes on some blusher –

her ten-year-old foundation has finally gone into the bin – and flicks a lipstick over her lips. That's grand.

'Lizzie? Are you decent?'

'Come in.'

Angela walks in, followed by Deirdre, who's holding her make-up box and looking embarrassed. Angela puts up a warning hand. 'Now, Lizzie, don't kill us – we thought you might like a bit of help with your dolling up.'

Deirdre chimes in, '*She* thought, Lizzie, not me,' and clicks open the box. Bottles and tubes and sticks of every description are neatly arranged inside.

Lizzie looks at it, then up at Angela. 'But I've just done my make-up – see?' She points to her face. 'And I've waxed my hair.'

'Exactly.' Angela nods, and turns to Deirdre. 'See what I mean?'

Deirdre looks helplessly at Lizzie. 'Sorry, Lizzie; I'm only following orders.'

Angela puts up a hand to shush her, and looks back at Lizzie. 'Look, pet, I know you'd like to look your best tonight' – she winks at Lizzie, back turned to Deirdre – 'and you know our Dee is always dying to try out her bits and bobs on someone. So I just thought you might like her to give you a bit of a makeover. What do you say? Don't be offended.'

Lizzie looks at them and laughs. 'I'm not in the least offended, don't worry – I know I haven't a clue, really.' She puts up her hands in surrender. 'OK. Deirdre, I'm all yours.'

Angela looks satisfied; she turns to Deirdre. 'Right, love, do your stuff. You've got ten minutes.'

When she's gone, Deirdre looks shyly at Lizzie. 'Are you sure you don't mind? It really was all her idea.'

'I have no doubt.' It never ceases to amaze Lizzie that any child of Angela's could be so quiet; Deirdre would never in a million years have suggested this. 'And I absolutely don't mind; I'm delighted.' Deirdre actually shows a real flair for doing make-up; she's done Angela's a few times, and it always looks great. Lizzie is only too happy to put herself in her hands.

As Deirdre cleanses and moisturises and begins to apply foundation, they chat. Lizzie doesn't see that much of Deirdre. She's out at school all day, and in the evenings she's busy in the restaurant, or studying for her Junior Cert. During the weekends she seems to disappear, with various pals, Lizzie presumes. Angela gives her a fair bit of freedom, not keeping too close an eye on her activities, as long as she's home at a decent hour. But then, Deirdre seems amazingly level-headed for a fifteen-year-old. Lizzie thinks that maybe teenagers in broken homes have to grow up quicker.

'You must be dying for the holidays.' The exams are just a month away.

Deirdre nods, patting powder on Lizzie's face. 'I sure am – can't wait.'

'Have you plans for transition year?' Lizzie only has a vague notion what that is; there was no such thing when she was at school. All she knows is that it's a kind of step sideways from the usual curriculum, a year of doing things a bit differently.

Deirdre nods again. 'Well . . . I'm hoping to do a beautician's course – there's talk of one being offered in the school for transition years; and then what I'd really like to do . . .' She hesitates, concentrating on what she's doing for a few seconds. 'I haven't talked about this to Mum yet, but I'd really love to get some work experience in England. The salons in London are supposed to be fantastic.'

Lizzie is surprised – she didn't imagine that Deirdre would be interested in leaving Merway. She can't see Angela turning somersaults at the thought.

'How could you do that with school, though?' She hopes she doesn't sound too like Mammy.

Deirdre shrugs. 'Well, you don't need the Leaving to work as a beautician – and that's what I really want to do.'

'Oh, right.' Lizzie digests this for a minute. She thinks back to her own great plans to travel the world, the disappointment she felt when Síle said she'd changed her mind. And she thinks of her own career dreams – all that time she wasted doing what others expected. Why shouldn't Deirdre go for what she wants?

She meets the girl's eye in the mirror. 'That sounds like a good idea; I'm sure London would be very exciting. You're still pretty young, though – I'd say you'll have a job persuading your mother to let you go.'

Deirdre smiles, nods. 'I'd say you're right there.' She strokes a liquid eyeliner carefully just above Lizzie's eyelashes. 'But there's a pal who might be interested in going as well . . . We'll see. I might manage to persuade her.' She looks anxiously at Lizzie. 'You won't say anything, will you?'

'Of course not.' She's touched that Deirdre would confide in her, maybe she doesn't have that many people she can talk to. It's certainly not something she could ask Angela's advice about – Lizzie can just see Angela hitting the roof at the thought of her innocent young daughter heading off to London.

She can see how much Angela cares about Deirdre; it's obvious whenever they're together – the fondness in her voice when she talks to her, the way she often reaches out and touches her. No doubt John does his bit too, when he takes her out for the day. Still, it must have been horrible for her when they split up.

When Angela gets back, she nods in approval. 'You'll do.'

And Lizzie has to agree. Deirdre has done something to her eyes that makes them look far more dramatic than they are; and her lashes, her pride and joy, look amazing. Deirdre refuses to take the credit. 'I didn't have to do much with them – just a curl and some clear mascara. You're lucky – they're gorgeous, so dark and long.'

She's made Lizzie's skin look smooth and even, not a freckle to be seen, a rosy glow just where it's supposed

141

to be. Her lips have been buffed and painted and blotted and sealed – she'll be terrified to eat or drink a thing. Angela reassures her. 'Don't worry, that lipstick will need to be scrubbed off tonight; it's going nowhere.'

Her hair has been properly waxed – Deirdre tentatively suggested that she add a bit more – and the highlights shine, and the layers are defined, and it looks twice as thick as it is.

Lizzie turns to Deirdre. 'Thanks so much, Deirdre. I'm really glad your mother bullied you into it. And please come shopping with me soon and help me choose make-up – I wouldn't have a clue what to buy.'

Deirdre smiles as she packs away her powders and paints. 'No problem; you look great. See you in a bit.' She heads out the door. 'Come on, Mum; your turn.'

Angela looks at her watch. 'Oh my God, they'll be here in twenty minutes. Lizzie, put some clothes on you quick and get your ass into that kitchen.'

'I'll be there in five minutes. Everything's ready, anyway; calm down.' As the caravan door closes, she calls, 'Angela?'

Angela puts her head back inside. 'Yeah?'

'Did I mention how amazing *you* look tonight?'

She does; wide-legged black linen trousers, cream-and-black linen top, glossy blonde hair – natural blonde, not like Lizzie's – and a turquoise-and-silver pendant that Lizzie covets every time she sees it.

'You didn't, and I know. See you in five.' And she's gone.

Lizzie shrugs off her dressing-gown and pulls on her new pale-blue low-rise cropped trousers. Then she takes out the white chiffon top that Angela made her buy to go with them, and puts it on. It's not the kind of thing she'd ever have bought on her own, but she has to admit that it looks good – dressy without being dressed-up. She likes the wavy neckband, and the fact that it's short enough to show off the band of darker blue around the top of the trousers.

She steps into the shoes that she bought in Footsie in Seapoint the other day. They're higher than she's used to, but they suit the cropped trousers; they make her ankles look slightly more slender, too, which they badly need.

Then she stands in front of the mirror and checks that the fake tan she put on her calves didn't streak. No sign of a giveaway line anywhere. She grabs her turquoise shawl and pulls it around her as she opens the caravan door. Tottering over the gravel on her way to the house, she tells God that she'd appreciate not falling flat on her face tonight, please; she'd really rather remember the night for quite a different reason.

Joe shows up at twenty past eight, one of the last to arrive. He makes straight for Angela and wraps her in a warm hug. 'Happy birthday, Ange. I must say you don't look a day over fifty-five.'

Angela steps back and looks at him, then turns to Lizzie, who's handing around a plate of canapés.

'Lizzie, give him no food. Or drink.' Then she pulls Joe back to her and hugs him again. 'You look great for ninety yourself. Where's my present?'

'I knew I wouldn't get in without one. Here.' He takes a small packet from inside his jacket and hands it to her.

Angela looks up at him and bats her eyelashes, raising her voice for the benefit of Maggie Delaney, who's standing nearby. 'Looks like an engagement-ring box. Are you planning to make an honest woman of me, Joe McCarthy?'

If she's trying to embarrass him, she's wasting her time. He grins. 'You wish. Open it.'

Angela opens it, and draws in her breath. 'Joe . . . that is absolutely amazing. Lizzie, come and see.'

Nestling in a little cardboard box lined with cotton wool is a life-sized wooden fuchsia on a thin silver chain. The detail is wonderful, each petal delicately carved and perfectly curved. Lizzie wonders briefly if he was working on this when she came to him with her demand for a frame. Was he under pressure, trying to get the two pieces finished on time? She decides to keep her mouth well and truly closed, just in case.

Not Angela. 'Joe McCarthy, you've really surpassed yourself this time. How did you manage it?' She holds it up and twirls it around. 'So perfectly formed, like myself . . . It's fantastic – thanks so much.' She reaches up and smacks a kiss on Joe's cheek, then rubs off the lipstick. 'And the frame is fabulous, too – look.' She gestures to the photo hanging on the wall.

He gives it an amused look. 'Where would you be without me?'

Angela digs him in the ribs. 'Don't start. Now, what are you having to drink?'

'What have you got?'

'Just about everything – except Guinness out of a barrel. But we do have cans of draught.'

'That'll do fine.'

Angela goes to get it, winking at Lizzie behind his back – 'Lizzie, entertain our guest' – and Lizzie watches as he peels off his blue-and-grey tweed jacket and drapes it over the back of a chair. Then she holds out the plate to him. 'Sir, can I interest you in a snack?' *And may I just say, sir, that you're looking dead sexy tonight?* He's wearing a faded denim shirt that somehow makes his eyes look even bluer, and khaki jeans. She could eat him up.

They're in the restaurant, which is closed to the public on Sunday nights. The tables have been pushed back to make a space in front of the fire, which is blazing away as usual. Apart from Angela and Deirdre, there are half a dozen people in the room already, including Dominic the artist and Big Maggie from Blooming Miracles. Sarah Vaughan, a favourite of Angela's, is singing softly in the background.

Joe eyes the plate of food and takes a salmon roll. 'Thanks – and, now that I have your ear, there's something I wanted to ask you.'

'What's that?' Lizzie looks innocently back at him, hoping he can't read her mind. *Whatever it is, the answer is yes. Especially if it involves any form of physical contact.*

'I wondered if you'd be interested in a bit of work.' He takes a bite of his roll. 'Mmm, very tasty.'

'Work? What kind of work?' Her first thought is that this is probably a joke. She can just see him figuring it all out in the shop earlier. She's determined not to be caught out tonight; she'll have to have her wits about her.

He wipes his mouth with the back of his hand. 'I need someone to help out in the shop, and I wanted to give you first refusal.'

Just then Angela comes back with a can and a glass, and Lizzie has a minute to think as Joe takes them and starts to pour. Is he serious? He seems to be – but then, Joe McCarthy is a master of the straight face. But why would he joke about a thing like that?

She decides to put him to the test.

'Angela, Joe has just offered me a job in his shop.' She watches his face for a reaction – nothing.

Angela gives him a fierce look. 'What – are you poaching my staff, Joe McCarthy?'

'No, no; I'm just looking for part-time help, two or three hours in the morning. You're free then, aren't you, Lizzie? I thought you might manage the two jobs.'

Angela looks puzzled. 'But, Joe, you don't need help, do you? I mean, the shop is hardly big enough for two working there.'

'That's true, but I want a bit of time off to carve. A pal has opened up a craft shop in Cork and asked me to supply some stuff, so I need someone to hold the fort to give me a break.' He looks at Lizzie. 'I'd still be on the premises, just in the back room.'

Angela's face clears. 'Joe, that's great. I always said you should be making money out of your carving. I'll leave you to negotiate with him, Lizzie. Just remember I need you in the afternoons. And you don't get out of bed for less than fifty euros an hour.'

When she's gone, Lizzie turns back to Joe. He's still looking at her, waiting for her answer.

So it's not a joke. Joe McCarthy is offering her a job in Ripe. She thinks fast. 'How many days a week were you thinking?' Please let her not sound as if this is the most exciting offer she's had in years.

'Let's see . . . say three days a week to start with, Monday, Wednesday and Friday, from maybe nine or nine-thirty, three hours a day. I'll pay whatever the going rate is. How does that sound?' He takes a swig from his glass and waits.

That sounds like music to my ears. Lizzie pretends to consider; easy does it. 'I think that would be fine . . .' She nods slowly. 'Yeah, I'll take it. Thanks. When would you like me to start?'

Joe beams at her. 'As soon as you like. Is tomorrow too soon?'

Not a minute. With great difficulty, she keeps a neutral expression on her face. Tomorrow she and the most fanciable man in Merway will be under the same roof for three solid hours. She'll be in the shop, and

147

he'll be only yards away, in the back room. She wonders briefly why the shifty-looking Charlie isn't helping out, then decides it's none of her business. 'That sounds fine. Let me get you another can to seal the deal.'

'Thanks. Oh, and by the way –' He picks another salmon roll off the plate. '– I did tell you about the uniform, didn't I?'

Lizzie grins. *Here we go.* She leans against the table and waits. 'Actually, no, Joe, you forgot to mention the uniform.'

He nods, studying the roll intently. 'Oh, yes, it's required by safety regulations. Black skirt, very short; little white frilly apron; very high heels – the ones you've on there would do fine; black top, very low-cut; and shiny red lipstick at all times.' Not a hint of a smile as he looks back up at her. 'Does that sound OK?'

She nods thoughtfully, biting her cheek to keep the smile away. 'Fine – except . . . .' Is she brazen enough for this? She is. 'The only low-cut tops I have are see-through as well; would they do?' God, she sounds like a right brazen hussy; Mammy would faint in mortification if she could hear her.

Joe gives her his best dirty-old-man look and leans towards her. 'I can see you're a quick learner. I look forward to doing business with you, Miss O'Grady.'

The party is a big success. Everyone stays till well after midnight, even Big Maggie, who's usually in bed by ten. Lizzie's baby quiches and savoury mini-muffins – parmesan and pine nut, cheese and bacon – and

Angela's salmon rolls, stuffed vine leaves and cheesy sesame squares are followed by a devil's-food cake and a hazelnut roulade, with one fat candle in the middle of each.

They drink champagne and wine and Guinness – Deirdre hides a glass of champagne from her mother, and Angela pretends not to notice – and Big Maggie, who brought Angela a begonia with giant frilly-edged leaves in a shocking-pink raffia pot, sings 'My Irish Molly', slightly off-key. Dominic the artist, who gave Angela a charcoal sketch of The Kitchen, recites 'If Ever You Go to Dublin Town' and makes them all join in on the 'Fol-dol-the-di-do' bit. Joe tells a totally ridiculous joke about a cross-eyed goose that goes on forever and has them all in stitches. Angela sings 'Someone to Watch Over Me' very sweetly. Marjorie, a friend of Angela's from Seapoint, shows them a trick with matchsticks that no one can figure out. Two of Angela's overnight guests, an engaged couple from Austria, attempt to teach Angela and Dominic a Viennese folk dance. Another guest, a retired landscape gardener from England, talks to Big Maggie about his prize-winning orchids, and promises to drop into Blooming Miracles in the morning for a look around.

Lizzie sits on the floor by the fire, shoes kicked off, arms wrapped around her legs, and watches them all. She thinks how much her life has changed in the past four months. She remembers opening the magazine in the dentist's waiting room and reading the words of the old woman from Kentucky and feeling that something was falling away from her, and being able to breathe again. She remembers picking up Pete the American in her blue Fiesta, and listening to him play the tin whistle, and wondering about staying in the tumbledown house in Rockford. She remembers walking into The Kitchen that first night and meeting Angela, and later stepping into the tiny caravan and feeling like she'd come home.

She looks across at Joe McCarthy, who's sitting the wrong way round on a chair, arms draped over the back of it, chatting to Dominic. As she watches him, he turns his head towards her and meets her gaze.

Lizzie looks back steadily, brave with wine and champagne. She sees him turn back to Dominic and say something; then he takes his glass and goes to the drinks table. He picks up a bottle of red wine and holds it up questioningly. She smiles and nods, and he walks over and sits on the floor beside her, long legs stretched out in front of him.

He pours wine into her empty glass. 'I probably shouldn't be doing this; you need a clear head for your new job in the morning.' At the thought of the job, her heart leaps. Joe puts the bottle on the floor and raises his glass. 'Here's to our new regime. May you never forget who's boss.'

'And may you never forget to pay me,' Lizzie says, laughing and clinking her glass against his. 'I hope you know I expect a good pension scheme, too, and holiday pay.'

He snorts. 'You'll be lucky. And you're the tea lady as well as the shop girl, in case I forgot to mention that. Tea at half twelve, when you finish up.'

She raises her eyes to heaven. 'I suppose I'll be expected to supply the biscuits to go with the tea.'

He looks at her over his glass. 'Why do you think I chose you, darling?'

Darling. Her heart is doing back-flips. She has to touch him. Her hand slides brazenly over and finds his on the floor. No one can see; the room is dim, all candles and firelight. 'I'll bring goodies on one condition.'

Joe makes no attempt to pull away. 'Are you trying to bargain with the boss, by any chance?' His face, warmed by the fire, is very close to hers. She looks steadily into the bluest eyes in Merway.

'I want free fruit and veg – and you do the washing up.' What a hussy all that wine has turned her into. *Sorry, Mammy.*

He leans over, and for a second Lizzie thinks he's about to kiss her. Then he puts his lips to her ear. 'It's a deal.' His breath against her skin is hot; her ear tingles when he draws away, and she lifts her glass to cover her flaming face.

She feels his eyes on her as she drinks, and she imagines walking into Ripe in the morning and being practically in the same room with him for three hours a day, three days a week.

And she wonders how long it will take.

Chapter Fourteen

Lizzie puts her head round the open door. 'It's twelve-thirty, Joe.'

He's bent over the workbench with something that looks like a chisel in one hand. 'Good – I'm ready for a break. Let's hope they leave us alone for ten minutes.'

Us.

He puts down the tool and the piece of wood he's been working on, and brushes the shavings from his faded grey flannel shirt and jeans. The floor around him is littered with bits of wood. The room smells like a forest. Then he stretches, arching his back and easing out his shoulders with a satisfied grunt.

Lizzie forces herself to look away from him. She's trying to be professional and not remember how she grabbed his hand the night before. Such a shame the party broke up just after that, when things were getting interesting.

She glances around the room; Joe showed it to her when she arrived at half nine, but she didn't get a proper look. It's fairly small, with a door at either end – one leading into the shop, the other into his house. His workbench, and two long presses above it, take up practically one entire wall, leaving just enough space at the other side of the room for a sink, a fridge, a small square table with a few chairs around it, and another press above the sink. Under the workbench are several crates filled with blocks of wood in varying sizes.

She takes the kettle from the top of the fridge and fills it. 'How's the work going?' Under the woody scent of the room she can smell his aftershave.

'Good. It's great to get a run at it like this, with no interruptions.' He's still loosening his shoulders, arching his back; it must be pretty tough to stay hunched over like that for a few hours.

She plugs the kettle into the socket beside the fridge and goes over to the bench. Taped to the wall above it, just under the long presses, are several sketches of pigs in various poses. A collection of wooden animals – elephants, monkeys, ducks, kangaroos – is scattered along it. She picks up a duck and runs her fingers along its curves. It feels slightly rough.

Joe takes a brush from where it leans against the wall and starts sweeping up the shavings. 'Watch out for splinters – those ones aren't sanded yet.'

'Where did you learn how to do this?' She's fascinated by his ability to take a block of wood and turn it into a thing that's full of charm.

He smiles, empties the shavings into the bin. 'Picked it up along the way, really. I liked drawing at school, but I always felt I wanted it to be more . . . 3-D, more solid than just a thing on a page. I think it was only a matter of time before I had a knife in one hand and a bit of wood in the other. Then I just . . . learnt as I went along.'

Lizzie is astonished. 'You mean you were never taught? Never went to woodwork classes or anything?'

He laughs. 'Woodwork classes in Merway? Hardly. We were happy to have maths classes.'

She puts down the duck and picks up the pig he was working on when she came in; it's still warm from his hand. The little chubby head is finished, poking out of the rest of the block. 'He looks like he's just about to wriggle out. But how do you know what to do? I mean' – she points at the pictures stuck to the wall – 'how do you know you have to work from a picture, and not just from your head? And do you draw the pictures from your imagination? And what kind of wood do you use? And where –'

He puts up his hands, amused. 'Steady on; one at a time – I'm still a bit addled from being bent over that bench for the past three hours.' He pauses, massaging the back of his neck. 'What was the first question again? Oh, yes – whether or not to work from a picture. Well, that depends; some things I can manage freehand, others I need help with. I get my images anywhere I can find them – books, magazines; the

Internet is a great source – and then I draw something simple based on those. Dominic has a good photo collection that he lets me use. And *National Geographic* is great for the animals, of course. The fuchsia I did for Angela's birthday – I found that in a gardening book in the library. The same book I used for the frame you wanted, actually.'

He picks up an elephant from the workbench and rolls it absently between his fingers. 'I get my wood from a few different sources – some locals have their own trees, a pal who's with Coillte gives me some. I mostly work with beech or sycamore, although occasionally I . . .'

Lizzie watches him rolling the little elephant backwards and forwards in his hand. His fingers are long and slender – craftsman's hands. His grey shirt is rolled up to the elbows, and the hairs grow black and thick on his arms. She looks at the triangle of skin above the opening of his shirt, and sees a few black hairs wandering up from his chest. She wants to slide her fingers in between the closed buttons and feel him catch his breath.

'. . . and I never really have to go too far to find it.' Joe drops the elephant. 'Now, I suppose there's no chance of a cup of tea?' The kettle is singing.

'Not yet.' She gestures towards the workbench. 'Why all the animals?'

'Noah's ark; almost done.' He opens one of the presses above the bench and Lizzie sees several more wooden animals, and more toys – trains, cars, puppets, boats, dolls. 'I'm just about to send off the first batch.'

'You've done an amount of work,' she says in admiration. 'It must have been hard, with no help in the shop. It'll be great for you to get paid for doing what you love – like me baking for Angela.'

Joe smiles. 'Provided the children of Cork decide they'd prefer wooden trains to PlayStations. We'll see what happens when this stuff is actually put out for sale.'

'Ah, go on – I'm sure it'll walk off the shelves.' Lizzie puts two cups out on the table and gets a little jug of milk from the fridge. 'Such a talent – you're lucky.'

He washes his hands at the sink, then takes two teabags from the box on top of the fridge and puts one in each cup. 'You're just as talented in your own way. It's not everyone who can bake like you.' He puts a hand on his hip and crooks his other wrist. 'I just can't get my scones to rise.'

She laughs, pouring the water into the cups. 'Ah, it's not the same, though. Most people could learn how to bake in a couple of months. What you have is special; and the stuff you make will be around for a long time. My baking doesn't last more than a day or two. Speaking of which –' She takes a Tupperware box from her bag. 'Here's some I made earlier. Hope you like ginger.' She puts the box on the table and sits down.

'I certainly do; thanks.' Joe sits down opposite her, takes a biscuit and dips it into his tea. 'Well, how did your first day go?'

'Fine.' And it did; she had no trouble with the till, thanks to O'Gorman's. The customers were friendly – she already knew most of them to see. All the prices were written up. If it hadn't been for Charlie, the morning would have been perfect.

The shop door opened at half eleven, and Lizzie looked up to see him standing in front of her.

'Hello.' With an effort, she arranged her face into a smile.

'Joe here?' No introductions, no niceties. He sounded like someone from *EastEnders*.

She cocked her head towards the back. 'In there.' If he wasn't going to waste his breath on conversation, neither was she.

Charlie went out to the back without a word. After a minute or so, Joe came in, went to the cash register and took out some notes. Lizzie pretended to be too busy arranging the apples in a Ferrero Rocher triangle to notice him. The money would probably go straight into Dignam's till; poor Joe.

Charlie walked out shortly afterwards. He winked at Lizzie – 'See you' – and was gone.

She looked after him as he walked down the street. Why on earth was he there? Had he some kind of hold over Joe? Then she shook her head – it was none of her business. And he was family; Joe felt an obligation, that was all. It was a pity he wasn't more friendly, though.

Walking home from Ripe, Lizzie hopes to God Charlie isn't planning to stay much longer with Joe. That afternoon she asks Angela about him again.

'When did he come here?'

'It was after I stopped the lunches,' Angela pauses, her knife poised over the chicken pieces on the chopping-board, 'so it must have been October, or maybe early November. It was a while before Christmas, anyway.'

'And you don't know why he suddenly appeared?'

Angela shakes her head and starts to chop again. 'Couldn't find out. I did my level best, but Joe wasn't giving anything away. For all his cod-acting, he's actually a very private person; when he doesn't want you to know something, believe me, you don't. Even Maggie didn't have a clue, and that's not like her.'

'How are Joe and Charlie related again?'

Angela considers. 'Charlie must be Tom's son, since he came from London. Tom is Joe's older brother – he left here when I was still a child and he hasn't been home for years, not since the parents died. Joe has two sisters, too, but they're both living in Ireland. I think one is in Cork, and the other . . . Clonmel, maybe?'

She dips the pieces of chicken into a bowl of spices and places them onto the hot pan. Then she says, 'You know, it wouldn't surprise me if that Charlie was on the run. I always think he's got the look of a criminal about him – those shifty eyes of his.' She shakes the pan, and the chicken leaps and sizzles. The spicy smell starts to drift around the kitchen.

Lizzie laughs, 'Ah, here, Angela, I think you're getting a bit carried away there. Just because he's not full of charm like his uncle, that's no reason to suspect him of robbing banks.' She divides her dough in half and reaches for the rolling pin.

For once, Angela doesn't joke back. She shakes her head and pokes the chicken around the pan with a wooden spoon. 'I hope I'm wrong, for Joe's sake, but I wouldn't be surprised, that's all.'

And that's that. For whatever reason, Charlie moved in, bag and baggage, with his uncle.

And just a few months later – a few weeks, really – Lizzie O'Grady arrived in Merway and fell headlong for Uncle Joe.

Well done, God. Great timing.

Chapter Fifteen

'You're getting on well at Ripe, are you, Lizzie?'

Lizzie smiles to herself. She figured it was only a matter of time before Maggie would be on the hunt for a bit of gossip.

'Grand, Maggie. I enjoy the work.' *Not to mention the company.*

'And yourself and Joe get on well together, by the looks of it.' It's not a question, but Lizzie is pretty sure she expects an answer.

'Fine; but I don't really see that much of him. He spends his time working on his carvings. That's why he took me on – so he could get away.' *No need to mention that 'away' is still near enough for us to share a radio. Or that it's only taken a few weeks for our tea break to stretch from ten minutes to nearer thirty.* And the fact that they never stop talking, once they sit down, is certainly none of Maggie's business. Sometimes Lizzie is amazed at the amount of conversation that flows back and forth between the two of them. They can talk about anything.

'. . . You should never eat a banana till the skin is spotty; that's when they're perfectly ripe. Most people eat them before they're ready – and then they wonder why bananas are supposed to be hard to digest. My favourite sandwich is mashed banana and peanut butter . . . What are you laughing at? . . .'

'. . . The first cake I baked was a disaster – I read the oven temperature wrong, and it came out weighing a ton and hard as a rock. Daddy ate three slices, the creature. I'd say he was up half the night with indigestion . . .'

'. . . I thought I was going to bleed to death – the chisel nearly took the top off my thumb. I had to wear one of those lovely leather thumb-covers for a month. Lucky I wasn't my brother – everyone would have called me Tom Thumb. Look, you can just about see the scar . . .'

She just about managed to resist the urge to stroke it.

'. . . Jones got into the kitchen once when my mother had left half a salmon on the table – we were having visitors that night, and she had just poached it and left it out to cool. He didn't eat again for almost two days, and every time she laid eyes on him she grabbed the broom . . .'

'. . . My first pet was a bee. I caught him in a jam jar and called him Buzzer and put him beside my bed when I went to sleep. In the middle of the night I knocked over the jar, and Buzzer flew out and stung me . . .'

'. . . I've always wanted to go to Greece – ever since I saw *Shirley Valentine*. I had no idea Tom Conti wasn't Greek; I'd never seen him in anything else. When I spotted him on telly in a car ad years later, I was dead impressed with his Welsh accent . . .'

'. . . My sister Bridget called me "Doe" when she was small; she couldn't manage "Joe". Tom changed it to "Dodo", and it stuck, until I was about eight. Then I put my foot down . . .'

'. . . For my confirmation I wore a lime-green suit and a matching straw hat. I looked like an American tourist on the way to the St Patrick's Day parade. I came across photos, years later, and begged my mother to let me burn them, but she wouldn't . . .'

'. . . Extra-cold Guinness is the invention of the devil – never let anyone talk you into it. It kills the taste; Arthur would turn over in his grave if he knew. The only thing worse was that Guinness Light stuff – what the hell were they thinking of? . . .'

'. . . Angela told some Austrian tourists that she was the great-great-great-granddaughter of Henry VIII. She said he really wanted to be a priest but was refused permission by the pope, so he married all those women to spite him. If you heard half the stories she makes up for the tourists – and they swallow every word, God help us . . .'

162

No, Maggie definitely doesn't need to know about the tea breaks. Or the crossword races, or the dimple in Joe's right cheek when he smiles. Or his habit of stretching his long legs out under the little square table and planting them on either side of Lizzie's while they have tea. Does he even know he's doing it? She feels deliciously trapped.

And so it goes. Three hours a day, three mornings a week, and tea and home-baked biscuits and talk, talk, talk around the small table in the back of Ripe. Sometimes she thinks: *This is enough; this can go on forever and I won't mind if nothing more happens.* Other times she wonders if he's forgotten the night of the party and the way they looked at each other, and she tries to calculate how long it'll be before she just has to knock back a few more glasses of wine and throw herself at him.

The only topic that never comes up is Charlie. Joe never mentions him, and Lizzie never asks about him. He wanders into the shop occasionally; he always goes straight into the back room, barely looking at her. She reminds God that Charlie has been scrounging from his uncle for well over six months now, and maybe it would be a good time for him to think about going back to London, if God wouldn't mind just planting the idea in his head.

And then three things happen that change everything.

Chapter Sixteen

'Angela, hi. I'm just off – see you about one. Can I get you anything on my way home?'

Angela is standing at the sink, her hands in the water. She turns and looks blankly at Lizzie.

Something's wrong. Lizzie goes over to her. 'Angela?' Her face is paler than usual; her eyes look empty. 'What's up?'

Angela takes her hands out of the water and wipes them on a towel. 'I got a letter.' Her voice is wobbly.

'A letter? Who from?' But she knows.

Angela goes to the table and sits down, leaning heavily against it as she does.

'He wants to come back.' She spreads her fingers on the table and stares down at them.

Lizzie sits down beside her. 'Hang on.' She takes her new mobile from her bag and dials Joe's number. 'Joe? It's Lizzie. I'll be a bit late today – can you hold the fort for a while?'

Joe doesn't ask any questions, and she blesses him for his sensitivity. Angela sits without moving, looking down at her hands. Her calmness – her blankness – is frightening.

Lizzie puts her phone back in her bag and takes Angela's hands in hers; they're warm from the washing-up, but they're trembling slightly. 'Now, what did he say?'

'He says . . . he realises he made a terrible mistake . . . and he wants to come back. And he hopes I'll have him.' Her voice is completely without expression – she could be reciting words in a foreign language that mean nothing to her. She is still looking down at her hands, limp and shaking in Lizzie's.

'Angela –' Is she in shock? 'Hang on.' Lizzie gets the brandy from Angela's press and pours a dollop into a glass. 'Here, take a bit of that – just a sip.'

Angela lifts the glass with both shaking hands, and gulps and splutters, and sets the glass down. But it seems to bring her back a bit.

'Thanks.' She takes a deep, shaky breath. 'Bit of a turn-up, isn't it?'

Lizzie hardly knows what to say. 'Had you no idea at all that this was coming?'

Angela shakes her head, and picks up the brandy glass again. 'None.' She takes another, smaller sip. 'The birthday card was a shock, but I just thought it must have been Dee's idea, or something . . . This was a complete surprise.' She shakes her head again.

Lizzie says nothing, just waits. After a few minutes Angela says, in a low voice, 'When he left . . . I was – it was worse than him dying, you know?' Lizzie nods. 'Knowing that he was with someone else, that he'd chosen her over me, that she was –'

Angela bites her lip, takes another long, ragged breath and finishes the brandy. 'I had to carry on, for Dee's sake. She was distraught; she couldn't understand why he'd left, although we both, separately, tried to explain to her that he still loved her, that that would never change . . .' She looks down into the empty glass. 'It took six months before I could think about him without crying.'

The colour is slowly coming back to her cheeks. 'The first few times he came to see Dee, I couldn't talk to him – I just pretended I was too busy, told her to run out to him on her own . . . I did a bloody good job of hiding my feelings; I'm sure everyone around here thought I was wonderful, how I recovered, turned everything around and got over him.' She sighs deeply. 'If they only knew how many nights I didn't close my eyes, how many times I cursed the ground he walked on . . . and in the next breath wished to God he'd just come back to us.'

She smiles faintly. 'I suppose, in a way, it made me more determined to make a go of this place. I wanted to show him that I could do it, that he couldn't destroy me.' She twirls the glass around and around by its stem. 'I hated him, even while I still loved him . . . I'd never realised it was possible to do that – love someone and hate them at the same time.'

Lizzie says nothing, just nods and listens. After a few seconds Angela says, 'It's been two and a half years now; I've moved on. Dee and I have survived. I'm making enough money to live on, and life is starting to look good again.' She puts down the glass and takes one of Lizzie's hands. 'You've helped, Lizzie, you really have. You've gone from being the lodger in the caravan to being a real good pal. In a way, the fact that you never knew John is great; you're part of my fresh start.'

Then her face hardens. 'And now he wants to sail back in here as if nothing had happened. How dare he? I've a good mind –'

'Angela, hold on.' Lizzie grips Angela's hand. 'I think you should do nothing; wait until this has sunk in a bit. You need to think about it. Please don't do anything rash that you might regret.'

'You don't think I'd consider letting him come back, do you?' Angela's face is incredulous. 'Lizzie, you can't imagine I'd do that.'

'I don't know – I can't know what's best for you. Only you can be the judge of that.' Lizzie holds on to her hand. 'But, Angela, for what it's worth, I do think you should give it some thought. Just sleep on it for a night or two – make sure you really come to the right decision here.'

'Sleep on it – that's a good one.' The ghost of a smile passes over Angela's face. 'That man has made sure that I'll have at least a week of lying in bed looking at the ceiling.'

She lets go of Lizzie's hand and stands up. 'Look, you need to get to work. Thanks for listening, and sorry for laying all that on you.'

Lizzie stands too. 'If you need to talk about it some more, you know I'm happy to do that.' She puts her arms around Angela and hugs her tightly. 'I'm not going anywhere; the lodger is staying put in the caravan. You'll have to kick me out.' She lets her go and picks up her bag. 'See you around one. Take care.'

She leaves Angela standing in the middle of the kitchen. Her heart aches for her; what a horrible position to be in . . . *At least she has me to listen to her, for what it's worth*. Angela has done so much for her since she got here – giving her a place to stay, not to mention the job she'd always wanted, and introducing her all around Merway. Lizzie is glad that she can do something in return, even if it's only being there when Angela needs someone to talk to.

As she walks down the street towards Ripe, she thinks about loving and hating someone at the same time, and wonders how it's possible. Who said, 'Love is akin to hate'? It sounds vaguely like Shakespeare, but it could have been anyone. Two of the strongest emotions, so close together that maybe sometimes they collide and cause all sorts of heartache.

When Lizzie reaches Ripe, Joe is standing in the doorway to the back room, arms crossed, looking thoughtful. The shop is empty.

'Morning,' he says.

'Hi, Joe; sorry about that – something came up.' She heads towards the counter, taking off her jacket as she goes.

'Did you sort it out?' He watches her.

'Yeah, it's OK now.' She looks at him. 'It's . . . not really something I can discuss, Joe. I hope you understand.' She drops her jacket on a chair behind the counter.

'That's fine; no problem.' Joe hesitates, as if he's going to say something else, then seems to change his mind. He turns. 'I'll be in the back if you need me.'

Lizzie looks after him, frowning; he's so serious this morning, not a bit like his usual self – not a hint of a smile, no smart comment. Could he be annoyed that she's late? She shakes her head – no, of course not. He'd assume she had a good reason.

She shrugs, and decides she's imagining things; that business with John's letter has her a bit anxious. It's a pity she can't talk it over with Joe, let someone else share the worry – and get a man's perspective. But of course she can't.

She busies herself tidying up, sweeping and polishing and serving and chatting with whoever comes in. Joe doesn't appear. Normally he puts his head around the door every so often with a smart comment – 'Just checking that you haven't made off with the takings.' But there's no sound at all from the back room. Even the radio's off.

He's just busy, that's all. Rushing to get this order out to Cork. Maybe he had a row with Charlie, and he's a bit fed up; he's entitled. Lizzie tries to concentrate on the crossword, to take her mind off the niggling worries, but the clues make no sense.

At twelve-thirty she goes to the back room. 'Joe? It's half twelve.' Maybe he doesn't feel like tea today. She'll leave it up to him.

He looks up and drops the wood he's holding. 'Right; thanks. We'll have tea.'

He still looks so serious. Suddenly Lizzie has to find out what's wrong.

'Joe, is everything all right? You look – upset.' She takes a deep breath. 'Is it something I've done?'

He gives her an odd look – she can't define it – and shakes his head. 'Not at all, Lizzie. Sorry if you thought that. I do need to have a word with you, though.' He gestures towards the table. 'Please sit down. I'll put on the kettle.'

As if I'm a visitor, and he has to be polite. As if we've never sat around the table, laughing at nothing. As if there's nothing between us at all. Her heart sinks further.

'No, thanks, not for me; I don't really feel like tea today.' It would probably choke her. She sits on her usual chair and waits. First Angela, and now this . . .

Joe sits down opposite her. 'Lizzie, I'm very sorry –'
Oh, no; she doesn't want to hear what's coming.
' – but I have to let you go.'

She looks at him, and can't think of a single thing to say. He laces his fingers together; she's never seen him like this, so uncomfortable. 'I'm sorry, Lizzie. It's been great having you here, but the fact is . . .' He stops, and meets her eye for the first time since he sat down. 'Charlie has offered to work here, and as he's family, I can't very well say no.'

This is the last thing Lizzie expected. Charlie is taking over. Sullen, scruffy Charlie is moving in and taking her place. Ruining everything.

'I see.' She forces a smile. 'That's fine, Joe. As you say, he's family. It makes sense to bring him in and let him help you out.' *Shut up. You don't mean a word of this; shut up.* She stops talking and stands abruptly. Her chair scrapes along the floor.

Joe stands too, then puts his hand in his back pocket and takes out an envelope. 'Here's what you're owed, Lizzie, and a week in hand.'

Lizzie is mortified, without knowing why. A memory of Julia O'Gorman handing her an envelope flashes through her head. She feels as if she might get sick at any moment.

Her face flames as she reaches out for the envelope – 'Thanks, Joe; I'll see you' – and practically runs out of the place, grabbing her jacket as she goes through the shop. Joe starts to say something, but she keeps going.

At the door, she nearly collides with Big Maggie coming in. 'Sorry, Maggie – I'm late for an appointment; Joe's inside.' There's no way she can stop and talk – least of all to the town gossip, who'll probably wonder to everyone she meets why Lizzie O'Grady was in such a flap coming out of Joe McCarthy's shop.

She walks quickly down the street towards The Kitchen, head down, blinking away tears and hoping to God she meets no one else she knows; and for once He listens. When she reaches her car she gets in and drives off towards Seapoint. There's no way she can go in to Angela, much as she's dying to talk to her; Angela has quite enough to think about without Lizzie crying on her shoulder. And she'd surely be spotted if she tried to sneak down to the caravan. No, she'll go and find a café in Seapoint and sit there with a coffee and try and pull herself together. She still has an hour or so before she needs to make a start on this evening's baking.

Her throat feels tight; her eyes are hot. As she drives towards Seapoint she forces herself to think positive thoughts.

It's not the end of the world. I've been let go because he needs to give Charlie something to do – to keep him out of trouble, probably. It's no reflection on how he feels or doesn't feel about me; he just can't afford to take two people on – and, anyway, there's no need to have two behind the counter in such a small shop. I'll still be meeting him around the place. Nothing's changed.

By the time she drives back to Merway, an hour and two cappuccinos later, she's almost persuaded herself.

As soon as Lizzie walks in the back door of The Kitchen, Angela stands up from the table and goes quickly towards her.

'Lizzie, I've been trying your mobile – I phoned the shop and Joe told me you were already gone –' Her face is pale. Something tightens around Lizzie's chest. *Oh, God, what now?* She doesn't want to hear, whatever it is; she can't face more trauma today.

But she has to. 'I switched off the mobile. What is it?' Can this day get any worse?

'Your mother phoned.'

Oh, God. Daddy.

'Your father had a fall. He's all right, though.' Angela holds out a bit of paper. 'Here, give her a ring – she left this mobile number, it's a neighbour who's at the hospital with her.'

The hospital. Lizzie's heart pounds. She looks at the paper, and the numbers dance. 'Will you dial, Angela?' Her voice is shaking.

She hears Angela's voice asking for Mammy. Then the phone is passed to her. She takes it with a hand that won't keep still.

'Mammy?'

'Lizzie, we're all right.' Mammy's voice sounds incredibly calm. 'Daddy had a bit of a fall. We're at the hospital, and he's having X-rays now. I'm in the waiting room with Claire.'

For a second, Lizzie can't think who Claire is; then she remembers – their next-door neighbour. For some reason she thinks of a cat.

'I'll come right back. I should be there in about two hours.' She's afraid to ask anything, for fear of what she'll hear.

'Drive carefully, love.' Mammy hangs up, and Lizzie is left holding the phone, and shaking. *Why didn't she tell me that there's no rush, that I could wait until tomorrow if I wanted?* A hand gently takes the receiver away from her, sits her down and places a steaming cup in front of her.

'I have to go – Angela, I can't –'

'Just drink a bit of this – it'll settle you.' Angela spoons sugar into the cup and stirs it. 'I've put an overnight bag together for you –' she gestures towards a bag sitting by the back door; Lizzie had walked right past it '– in case you can't come back straightaway.'

What's she talking about? Of course I'll be back straightaway. Daddy will be fine when I get there. He just had a fall; it's nothing.

Angela lifts the cup, puts it into her hands. 'Take it, Lizzie. You need something before you can drive.'

The tea is sweet and very hot – she burns her tongue. But her heart slows down a little and she feels a bit steadier. After she's forced down half a cup, she goes and picks up the bag.

'Now you take your time; you won't be much good to anyone if you have an accident.' Angela hugs her quickly. 'Ring me when you've news – and take care, Lizzie. We'll look after Jones till you get back.'

Jones – she'd totally forgotten him. 'Thanks, Angela.'

They go out to the car, and Lizzie gets in and drops the bag on the seat beside her. A memory nudges inside her head – saying goodbye to Mammy and Daddy when she left Kilmorris. Packing up the Fiesta and heading off to start her life.

And never going back to see them since, not once; although they asked her and asked her. Putting it off every time she thought about it. Making every excuse she could think of.

She fights down a feeling of panic and starts the engine. *Daddy will be fine. He's had a fall, that's all; his bad leg gave way, probably. Maybe now they'll fix it once and for all – no more Deep Heat.*

She puts her head out of the window. 'I'll call you when I have news.' Angela nods, and waves as Lizzie drives off.

As she passes Ripe, she sees Joe's black Land Rover outside the door. She puts her foot on the accelerator and drives out of Merway.

Chapter Seventeen

Daddy has cancer. Daddy is dying.

Lizzie sits beside Mammy, holding her hand. Mammy's hand is cold and rough. It's twenty past midnight, and they've just been told that Daddy has enough cancer in his body to make sure he's dead within weeks.

Daddy's bad leg. For the past year and a half they've called it *Daddy's bad leg*, in the same tone of voice they'd use to talk about *Daddy's best suit* or *Daddy's gardening gloves.* Daddy limping around the house, wincing if he banged his knee against anything, saying, 'It's at me today a bit.' Mammy and Lizzie taking turns to rub Deep Heat into Daddy's bad leg. And all the time it was filling him up with poison, spreading the poison around his body till he was eaten up with it. Trying to cure cancer with Deep Heat. Like trying to put out a blazing building with a watering can.

How could they not have known? How could they not have noticed that Daddy's bad leg was slowly killing him? Why was there no sign, no warning that in the middle of one night they'd be sitting close together in a doctor's office, holding hands and trying not to hear the words coming out of the doctor's mouth?

Lizzie can't remember the last time she held Mammy's hand. The skin is rougher than she thought it would be – all that scrubbing and polishing and scouring. Mammy stares straight ahead – she hasn't said a word since they sat down – and her empty face doesn't change as tears start to pour slowly down her cheeks. She makes no effort to wipe them away; it's as if she doesn't know they're there. They fall off her chin and drop one by one onto the handbag in her lap. The sound they make is tiny, a little, gentle *plup*. Lizzie watches them and thinks: *Daddy is dying. Daddy has cancer.* She lets the words fall like the tears; but they're heavy, and black.

They're taking Daddy home tomorrow. The hospital will arrange for a nurse to visit the house each day and inject him with enough morphine that he won't be in pain. Or not in too much pain.

'I'm so sorry; it's quite clear from the X-rays that there's nothing we can do for him.' The doctor looks too young and too tired to have to do this terrible thing. Lizzie looks at him and wonders how often he has to smash people's lives with a few sentences. Does it get easier every time he does it? After a few years, will he be able to break hearts and then go home and eat his dinner? She wants to hate him, but she can't. All she can do is hold Mammy's hand and watch the tears leaving dark splotches on the cracked brown leather. *Daddy has cancer. Daddy is dying.*

Daddy is sixty-nine.

They go to sit with him in his room. He's sleeping, his mouth slightly open. His false teeth are sitting in a glass on the locker, giving his face a defenceless look that makes Lizzie want to wail out loud. He's wearing his own pyjamas, which their neighbour Claire brought to the hospital at some stage. Lizzie wonders who put them on him. There's a needle attached to the back of his hand – *Were his fingers always that thin?* – with a tube going into it from a see-through bag of clear liquid. Something is beeping. The room is warm and smells of medicine.

They sit on either side of the bed and look at him. Lizzie feels wide awake. She watches Daddy's chest rising and falling under his pyjama top. She imagines him not being around any more, and has to push the thought away quickly because it makes her feel like getting sick.

She remembers a one-man show she saw once, years ago, in Dublin. She and a pal were up for a few days, staying in a B&B near the theatre, and they decided to check out the show for the laugh. The actor was Australian, and he pranced about the stage and spoke in rhyme about his speckled life. One line stuck in

Lizzie's head: 'He dragged me from happy and pushed me to sad.'

Now she knows what he meant. She feels as if some brutal hand has reached out and wrenched her from the happy place she lived in until this morning, and shoved her into someplace dark and cold.

I'm frightened, here in the dark.

She tries to remember Daddy when she was young, but all she can find in her head is a black-and-white photo: the two of them on a beach somewhere, sitting on a rug. She's half-wrapped in a big towel – the straps of her togs are just visible above it – holding a bag of Taytos and looking straight at the camera, unsmiling. Her hair is wet and plastered to her head. A bucket and spade are beside her. She looks about four.

Daddy's hair is black, and he's smiling and looking at her. He wears dark trousers and a white short-sleeved shirt, and his feet are bare. He sits with his legs out in front of him and leans back on his palms and looks at his little daughter.

Just at the edge of the photo, someone – her? – has built a higgledy-piggledy sandcastle with a moat. A few shells have been stuck haphazardly into its sides, and a lollipop stick pokes out of the top. The bit of the sky that's visible is very white – too white to have been blue in reality. The day must have been cloudy. Some long-forgotten holiday; she knows they went to Donegal a few times when she was small.

The night lasts a million years. Only Daddy sleeps. Mammy sits beside him and holds the hand that's not attached to a tube and cries very softly. Lizzie sits for a while, and then gets up and leans on the radiator and rests her hot cheek against the window and tries not to think. About anything.

In the morning, Mammy and Lizzie go to the canteen and push toast around their plates. When they get back, Daddy is having breakfast – two thin sausages and a rasher, and homemade brown bread, and a cup of tea. He eats nearly one sausage and half a slice of bread. Mammy pours him more tea.

As if they're having breakfast at home. As if none of this nightmare is real.

They talk about the weather – typical Irish summer – and about how nice and warm it is in the room. Lizzie's eyelids are like sandpaper rasping up and down over her eyes. Her legs are heavier than lead, but her head feels light. Daddy says they should think about getting central heating in the house. He doesn't ask them about his leg, doesn't ask any questions. He seems glad to be going home. Lizzie wonders if the doctor told him.

After breakfast, they have to wait in the corridor while he's given medication and dressed. Then they put his pyjamas and his Steradent and his comb and his razor back into the bag Claire brought the day before. He's wheeled to the car in a wheelchair and manoeuvred in by Lizzie and one of the nurses. It's shocking how feeble he suddenly seems to have become, like an old man.

His hand trembles as Lizzie gently guides him in. 'Thanks, love.' She wants to cry, just looking at him; she blinks fast and hard.

He's given a stick to use when he gets out of the car, to get him to his bed. Hopefully he'll be able to manage the stairs, the nurse says; otherwise they'll have to move a bed downstairs.

Daddy makes no comment when he realises that it's taken for granted that he'll go straight to bed when he gets home. He says nothing, just nods, when the nurse tells him that one of them will be calling in to see him the next day. Mammy gets in beside him and puts her arm through his and pats his hand.

Lizzie looks at him sitting quietly in the car, and knows he knows. On the drive home, he doesn't speak. She watches his eyes droop in the mirror.

Dragged me from happy. Pushed me to sad. She keeps having to swallow.

When they've got Daddy upstairs and settled in bed, he falls asleep again almost immediately. They go down to the kitchen, and Lizzie makes tea and Mammy tells her what happened.

'I came home from town and walked in and saw him lying there.' He'd missed his footing near the top of the stairs and come tumbling down. 'He wasn't unconscious, but he couldn't get up, couldn't put the weight on the bad leg.'

Lizzie's heart clenches as she pictures him lying in pain at the bottom of the stairs. She sees Mammy dropping her bags and running over to him, front door swinging wide open.

'I rang for an ambulance, and then I ran out for Claire.' Peter O'Driscoll grew up next door to the O'Gradys, and Claire married him and moved in when Lizzie was about eight. They had no children, just the odd cat who spent his time avoiding Jones. Claire would wave and smile whenever Lizzie passed her in the garden, but generally the O'Driscolls kept to themselves. When Lizzie walked into the hospital, the night before, she wondered for a second who the woman sitting beside Mammy was.

'She was great, Lizzie – insisted on coming to the hospital, brought Daddy's things, stayed till you came . . .' Mammy's voice trembles; her eyes fill with the tears that keep appearing. 'You never know how good people are till you need them.'

Lizzie hands Mammy a tissue and sits beside her while she cries hopelessly. The tea they made goes cold. Neither of them wants to move – what is there to do that can't wait until later?

Lizzie looks around the kitchen. It hasn't changed since she left – not that she expected it to. She thinks, *Something is missing*, and then realises that it's Jones; normally he'd be wandering around, getting under Mammy's feet as she swept and washed up.

Mammy's good friend Julia O'Gorman calls later that day – she met Claire in town. Lizzie answers the door.

'Lizzie, my dear, I just heard Jack had a fall; how is he?' There's no sign of the coldness Lizzie remembers from their last conversation. It's amazing what a little tragedy will do.

She opens the door further. 'Julia, come in. Thank you for coming. Mammy is just checking on him.' She gives Julia tea, and they spend ten minutes talking about nothing at all, and manage not to mention Tony's name once. Julia doesn't ask Lizzie about where she's been, and she doesn't tell Julia that she knows about Pauline Twomey. Then Mammy comes down and Lizzie escapes.

Later she phones Angela and tells her the news.

'Oh, God, Lizzie, you poor creature. I'm so sorry.'

The sympathy in her voice makes Lizzie want to burst out crying. She bites her lip, hard. 'Angela, I don't know when –' When what? When she'll be back? When Daddy will die?

'Of course you don't, pet; you'll stay there as long as you need to.' Angela's voice is strong and steady, and Lizzie clings on to it. 'Don't give another thought to anything here – your stuff will be fine, Jones will be well fed. Dumbledore has promised to mind him till you're back. And I'm sure Joe will manage fine without you too.'

'Actually, he let me go.' Lizzie tries to sound casual. 'Charlie has offered to work for him.'

There's a slight pause; then Angela says, 'Oh, right . . . Well, your baking job is still here for you; I've no intention of sacking you.'

Lizzie tries to laugh, and something that might be a sob comes out instead. 'Thanks, Angela . . . I'll call again in a few days.' Suddenly she remembers John's letter. 'Angela, what about you? How are *you* doing?'

'We're fine here – don't give us another thought. Just look after yourself, and your mam.' Angela clearly doesn't want to talk about John. 'Look, I won't keep you. We're all thinking of you.' And she's gone.

Over the next few days, they accumulate enough casseroles and apple tarts and fruitcakes to last them a month. Hardly half an hour goes by without someone calling to see how Daddy is – neighbours, friends, people from his work, even though he retired four years ago. It's exhausting, but Lizzie is glad of it; it keeps the darkness away for a while.

She's terrified at how quickly Daddy has deteriorated since he came home. Now she understands what people mean when they talk about someone 'going downhill'. It's as if Daddy was teetering at the top of a steep slope for the past eighteen months, and one day someone came along and nudged him gently in the back with a finger, and off he went.

He sleeps a lot; there must be some kind of sedative in the injection he gets from the nurse who calls in the afternoons. He doesn't seem to be in pain – not that he'd say if he were – but he eats very little; a slice of

Lizzie's lemon sponge, one of his favourites, comes back downstairs barely touched. He takes Complan, and a little stewed apple sometimes, and occasionally one of Mammy's egg flips, dolloped with sherry.

They take it in turns to sit with him when he's awake, and when it's Lizzie's turn she reads him bits of the paper – the main news, the sports, anything she thinks will appeal to him. He lies there and listens, smiling gently now and again. Sometimes they do the crossword. Sometimes she just sits in the room with him, listening to the rain outside.

And sometimes they talk. He asks her about Merway.

'You must have made a lot of friends there.' His voice is low; Lizzie has to bend her head a little to hear him.

'I have.' She tells him about Angela, and working in the restaurant, and how Jones and Dumbledore manage to share the garden fairly happily. She describes Merway's main street and pebbly beach, and Big Maggie's garden centre, and Dominic painting by the sea with his rickety easel, and Rory and Aisling in the laundrette, and Gráinne in the newsagent's.

She leaves out Joe, and Ripe, and Charlie.

At night she lies in her old single bed and hates herself. Why didn't she come back to visit them? Why did she keep putting it off? What was so important about her wonderful new life in Merway that she couldn't spare one weekend to get into the car and go home?

She thinks of Daddy asking on the phone when she was going to come and see them, and she has to turn her head into her pillow to try and smother the grief. She misses Jones's bulk, the weight of him on her legs, the buzz of his purring when she reaches out and strokes his head.

One night, when Mammy has gone to bed, Lizzie goes out into the back garden and walks down to the end. She sniffs: the saltiness of the Merway air is missing. No waves rattling the pebbles. The moon is out, though – she can make out the shapes of the shrubs, the shiny leaves of the red robin catching the cool white light, the last of the clematis draped over the stone wall.

The garden was always Daddy's territory. Lizzie can see him, in his old blue shirt and grass-stained grey trousers, trowel in hand as he squats beside his flowerbeds, digging out weeds and slinging them into a green plastic bucket. On his head is an ancient grey-white baseball hat that Mammy hates – 'If you could see how ridiculous you look' – but that he quietly insists on keeping. He found it on a golf course years ago and has worn it for gardening ever since. Lizzie wonders where it is now.

She looks at the sky and ignores God. She's been ignoring Him since she came home. The stars go blurry, and she puts up her hand and wipes her eyes. She wonders where people go when they die, and hopes Daddy will be happy when he gets there. More tears flow out and she feels them sliding down the sides of her upturned face and into her ears.

After a while her neck starts to hurt, and she stops looking at the stars and pulls her head back up. She stands at the bottom of the garden, hands in the pockets of her jacket, and wishes again that she'd brought Jones home with her. She wants to hug his furry warmth and bury her face in him.

Or Joe would do instead. He could hold her and tell her everything will be all right, and she'd close her eyes and lean against him and believe him.

She goes back to the house and locks the door for the night, and goes upstairs to lie in bed and stare at the bedroom ceiling until it's time to get up again.

It takes Daddy nineteen days to die. He does it quietly, like he did most things, in his own bedroom, in the middle of a sunny afternoon in June, when Lizzie is in town shopping for groceries and Mammy is hanging out the washing. The only person with him is Gary O'Rourke from the end of the road. Gary is studying to be a nurse and has been sitting with Daddy for a couple of hours a day. He hears the change in Daddy's breathing and calls to Mammy out the window, and she drops the sheet she's holding and runs in with two clothespegs still in her hand, and by the time she gets up to the room Daddy is dead.

Daddy is dead.

Lizzie arrives home forty minutes later and hears what sounds like singing upstairs. Then the kitchen door opens, and she looks at Gary and she knows that it's not singing. She drops her bags on the floor and covers her face with her hands as he walks towards her with his arms out. Two oranges roll across the hall carpet.

The first person Lizzie phones is Angela. Three hours later, just when The Kitchen would be getting busy, Angela rings the bell. She brings a mountain of sandwiches in a roasting tin and two still-warm chickens, and she walks past the group of neighbours in the hall and straight into the kitchen, where she drops everything on the table. Then she finds Lizzie and wraps her arms around her and hugs her tightly and rocks her as she bawls.

Later, she hands around sandwiches and makes tea while Lizzie phones the undertaker and talks to the priest.

All through what's left of the day, Mammy sits in a chair beside the bed. People come and talk to her in low voices and hold her hand and go away again, and she sits and nods and doesn't cry and rubs at her arms every now and again, as if she's cold, although the day has been unusually warm.

Later still, when everyone else has gone, and Daddy has been taken away to the funeral parlour, Lizzie and Angela leave Mammy and her sister Rose upstairs together and go down to wash up and clear away the remains of the comings and goings of the day.

Then they sit at the table with more cups of tea. Lizzie's head feels light, as if she's had a few glasses of wine, although she's drunk nothing but tea all after-noon. She keeps forgetting about Daddy, and then remembering, and every time it happens she feels like her heart is simply going to stop beating, because there's no sensible reason for it to carry on.

She looks across at her rock. 'Angela, I never even asked you how you managed to come, with the restaurant.'

Angela waves a hand. 'Trish stood in for the night – you know, the one who does the lunches – with Dee as her assistant. They'll be grand; Trish is well able. I had everything ready to go, anyway.' Then she looks across at Lizzie. 'You're exhausted. D'you think you'll sleep?'

'Maybe, in a while.' Lizzie yawns and rubs her hands across her eyes. 'But tell me about you. What's happening with John?' It's been nearly a month since Angela got his letter.

Angela dips her finger into a drop of tea on the table and starts making circles with it. 'Oh, I wrote to him and told him I didn't want him back.'

'And he hasn't been in touch again?'

'Nope. Not a word.' She shakes her head. 'It's in the past – and I think it's better that it stays there.'

Then she reaches over and puts her hand over Lizzie's. 'Now, tell me what happened with you and Joe. He's been going around with a face as long as a wet week since you left, but I can't get anything out of him.'

'There's nothing much to tell. He decided he should give Charlie the job instead of me, that's all,' Lizzie says. 'It makes sense, doesn't it? He's family, I'm not.'

Angela shrugs. 'Actually, I've never seen Charlie working there; Joe's the one I meet any time I go in.' She smiles faintly. 'We're a right pair, Lizzie.'

Lizzie tries to smile back. 'We are.'

After a minute, Angela stands up. 'I'd better get back, I suppose.'

Lizzie walks to the car with her, and hugs her at the door. 'What would I do without you?'

'Ditto, my dear.' She gets into the car. 'Lizzie, mind yourself. You've a busy few days ahead of you; try to sleep, and don't worry about anything in Merway. See you soon.'

Lizzie stands on the path, waving, as Angela drives off. *Six months ago Daddy stood here and waved me off.* She wonders how she can possibly go on producing so many tears.

Two days later, Joe McCarthy comes to Daddy's funeral.

Lizzie doesn't know he's there until after the Mass, when people are lining up to shake her hand and tell her they're sorry for her troubles. Tony O'Gorman is there, with Pauline Twomey, and all of her old friends, and some of her regulars from O'Gorman's, and friends of Mammy's whom she's known for years. Lizzie is standing beside Mammy and nodding and saying thank you and telling people to come back to the house afterwards, and then she sees the next person and it's Joe.

She looks at him and bursts into tears. He reaches out and gathers her into his arms, there in the church

190

in front of everyone, and holds her. 'I'm so sorry, Lizzie,' he says. She smells his spicy aftershave and feels the rough cotton of his shirt against her wet face, and she doesn't know what he's sorry for, and she doesn't know what she's crying for most. She wants to stay wrapped up in him for a long time; it feels like the safest place for her to be, with his arms tight around her. He keeps the dark away.

Then she remembers Mammy standing beside her. She takes a deep breath and makes the tears stop, and stands back from him, and says, 'Thank you for coming, Joe.' He slips something into her hand and moves off, and she puts it quickly into her pocket and turns to the next person in the line.

She can still feel his arms, wrapped around her and holding her tight.

She sees him again at the graveside, standing next to Angela and Deirdre. The day is showery; someone holds an umbrella over her as they watch Daddy disappear into the ground. She hangs on to Mammy and tells him goodbye and carries on ignoring God.

They go back to the house, and Lizzie busies herself passing around sandwiches, finding plates for buns that someone brought, making pots of tea, opening bottles of whiskey and gin and vodka and wine. Angela is everywhere, making sure everyone has a drink and something to eat. Deirdre spends her time at the sink, recycling the piles of cups and plates that keep appearing. Sometime during the afternoon, Lizzie sees

Angela touch Mammy's arm and say something, and she watches Mammy's face break into a careful, grateful smile.

Joe doesn't come back to the house. When there's a lull in the afternoon, Lizzie finds her jacket and puts a hand into the pocket. She pulls out a chubby little wooden cat, his head cradled in his paws, his tail curled around him, fast asleep. There's something poking out from under one paw. She looks closer; it's a tiny fish-tail. She pictures Joe bent over his workbench, carving it.

But Charlie is never in the shop.

Lizzie serves food and drink, and mourns.

Chapter Eighteen

And life goes on.

Nights are there to be got through. Days are measured in meals: prunes and Bran Flakes in the morning, a sandwich and a cup of tea around midday, dinner in the evening. Mammy still cooks all the dinners. Lizzie has offered to help, but Mammy won't hear of it.

'Thanks, love, but I prefer to keep busy. You go and read your book, and I'll call you when it's ready.' Lizzie wishes she could concentrate on a book; it might make the hours seem less like years.

Conversation is difficult. Lizzie does her best.

'I passed Johnny McDermott in town today.' The McDermotts live at the end of the road.

'Is that right.' It's far too flat to be a question.

'I hardly recognised him, he's got so tall. He must be – what, eighteen now?'

'I suppose, about that.' Mammy pushes a bit of bacon around her plate.

'He was smoking. It's a pity, isn't it, when they start?' Surely that'll get a response.

'Mmm.'

Sometimes Lizzie talks about the people she met in Merway.

'He's an artist – I think I told you about him on the phone. He paints outside every day, whatever the weather – unless it's absolutely lashing. You should see his paintings; they're great. And his house is just by the beach, practically on it.'

'Really.'

Every morning after breakfast they walk to the grave, about a mile away. They stand beside the fresh earth, still piled with wreaths. Mammy prays quietly, and Lizzie thinks about Daddy and doesn't pray.

Sometimes they call into the supermarket on the way home, and Mammy fills a basket with the same foods they've always eaten – chops, sausages, eggs, oranges, potatoes, carrots, peas. Lizzie looks on the shelves and sees salami and melons and asparagus. Once she asks Mammy if she'd like to try some hummus – 'Just for a change; you can spread it on bread or crackers' – but Mammy just shakes her head. 'I don't think I'd like it, love. You get it if you want.' Lizzie doesn't bother.

In the afternoons she tries to read, and pulls weeds from Daddy's flowerbeds, and mows the lawn he always mowed, and answers letters of condolence. And walks.

One evening, after dinner, Mammy gives her Daddy's watch. He was presented with it at his retirement, four years ago, after working for forty-one years in the same insurance office in town.

'I want you to take this, Lizzie. I know Daddy would have wanted you to have it.'

It's a beautiful gold watch, with a black face and thin gold hands and Roman numerals. Daddy didn't wear it for about a year after he got it. It sat on the dressing-table, in its shiny black box, and he kept wearing the old watch with the battered brown leather strap that he'd had for years, until Mammy wore him down – 'For goodness' sake, Jack, would you ever give that old thing to charity and put the new one on? What are you saving it for?' But even after he started to wear the new watch, he always put on his old one when he was gardening or doing any kind of rough work; and he'd still be wearing it at bedtime.

Lizzie looks at the beautiful watch that Daddy never grew fond of, and feels miserable. 'Thanks, Mammy.' She takes off hers and puts on Daddy's. It looks good on her wrist, big and solid – she's always liked big watches. But it doesn't remind her of Daddy.

She thinks it might be better not to tell Mammy that she's already got something much more precious to remember him by.

After the crowd left on the day of the funeral, she went out to the shed and found his old baseball cap poking out from under one wheel of the lawnmower. It was splattered with paint and covered with dried earth, and it smelt musty. She keeps it in the drawer of her bedside locker, next to the little wooden cat.

She lies in bed every night and hears Mammy crying in the next room. Lizzie's heart breaks for her – the life has gone out of her as surely as if she'd been buried next to Daddy. How can Lizzie possibly leave her like this and go back to Merway? She'll stay a month or two, and then see.

And her heart sinks as she feels her old life wrapping itself around her again. *Why, Lizzie, you're back; how nice to see you. You make sure you stay this time, right?*

No way. She'll just keep Mammy company till she's able to be on her own.

Mammy, who's never lived alone in her life – who moved straight from her family home to married life with Daddy. Who doesn't drive, barely knows how to change a light-bulb, has never replaced the battery in the smoke alarm and couldn't find where to turn off the water supply if her life depended on it.

And slowly, *when I go back* turns to *if I go back*. Standing in the garden one night, Lizzie makes herself face the possibility that she may never again live in Merway. Never wake up and hear the seagulls. Never step outside the caravan door and breathe in the salty air. Never knead a ball of dough on Angela's big kitchen table, up to her elbows in flour, giggling away at something Angela has just said.

Never open the door of Ripe and see Joe McCarthy smiling at her.

For the first time since Daddy died, Lizzie lets herself think about Joe – and immediately, a single question buzzes around her head: why did he tell her he had to let her go to take Charlie on? Angela said Charlie is never in the shop; it's always Joe she meets when she goes in. And this brings a new and unpleasant notion drifting into Lizzie's thoughts: was Joe trying to get rid of her? Did he realise that she was falling for him, and decide he had to put a stop to it? The night of Angela's party, when he flirted like mad with her, whispered in her ear – was that just the Guinness talking? All the times they sat around the table in the back room, all the gentle teasing that she pretended to hate – could that really have meant nothing to him?

And then she thinks about the way Joe chats and laughs with anyone who comes into the shop. The way he makes old Mrs McLaughlin raise her eyes to heaven and sympathise good-naturedly with Lizzie: 'God help you, dear, having to put up with his *ráiméis*.' The way he can even raise a reluctant smile from grumpy old Gráinne in the newsagent's. What ever gave Lizzie the notion that she was special? Just because he offered her a job doesn't mean he fancied her, for God's sake.

The fact that he came to her father's funeral doesn't really prove anything either; isn't that something any friend would do? And the little carved cat – well, that was just Joe. That's what he does. For everyone.

The more she thinks about it, the worse Lizzie feels. If Joe could see how she felt about him – if she was that pathetically obvious – who's to say that half of Merway didn't see it too? God, was Big Maggie telling all and sundry how Lizzie O'Grady was making a fool of herself over Joe McCarthy? She cringes at the thought of them all having a great laugh at foolish little Lizzie.

Wrapped up in her grief and loneliness, she comes to the conclusion that she was sadly mistaken about Joe. He needed someone to take over for a few hours in the shop, and she was available; that was all there was to it. Not that it matters, anyway, if she's not going back to Merway.

She wishes she'd told Daddy about Joe. Even if it has come to nothing, she's sorry Daddy never knew that, at the age of forty-one, his daughter had finally discovered what it meant to be in love.

One morning, about three weeks after Daddy's death, Lizzie looks out her bedroom window and sees Mammy hanging clothes out on the line. She's bending to the laundry basket like an old woman, fumbling with the pegs that she keeps in a biscuit tin. When did her hair go that grey? How can Lizzie even consider deserting her?

After dinner that night, she tells Mammy that she's not going back to Merway. Mammy is delighted, and they live happily ever after in Kilmorris until Mammy's death twenty-three years later. Lizzie makes her peace with God and enters a convent the day after Mammy's funeral, and dies in a state of grace at the age of ninety-six, just after benediction. The other nuns miss Sister Elizabeth's spicy fruit scones and rhubarb crumble.

Except that's not what happens at all.

Lizzie is about to clear the plates from the table – she'll wait till they've settled down for the night to talk about her decision – when Mammy puts a hand on her arm to stop her. 'Hold on a minute, Lizzie. Will you sit down again, please? I want to say something.'

Lizzie puts the plates back on the table and sits down beside her.

'What is it?'

'Lizzie, don't you think it's time you went back to Merway?' Mammy looks steadily at her, hand still on her arm. 'Angela will be missing you for the baking.'

Lizzie's eyes sting. She puts her hand on Mammy's. 'Mammy, I'm not going back – of course I'm not. I'm staying here to look after you and keep you company. I was going to tell you tonight.'

Mammy shakes her head, smiling faintly. 'You don't have to do that, love; I don't need looking after.'

'But I don't mind.' Since she's not talking to God, she doesn't imagine a lie will do much harm. 'I couldn't leave you here on your own. My place is with you now, and I'm happy to come back, honestly.' Mind you, it *is* a fairly big lie. A colossal lie, really. But still, as long as she's not talking to Him . . .

Mammy is shaking her head more firmly. 'No, Lizzie, your place *isn't* here; not any more.' She presses Lizzie's arm gently. 'You have your own life to lead now. You go back to Merway; you liked it there, didn't you?'

As Mammy speaks, Lizzie watches her face. The lost look that's been in her eyes since Daddy's death is still there – she misses him terribly. Grief has crisscrossed her forehead, and the skin on her cheeks looks tauter, the cheekbones more pronounced. A new collection of faint little vertical lines runs from her nose to her mouth. The man she expected to grow old with is gone, and now she faces the prospect of doing it on her own. It must be terrifying.

And yet here she is, sitting beside her only daughter – the daughter who's just offered to come back and live with her – and letting her go. No, *insisting* that she go. She mustn't know what she's saying; she can't have thought it through.

'But, Mammy,' Lizzie says gently, 'you've never been on your own. How would you manage?'

'Better than you'd imagine,' says Mammy crisply, and Lizzie sees a flash of the old Mammy, the one you didn't dare face without whatever she'd sent you for. 'I'm not completely helpless, you know. And haven't I got plenty of friends and neighbours I can call on? There's Peter and Claire next door, and Julia, and the McDermott lads are always around the place for odd jobs; and Rose is going to come and stay for a few days every now and again.'

Aunt Rose, Mammy's widowed sister in Cork, already lined up to come and visit . . . Maybe Mammy *has* been thinking it through. A tiny flicker of hope leaps in Lizzie's chest, but still . . . she has to be sure.

'Well, yes, of course Rose will come, but –'

Mammy doesn't wait for her to finish. 'Look, Lizzie . . .' She looks at the table and says nothing for a minute, and then she looks back at Lizzie. 'I know it hasn't been easy for you, seeing all your friends go off and get married, or go abroad somewhere, making something of their lives, while you . . . well, you never really got to do what you wanted, did you?'

She shushes Lizzie's protests. 'No, you didn't. You took the waitressing job even though it wasn't what you wanted; you wanted to be a baker, and we never really listened to you or tried to help you.'

This can't be Mammy talking – Mammy who was so adamant that baking was no sort of a career, Mammy who had her heart set on me getting married and having children and taking over O'Gorman's someday . . .

'You got engaged to Tony because you knew it was expected of you,' Mammy says gently, 'and he wasn't right either.'

Tony O'Gorman, son of Mammy's best friend Julia – the most eligible man in Kilmorris, as far as Mammy was concerned . . . Lizzie remembers Mammy's face the day they told her they were engaged; she was thrilled.

'All your life, you did things that weren't really what *you* wanted – maybe you felt we wanted them for you, or maybe you just thought they were things you should do . . . Anyway, that doesn't really matter now.'

All Lizzie can do is sit and listen while Mammy says things she never expected to hear her say.

'When you came home that day and told us you'd broken off the engagement and you were going to head off to God knows where, I couldn't believe it.'

Don't I know it; and didn't you make no secret of how you felt. But Lizzie feels no bitterness; she's too stunned to feel anything. She suddenly notices that Mammy's eyes are full of tears.

'I'm ashamed to admit it, Lizzie, but I had no idea you were unhappy – and you must have been, for a long time. I just never thought beyond what I wanted for you – or really, I suppose, what I wanted for me.' Mammy blinks, and a tear rolls from each eye and races down her face, veering sideways when it comes to a line. She pulls a tissue from the box on the table that keeps having to be replaced.

'Mammy, don't feel bad, please; I really didn't know myself what I wanted.' Lizzie squeezes Mammy's hand. How hard must it be for her to lay herself bare like this? She's admitting that maybe she got it wrong all those years . . . and doing it without the comfort of Daddy beside her. Lizzie speaks gently, 'Something just – woke me up one day, and I knew that it was all wrong . . . and that I had to stop, and get away . . . It's hard to explain.'

Mammy nods, dabbing her eyes. 'And I made it as hard as I could for you to go. I'm mortified now when I think of how selfish I was, worrying about what people would think, never giving a thought to you and your happiness.'

Lizzie shakes her head, but Mammy goes on: 'Lizzie, it's taken Jack's death to make me realise how short life is, and how silly it is to worry about what others think . . . and how we must make *sure* to make the best use of it that we can.' She grips Lizzie's arm urgently. 'You have to promise me that you'll go back to Merway.'

The spark of hope bursts into a tiny flame. Lizzie chooses her words carefully. 'I *have* been happy there – happier than I'd been in a long time.'

Mammy smiles. 'I know, love, and I'm glad you finally found the courage to make the break, despite your stubborn old mother.'

Lizzie starts to say something, but again Mammy stops her. 'Hold on – there's something else I have to tell you.' She presses a hand to her mouth for a minute, then goes on. 'Your father had a life insurance policy from his work, and he kept paying into it after he retired.' She takes an envelope from her bag and puts it between them on the table. 'I got this in the post today.'

Lizzie takes the letter out and discovers that Daddy, who always provided for them, made sure that they'd be well taken care of after his death too. The words on the page blur together.

'Lizzie, that money is for you; he always said so. He invested his retirement lump sum; I'll have plenty from that, and the pension.'

Lizzie thinks of Mammy's careful spending – the chops and the cabbage and the white pudding, and the homemade brown bread. She thinks of the long-ago caravan holidays, and the rented houses in Kerry and West Cork and Connemara when she was a bit older – the pub lunches, the dinners Mammy cooked in the rented kitchens. They had nothing expensive, nothing extravagant, not even when Daddy retired. Mammy and Daddy never stayed in a hotel, not once – never ate in a fancy restaurant, except for the few times when Lizzie and Tony insisted on bringing them out to dinner. They never had a foreign holiday. They were saving all the money for some distant future, when only one of them would be around to enjoy it.

Mammy gestures towards the letter. 'Would it be enough, I wonder, to start your little bakery in Merway?'

Oh yes, Mammy, it would. Lizzie smiles over at her and nods, and silently tells God she's sorry for fighting with Him.

Later that night, she phones Angela.

She stays another week with Mammy, sorting out a list of numbers for her to keep beside the phone – doctor, plumber, electrician, handyman. Unknown to Mammy, she calls in to Claire next door and thanks her again for all her help, and leaves her mobile number with her in case of any emergency. She finishes replying to the letters of condolence, and arranges for Cian McDermott, Johnny's younger brother, to mow the back lawn once a week till the end of summer. She shows Mammy where the water turns off and where the fuse-box is and how to read the meter, and she makes sure that Mammy has a drawerful of candles and a torch. She checks the batteries in the two smoke alarms and shows Mammy how to do it too. She gets a man out from Eircom to run a phone line into Mammy's bedroom, even though Mammy thinks it's the height of nonsense.

'It's not for you, Mammy, it's for me; it'll help *me* sleep, even if it does nothing for you.' Then she smiles faintly; it's the first time she's felt more like Mammy's mother than her daughter.

On the day she's heading off again, Lizzie stands by the car. 'I'll phone twice a week, Wednesday and Sunday, and you have my mobile number if you need me.'

Mammy nods.

'And I'll come and visit often, I promise; and you have Rose coming at the weekend.'

Mammy nods again.

'And you'll remember to –'

Mammy stops nodding. 'Lizzie, for goodness' sake, I'm not a child. Get into that car, and give me a ring to let me know you're safely landed.'

So Lizzie hugs her and drives away, and tries not to remember the last time she drove off, with her head full of dreams and Daddy standing beside Mammy on the path, waving.

When she comes to the place where she picked up the American hitchhiker, she wonders what's become of him. Is he still in Rockford, in the house with the holes in the roof? She can hardly remember what he looks like.

She drives on towards Merway.

Chapter Nineteen

When Lizzie pulls up outside The Kitchen, she sits in the car for a minute. It's been less than two months since she was here, but it feels like another lifetime. She winds down her window and breathes in deeply, smelling salty air and garlic: Angela has started the dinners. A wave of something peaceful washes over her.

She takes her bag out of the car and walks around to the back of the restaurant, feet crunching on the gravel. The kitchen door opens as she approaches it.

'Lizzie – there you are. Good to see you.' Angela gives her a hug, then steps back and looks at her carefully. 'You've lost weight. How are you?'

'All the better for seeing you, my dear,' smiles Lizzie. 'How are you?'

'Fine; I'll be telling you all later on.' Angela goes to the cooker and gives the pan a shake, making something sizzle loudly. 'Why don't you settle back in and come up when you're ready? I've your duvet airing in the hot press here – you can take it down when that rain stops.'

On the way to the caravan, Lizzie spots a familiar ginger bulk poking out from under a bush. 'Jones, hi.' She crouches beside him and scratches the back of his neck, and he yawns hugely at her. 'Well, I'm really glad you missed me too.'

She opens the door of the caravan. *I'm home.* The familiar space feels so right – the small kitchen, the shelves with her cookery books, the rug in front of the fire, the bowl of shells on the coffee table; the vase she always kept filled with flowers, full of flowers now – *thanks, Angela.*

She drops her bag on the bed. A shower and a change of clothes, and maybe a short walk on the beach, and then she'll go back up to Angela. Might as well get stuck in.

But first . . . She puts a hand into a side pocket of the bag and takes out the cat and the baseball cap. She puts the cat on the little shelf beside the window and the cap under her pillow.

A little later, crunching along the pebbles next to the water, Lizzie wonders about Angela. Of course she seemed glad to see her, but was there something . . . subdued about her? She wasn't her usual bubbly self, was she?

Lizzie shakes her head impatiently. *I'm imagining things; Angela was perfectly normal. She was hardly talking to me for more than a minute, for goodness' sake. And, anyway, she knows I'm not able for bubbly just yet.* She turns back and heads towards the restaurant.

But by the time they've cleared away the last of the dinners, Lizzie's decided that her first instinct was right: something is definitely up with Angela. She's been distracted all evening, going through the motions of cooking and dishing up and serving, but clearly a million miles away.

Lizzie waits until they're sitting down with tea.

'Want to talk about it?'

Angela gives her a half-smile. 'How well you know me.'

'It's John, isn't it?'

'Yeah.' Angela takes a deep breath. 'You know I wrote to him and said I wasn't interested in getting back together again.' Lizzie nods. 'I feel I made the right decision; that part of my life is over, I just want to move on . . . To be honest, I don't think I'd ever be able to trust him again.'

Lizzie passes her the milk. 'That letter can't have been easy to write.'

'About as easy as pulling teeth from a rabid elephant, if there's such a thing,' Angela says. 'Anyway, I heard nothing for a few weeks after that. I was beginning to think that was the end of it – and wondering if he'd stop coming to see Dee, just to spite me . . . Then he turned up out of the blue, about a week ago, and told me that, if I wanted to make a clean break, then he'd rather we made our separation . . . official.' She makes a face.

'But isn't that better, Angela? Isn't that what you want too?' Lizzie says gently. She can imagine that Angela's feelings must be terribly mixed; it's one thing to say you want to put your marriage behind you and make a fresh start, and another to actually do it.

'He said we should get a divorce.' Angela picks up her cup, then puts it down again. 'He said we should do it properly – get a solicitor each, and divide everything up between us.'

'I suppose it makes sense, really – as long as he keeps up the contact with Deirdre.' Dee is obviously close to her father; it would break her heart to be cut off from him.

Angela frowns. 'Yes, I'm sure he'll see her like he always has; that's not what I'm worried about. But Lizzie, if we divide everything up between us, that includes this place – the restaurant. My livelihood. He's probably entitled to half.'

Lizzie looks at her in alarm. 'Half this place? But – no, he has no right. This is all *your* work, *you* set it all up.'

'Yes, yes, I was the one who opened the restaurant,' Angela says impatiently, 'and I was the one who stayed up half the night for the first six months, trying to make a go of it. But it was his place to begin with; he already had the house and the video shop when we got married. I just moved in.'

She pulls a hand through her hair, and Lizzie suddenly sees how tired she looks. 'I don't know exactly what he's entitled to at this stage, but one thing's for sure – there's no way in the world I can afford to buy him out, whatever his rights are.'

'But he can't just come along like that and demand –'

'Actually, I'm afraid he can. I haven't really talked to my solicitor yet – I'm meeting her in the morning – but on the phone she didn't hold out much hope. She said he'd definitely be entitled to "a substantial share", whatever that is.'

Lizzie's head is buzzing. Everything Angela worked for, all her efforts to keep going after John walked out . . . It seems incredible that he might be able to come along and claim half – and, in the process, ruin her. What kind of justice would that be?

No wonder Angela seemed distracted; she must be going out of her mind with worry.

Lizzie tries to gather her thoughts. 'Look, wait and see what the solicitor says when you meet her. It mightn't be as bad as you think; I mean, surely a lot would depend on what kind of income John has now, wouldn't it? And Deirdre is living with you, so that'll be taken into account . . .'

But, even as she says it, she knows that Angela is probably right: if this place originally belonged to

John, he must have a strong case for claiming at least half. And, of course, he walked out on his livelihood – the video shop – when he left, so chances are he's not rolling in it now.

Angela smiles thinly. 'Watch out, Lizzie – Dee and I could well end up moving into the caravan. You might have to make room.'

Even though it's meant to be a feeble joke, Lizzie feels a very selfish stab of fear at the thought that the caravan might be taken from her. Mammy sends her back to Merway, and she's evicted a week later . . . how ironic would that be?

She lifts the teapot, but Angela shakes her head. 'No, thanks; I think I'll turn in. Sorry – not much of a welcome back for you, was it? . . . Oh, and not a word to Dee – I haven't mentioned this to her yet. I dread to think how she'll take it, actually.'

'I wouldn't worry too much about that – kids are resilient.' *Except that she's not a kid any more; she's a teenager, probably full of the insecurities and uncertainties that I remember from that age*. 'If there's anything I can do to help, I will; you know that. Now that I'm not working in Joe's any more, I can be around here as much as I'm needed.'

Angela gives her another weak smile. 'I know, pet. Unfortunately, I don't think there's a darn thing you can do to get me out of this one.'

As she goes through the door into the hall, Lizzie looks thoughtfully after her. *Actually, you might just be surprised.*

212

The following morning, Lizzie walks to Blooming Miracles after breakfast. Big Maggie's head pops up from behind a display of seed packets as the door opens.

'Lizzie, how lovely; Angela said you were coming back this week. Any excuse to take a break from cleaning is very welcome.' She takes Lizzie's hands and presses them gently between hers. 'My dear, I'm so sorry about your poor father.'

Lizzie is touched. 'Thank you, Maggie – and thanks for your Mass card; it was very thoughtful.'

'Not at all, dear – the least I could do. I wanted to come to the funeral, but I had a big wedding order that day.' She drops Lizzie's hands. 'Now, have you time for a cup of tea?'

'That'd be lovely, Maggie. I think I could spare a few minutes – and you can bring me up to date on what's been happening around Merway.' *Because if anyone knows, you will.*

So Lizzie hears the news – a spate of break-ins within days of one another; a new boutique about to open; a near-drowning a few miles down the coast; Maggie's own plans to redecorate and possibly extend the garden centre.

Lizzie wonders how long before the name she's waiting for comes up. 'Anything else strange?'

'Well, I suppose Angela has already told you that Dominic is off to the States next month. Some big offer of work from the man he deals with there.' Lizzie hadn't heard; Angela had other things on her mind the night before. 'Yes, it seems he could be gone quite a while – two or three months, maybe. He told me he's asked Joe McCarthy to keep an eye on his house for him.'

With an effort, Lizzie looks innocently over at Maggie. 'Oh, I see.' And then she waits.

Maggie leans over and puts a hand on Lizzie's arm. 'I hope you're going to be working with Joe again, dear, now that you're back. Take your mind off things.'

And give you something fresh to talk about. Lizzie shakes her head firmly. 'Oh, no, Maggie – that was only a temporary arrangement, just to give Joe a hand for a few weeks. No, I'll be helping Angela out more in The Kitchen, actually; I'll have my hands full there.'

'Oh, I see.' Maggie looks faintly surprised. 'I thought you were a permanent fixture in Joe's shop; you seemed to get on very well.'

'Ah, no, I wouldn't really fancy that kind of work; not my cup of tea at all.' Lizzie smiles. 'I'm much happier baking for Angela . . . Anyway, Joe has Charlie to help him if he's stuck.'

'That fellow?' Maggie says in disbelief. 'He wouldn't last a day there; he doesn't know the meaning of work.'

So Lizzie was right: Charlie was simply Joe's excuse to let her go. It's painful for her to accept the truth – but at least now, she hopes, Maggie doesn't think she's pining for Joe.

They talk some more, and then Lizzie looks at her watch and remembers that she should be getting back to help Angela. She thanks Maggie for the tea, and buys two bunches of freesias.

She heads towards the beach; she'll walk back to The Kitchen that way. She's not in as much of a hurry as she led Maggie to believe, and the day is fine.

It's got nothing to do with the fact that, this way, she won't have to walk past Ripe. As she crunches across the pebbles, she tells herself that she's not avoiding Joe; of course not. It's just that she's not quite ready to face him yet. Give her a week or so, to get back into the swing of things in Merway, and she'll be able to chat away to him and be perfectly friendly and natural.

She hopes.

As luck would have it, every time Lizzie turns around, over the next week or so, Charlie is there. He saunters past The Kitchen one afternoon, hands in the pockets of the one pair of scruffy jeans he seems to own. She sees him coming out of Doherty's another day, and heading into Dignam's one evening. If he sees her, he doesn't let on, and she's glad that she doesn't have to pretend to be friendly.

One day she drives past a chipper in Seapoint and sees Charlie talking with a girl in a blue top. She looks awfully like – Lizzie slows down and cranes out the window – yes, it's definitely Deirdre, deep in conversation with the most unsavoury character in Merway. She's sharing his newspaper bundle of chips, or whatever, and laughing at something he's saying. Lizzie is amazed that they even know each other, but then she thinks: *Why shouldn't they? They've been living in the same village for nearly a year.*

After deliberating for a while, she decides to say nothing about it; Angela has other things on her mind these days.

Or, at least, one other thing.

Today she's visiting her solicitor for the second time in a week. Today she'll be told whether John Byrne is going to bring about the end of her business. Lizzie wants to go with her, but Angela insists on going alone.

'If I'm delayed, you'll need to make a start on the dinners – Dee will be around to give a hand if you need her. At least, I hope she will; she's been out a lot lately.' Angela looks pale and worried, and Lizzie feels a knot of anxiety for her.

'Look, just wait and see; it mightn't be as bad as you're thinking.'

Even as she says it, Lizzie knows that this is a fat lot of good to Angela, who has a head on her shoulders and a pretty good idea what her solicitor is going to say. But Angela nods and climbs into her car.

Later, as Lizzie comes out of the caravan, she sees Deirdre coming through the gate from the beach.

'Hi, Lizzie.' Her usually pale cheeks are slightly flushed, presumably from having rushed home from wherever she was. She looks up towards the house. 'Wonder if Mum is back yet.'

Lizzie shakes her head. 'She said she'd ring me when she's on her way home. I was just about to go and make a start on the bread.'

Deirdre nods – 'Shout if you need me; I'll be in my room' – and walks quickly up to the house.

Looking after her, Lizzie wonders how much she knows, or guesses, about what's happening between her parents. She's been out more than in since Lizzie got back. Maybe she prefers the company of her friends at the moment, with Angela so distracted – and who could blame her, poor thing? As long as she's not seeing too much of Charlie McCarthy . . .

She glances at her watch: two-fifteen. If Angela gets back in the next half-hour, they'll have time to chat before they get too busy.

Enough time, Lizzie hopes, for her to find out what she needs to know.

Chapter Twenty

'You must be out of your mind.'

Angela looks incredulous. Lizzie smiles gently back. It's eleven o'clock that evening, the clear-up is finished and they're in the kitchen.

'I knew you'd say that. You're so predictable. And I'm not out of my mind, I'm perfectly sane – as well you know.'

Angela shakes her head slowly. 'No, you've definitely flipped.' Then she smiles. 'Look, Lizzie, don't think I'm not grateful; it's the most generous offer I've –'

'Generous, my foot. Now you listen to me, Angela Byrne.' Lizzie sits down across from her, and the look on her face makes Angela think that it might be wise to listen. 'That money is mine to do as I please with. It's not up to you how I spend it; it's up to me. I'm so bloody tired of everyone telling me what I can and can't do.'

Angela looks at her in amazement. 'Of course, I know that, but –'

'Hang on – I'm not finished.'

Angela hangs on.

'Just listen, right?' Lizzie holds out her fingers and counts on them: one. 'I've always wanted to bake for a living – and this is the first place where I've managed to do that.' Two. 'We've got on well together since we met.' Three. 'Now, you need money to stay in business; you've been told that John is probably entitled to forty per cent of this place, right?' Angela nods.

Four. 'You've worked out roughly how much that would be, and I have that money – or near enough.' Five. 'It's not just going to help you – it's going to help *me*, too, to do what *I've* always wanted.'

She runs out of fingers and stops counting. 'Angela, I'm talking about a partnership. You and me, running The Kitchen and sharing the profits; paying John off and making a fresh start. Working together – really working together, not this half-assed arrangement we have now. Think about it, please. Daddy has given me this wonderful chance, and this is the way I'd love to use it.' Her voice wobbles and she takes a deep breath. 'At least say you'll think about it – don't dismiss it out of hand. Sleep on it.' *And then say yes. Please say yes.*

Angela finds her voice. 'God.' She stares across at Lizzie. 'Partners.'

Lizzie nods furiously.

'John paid off and The Kitchen still going strong.'

More nodding.

'God,' says Angela again, her eyes wide, 'd'you really think it could work? Really?'

Lizzie feels a smile start somewhere inside her; Angela is beginning to believe in her brilliant plan. 'What do you mean, do I think it could work? Isn't it working now? The only difference would be that you'd have someone to share all the hassle, and the security of knowing that no one could take the place away from you – and I'd get to share the profits.' She's home and dry; she can tell. 'What did you call us – a match made in heaven, the baker and the chef? We're still that.'

She gets up and goes to the fridge. 'And now I really need this . . .' And she hauls out a bottle of sparkling wine she snuck in earlier.

'Hey, poor man's bubbly – lovely.' Angela takes down two glasses.

'So you'll think about it,' Lizzie says, easing out the cork.

'Yeah, I'll think about it.' Angela puts the glasses on the table. 'Now, don't be getting your hopes up too much, Lizzie – I do need to think carefully about it – but I will say that, in theory . . . your daft idea is slowly beginning to make a tiny bit of sense to me.'

Lizzie pours two glasses and lifts hers. 'I'll drink to that.'

Angela takes less than a week to agree to the partnership. She writes to John to let him know that she's buying him out.

'It's only fair – and I want to avoid bad feeling if I can, for Dee's sake. If I keep him informed right from the start, he can't turn around later and say I sprang it on him.'

Two days after that, John turns up at the restaurant, just as Angela and Lizzie are finishing the lunch clear-up.

He walks straight in the back door. 'Ange.'

She spins around from loading the dishwasher, then just stands looking at him. Lizzie places the cutlery she's holding on the table and wonders if she should leave – or will Angela need some support?

She doesn't have long to wonder. 'Lizzie, could you give us a little while, please?' Angela's face is expressionless, but the colour has drained from it.

'Sure.' Lizzie nods at John and walks past him, out the door and straight down the gravel path to the pebbly beach. John doesn't even glance her way. She's gone about a hundred yards before she realises that she's still wearing her apron, the one that Angela got her with the giant ice-cream cone on it.

She gives them an hour. Apart from that night in the hospital with Mammy, when each minute seemed to go on forever, it's the longest hour of her life. She paces across the pebbles, holding the apron by the strings and trying not to panic.

Two little children are paddling; an older woman – Granny, maybe – is perched precariously on a canvas chair, watching them. At Granny's feet is a tartan rug strewn with little buckets and towels and clothes and sandals; it reminds Lizzie of the rug in the photo of her and Daddy on that long-ago holiday. She smiles absently at the woman, her mind full of what could be happening a little way away.

What if John changes Angela's mind – persuades her, even at this late stage, to take him back and make a new start? Lizzie would be happy for Angela if it worked out – of course she would – but what if he comes back and it all goes wrong again? What if he decides, three months later, or six months later, that he's made a mistake, and walks out for the second time?

And what about the restaurant? Would they keep it going – or close it down and open a video shop again? Surely not – The Kitchen is ticking over, quite healthily, by the looks of it; but with the two of them there to run it, Lizzie could forget about having anything to do with it. She wonders what John's baking is like.

And of course she'll have to leave the caravan. She doubts that John would take kindly to the person who almost bought him out living in his back garden. So she'd be jobless *and* homeless.

She crunches over the pebbles and tells herself to calm down. She might as well tell the Atlantic to part.

After an hour, she goes back. She stands outside the kitchen door and hears nothing. She knocks and waits. After a few seconds, it opens.

'What are you knocking for?' Angela looks pale, but she's dry-eyed and seems calm.

'I didn't want to walk in on you and John.' Lizzie follows her in; no sign of him.

'He's gone about twenty minutes.' Angela goes to the sink and turns on the tap. 'I was just going to make a start on the spuds; I know we've time enough, but I felt like being busy.' She hauls up a bag of potatoes and empties them into the sink.

Lizzie stands there helplessly. Should she ask how it went? Angela seems so calm . . . could it really have been that civilised?

'Nothing's changed, in case you're wondering,' Angela says, over the running water. 'I told him that we're serious about buying him out, and that I've already told my solicitor that I intend to file for divorce when the time comes.'

But she's so calm . . . is that natural? 'How did he take it?'

Angela lifts her shoulders, picks up a potato and starts to scrub it. 'Well . . . it appears his looking for half of everything I have was a big fat bluff – he thought I'd get such a fright that I'd crack and agree to have him back. Not that he admitted it in so many words, of course. But I could tell.'

She puts the scrubbed potato on the draining board and starts on another one, head bent; Lizzie can't see her face. 'He must have got a right shock when he got my letter. He never for a minute thought I'd be able to buy him out – why would he? So, once he realised I was serious, he tried to change my mind. He repeated everything he said in his first letter – he must have been out of his head to leave me, he realises that now, blah blah blah – but I was having none of it.'

By now she has half a dozen potatoes done; they sit all higgledy-piggledy on the draining board. 'I stayed very calm and told him my mind was made up. I said my solicitor told me he'll probably be entitled to forty per cent of this place; he didn't comment. I told him I wasn't interested in a reconciliation, thank you very much, and then I said he'd have to leave because I had to get started on the evening meals.'

She puts the scrubber down and empties the earthy water out of the basin. 'I suppose he took it fairly well, considering. Very polite and . . . civilised . . .' She trails off, watching the water vanish through the plughole. 'He even arranged to come and take Dee out next Saturday.' Then she runs fresh water into the sink and sloshes it around.

Lizzie stands where she is, watching Angela's hands in the water. 'Are you OK?'

Angela turns to her then, and Lizzie sees her eyes are bright with tears. But she nods. 'I will be. But it's just . . . very sad. How it can all . . . go wrong like that. When it was so right for so long.'

She rubs a hand across her eyes, turns back to the sink and picks up another potato. 'Life will go on, and hopefully it'll be better – eventually.' She scrubs hard, shifting little clods of earth under the running tap.

Lizzie shakes out the apron she's still holding and puts it on. Her heart goes out to Angela, trying to scrub away her heartache – and then a thought strikes her. She and Angela are both in mourning: her for Daddy, and Angela for her marriage.

Maybe it's a good thing they're joining forces; they can help each other through, maybe.

The next three weeks are a flurry of phone calls and solicitor's appointments and 'Sign here, please' and trawling through inventories and getting valuations. Lizzie is relieved to discover that they don't have to come face to face with John during the process – she isn't sure what reception he'd give her. Luckily, their solicitors do all the liaising.

And six days before her forty-second birthday, Elizabeth Mary O'Grady uses Daddy's money to make a cheque out to John Byrne, and becomes a partner in Angela Maureen Byrne's restaurant business.

That evening she phones Mammy, and cries.

Chapter Twenty-one

Lizzie and Angela decide a quiet birthday celebration is in order; there's a session in Doherty's on Sunday night. 'But if you tell anyone my age, I'll kill you.' Lizzie scrunches her newly trimmed hair and turns her head to check the sides.

'Well, that's just lovely,' Angela says, 'when the whole of Merway knew the day I turned forty.'

Lizzie pulls the door of the caravan closed and they walk up the gravel path. 'Forty is different. Forty is – special. There's nothing special about forty-two.'

Angela links her arm. 'Relax, Granny – your little secret is safe with me. Not that you've anything to worry about, anyway – who'd believe me?'

'Thanks,' Lizzie says, grinning at her. 'You don't look too ancient yourself.'

'Well, I should hope not – I'm years younger.'

As they approach Doherty's, Lizzie looks at Angela. 'Now remember – Johnny Morris is mine.'

Angela sweeps past her into the noisy, crowded pub. 'Not if I see him first.' She makes for the bar. 'You find seats, I'll get the jars.'

Lizzie weaves around a group of young tourists in bright-coloured raincoats and spots two stools and a table at the back. She makes straight for them – they won't be free long – and one of the tourists steps backwards and bumps into her, sending her colliding into a man on his way to the bar. 'Oops –'

He puts a hand out to steady her. 'Are you OK?'

American. She steps back and looks up at him. 'Sorry about –' She stops, has another look. 'Hey, I know you.'

After a second his face breaks into a wide grin, and she remembers the lovely white teeth. 'Yeah . . . hey, yeah; the lady with the cat.' He snaps his fingers. 'Lizzie, wasn't it? Headin' off on your adventure.'

She's ridiculously delighted that he remembers. 'Wow, I'm impressed. And you're . . . don't tell me . . .' What was it? Mike? Dave? Some short name – Paul? Suddenly she remembers. 'Pete – the only man in Ireland wearing sandals in January.'

'That's me; eccentric Yank,' Pete says, amused. 'Actually –' He takes a step back and points downwards, and Lizzie sees the same sandals, minus the thick socks.

She laughs. 'Sandals in the rain – yes, still daft. Are you on your own?'

'Yup. Came for the session.' He reaches into the back pocket of his jeans and pulls out his tin whistle, and she remembers him playing it in the car. 'Are you livin' here now?'

She nods. 'Yes, this is where I ended up – and you?'

'I'm workin' just outside Seapoint.' Seven miles away.

'What are you doing there?'

He shrugs lazily. 'Farmin', mostly – bit of this, bit of that . . .' Lizzie smiles, remembering how much she liked his easygoing manner.

'How did you get here from Seapoint?'

He grins. 'Hitched, of course; how else?'

'Of course.' She makes a silly-me face. Then she gestures towards the two stools at the back. 'Look, I'm going to grab those seats for me and my pal – why don't you see if you can find another stool and join us, till the music starts?' Angela will get a big kick out of Pete.

'Sure, that'd be great; thanks. See you in a bit.' He disappears into the crowd at the counter, and Lizzie goes to claim the stools.

Imagine bumping into Pete again out of the blue – just when she could use a bit of diversion, to get her mind off Joe.

It's one thing to accept that there's nothing between them, and quite another to get Joe out of her head. She finds him drifting around there every now and again; in the middle of kneading dough or icing a cake or rolling out pastry, she'll remember something he said that made her laugh, or how that blue shirt he wears is so exactly the colour of his eyes. Walking along the beach in the rain, she sees him bent over a piece of wood. Scooping out cat food for Jones, she remembers how good he smells: cotton and spice.

She shakes her head crossly; there he is again. *Enough; get out of my head, Joe McCarthy*. Thankfully, she hasn't come face to face with him since she's been back; a few times she spotted him in the distance, and once she passed him in the car. She hasn't been into Ripe, either – stupidly, she still can't bring herself to go in.

'What are you shaking your head at?' Angela plonks two gins and a bottle of tonic on the table.

Lizzie picks up the tonic and divides it between the two glasses. 'Nothing. Hey, you'll never guess who's joining us in a minute.'

Angela scans the pub. 'No one springs to mind. I give up.'

'Pete.' Angela looks blank. 'Remember the American I gave a lift to when I was coming here in January? I told you about him – smoking pot; and the house I brought him to, that was practically falling down.'

Angela grins, delighted. 'Oh yeah – he's here? I bags him.'

'You're such a hussy,' Lizzie laughs. 'He's just getting a drink; then he'll come over. He's working in Seapoint, would you believe.' She looks over at the bar and waves. 'Here he is.'

Angela watches Pete manoeuvre around the tables towards them, stool in one hand, pint in the other. 'Yes, I definitely bags him.'

'Stop that,' Lizzie shushes her as he arrives, drops the stool and puts the pint on the table. 'Pete, this is my friend Angela.'

He wipes his hand on his jeans before shaking Angela's. 'Hey.'

'Hey yourself. Welcome to Merway. Lizzie tells me you're staying in Seapoint.'

'Yeah – doin' some work for a farmer there, Donal Harris.'

Angela considers. 'Harris . . . mm, I think I know where that farm is – a mile or two this side of Seapoint, in off the coast road a bit?'

'That's the one,' Pete says. 'You from round here, then?'

'Born and bred.' She smiles at him. 'I'd say you're from a bit further away yourself.'

'Yeah.' His face doesn't change. 'I come from Tipperary.'

Angela is well able for him; she nods, unsurprised. 'You'd always know the Tipp accent, wouldn't you, Lizzie?' Pete grins at her over his pint.

Over the next half-hour they discover that Pete has been living in the general vicinity of Merway for over a month now; before he started with Donal Harris, he was with a builder about twenty miles away. His potter friends are still living in Rockford – he hasn't seen them in a while.

He admires Lizzie's hair – she forgot it was different when she met him first – and he's very impressed to hear that she's living in a caravan now. 'Cool, you're a gypsy.' He asks if Angela serves pizza in the restaurant, and she tells him it's much more upmarket than that. He gives her a pitying look. 'Guess you can't manage the base, right?' She laughs, and Lizzie thinks: *She's met her match.*

He asks about Jones, and Lizzie says, 'It took him a while, but he's settling in fine now.' They tell him about Lizzie's new baking career.

'Actually' – Angela lifts her almost-empty drink – 'we're celebrating tonight. We've just become business partners; Lizzie's decided to invest in the restaurant.' No mention of John, of course.

'Hey.' Pete turns to Lizzie, raising his eyebrows. 'No kiddin'? That's great.' He clinks his glass against theirs, drains it and stands up. 'Let me buy you ladies a drink to congratulate you.'

'No way,' Lizzie says. 'It's my turn; I insist.' She gathers up the glasses and turns towards the bar, weaving around the tables, smiling at people she knows.

Dominic is at the counter, with a newspaper open in front of him. She peers over his shoulder; he's doing the crossword, and he's filled in about a quarter of it.

'You look like you need some help.'

He turns and smiles at her over his glasses; she's seen him a few times in the restaurant since she got back. 'Lizzie, hello there – are you any good at them?'

'Not bad; let's see, now.' She puts the glasses on the counter and starts to read the clues.

'Don't mind her, Dominic – she's no good. She'll put you all wrong.'

Lizzie turns and there he is, peeling off a raincoat, looking just as good as she remembered. No, better – he hasn't shaved in a couple of days, and she's always been a sucker for a bit of stubble.

She wills her heart to slow down. 'Hi, Joe.'

He smiles the smile that she thought she'd got over. 'How are you, Lizzie?'

'I'm doing OK. It's good to be back.' *Not to mention seeing you again.*

She looks into the bluest eyes in Merway. He's wearing her second-favourite shirt – the khaki – and dark-blue jeans she hasn't seen before. His hair is shorter than she remembered it; he must be just after a cut. She can smell his scent. How in God's name is she supposed to get over a man who smells as good as that?

She turns back to Dominic; normal conversation is called for. 'You must be getting ready for the big American adventure.' He's due to leave in a few weeks, for at least two months.

He nods, folding up his paper. 'I'm just about getting around to it now; I'm giving Joe a few instructions – he's going to be on duty while I'm away.' He catches the barman's eye and holds up his glass. 'You'll have a pint, Joe – and Lizzie?'

'No, thanks, Dominic; I'm with a few over there.' She gestures towards the back; they both look over,

232

and Angela spots them and waves. *Have they seen Pete beside her? Of course they have – good.*

Once Lizzie has ordered, she decides she may as well tell them the news, now that it's official. 'Actually, we're celebrating. Angela and I are going into partnership in the restaurant.' It sounds good; she hopes she gets lots of chances to say it.

'Lizzie, my dear, that's wonderful,' Dominic exclaims, beaming. 'All the very best to you both.'

The drinks he ordered arrive, and he turns around to pay for them. Lizzie makes herself look over at Joe again, and waits for him to speak.

'So you're here to stay, then.' His expression is hard to read – not that it matters, of course; she didn't come back for him. Still, it would be nice to feel that he was pleased at the prospect of her living here long-term.

Then he smiles slowly. 'Good. I've got used to you around the place.' The dimple is still there; the smile still has the power to play havoc with her heart rate.

And then her drinks are there, and she has to pay for them and gather them up; by the time she turns and tells Joe and Dominic that she'll see them around, she's nearly calm and composed again.

When she gets back to the table, Pete is standing. 'Time to tune up.' He's still calling it 'toon'. The musicians are getting ready. Lizzie hands him his pint and watches him stride over to them, pulling his tin whistle out of his back pocket.

Yes, I badly need a diversion.

She looks across at Angela. 'Well?'

Angela looks blankly back. 'Well what?'

'Angela Byrne, do I have to torture it out of you?' Lizzie demands in exasperation. 'What do you think of Pete?'

'He's lovely.' Angela looks over at him, settling down beside Johnny Morris. 'Gorgeous, funny, just younger enough to be interesting . . .' She looks back at Lizzie. 'And I have no intention of getting romantically involved with another man for at least ten years.'

Lizzie shakes her head, laughing. 'Not for you, silly – for me. Don't you think it's high time I had a fling? Haven't you been telling me that since I arrived in Merway?'

Angela considers for a minute, smiling faintly. Then the music starts and she leans closer to Lizzie.

'Did young Joe McCarthy have anything interesting to say for himself?'

Lizzie shakes her head, glad that the music prevents too much chat. She knows exactly what Angela is getting at.

She taps her foot in time to the music and watches Pete as he plays the tin whistle. His hair is slightly longer than it was in January, just tipping his shoulders. He's got a bit of a beard now, too – it suits him. His fingers fly over the holes in the tin whistle, his head bobs up and down in time to the lively air they're playing. Great cheekbones, clear tanned skin. His legs are crossed; one sandaled foot taps in rhythm.

He looks up and winks at her. Lizzie lifts her glass and grins back, and tries not to wonder whether anyone at the bar noticed the wink.

Not that it would matter, of course. Not at all.

At the end of the night they bring Pete and Denis – a quiet, middle-aged musician from Seapoint who promised Pete a lift home – back to The Kitchen for toasted cheese sandwiches and tea. Pete plays a few more tunes on the tin whistle, and Denis sings 'Blackbird' in a surprisingly strong voice, before Angela hunts the two men out the door – 'My partner and I have a business to run in the morning.'

When she comes in from seeing them off, Lizzie is washing up.

'Pete's coming back for dinner next Wednesday night,' Angela says. 'With any luck it'll be fairly quiet inside, and I'll bribe Dee to go on duty – I'm sure she won't mind.'

Deirdre has had a lot more time off since the partnership arrangement kicked in; after dinner, she often disappears until quite late. Angela doesn't seem too bothered – 'She's with some pal or other, she's fine.' It's great, the trust she has in her daughter.

'That's nice.' Lizzie's head is beginning to throb faintly; one too many gin and tonics.

'Look at her, pretending not to care, when I'm doing my level best to matchmake.' Angela picks up a tea towel.

'Are you now?' Lizzie takes a cup out of the soapy water and puts it on the draining board.

'Ah, not really; but . . .'

When Angela says nothing else, Lizzie turns around. 'But what?' But she knows what.

Angela picks up a plate and starts to dry it. 'Lizzie, what about Joe?' she says gently, no laughing now.

Damn – even his name makes her heart skip a beat, blast it. She feels around in the soapy water and fishes out two teaspoons. Then she empties the basin and wipes her hands on a towel.

'I'm still mad about him, of course.' She can't lie to Angela. Her mouth feels dry, even after the two cups of tea she's just had.

Angela says nothing, just goes on drying.

'But I'm pretty sure he doesn't feel the same.' The throbbing is getting stronger. Lizzie rubs her temples. 'He told me Charlie offered to work in the shop, but he's hardly ever there.'

'Lizzie, that doesn't prove anything –'

'He's never there, Angela. Joe said I had to go because he had to give Charlie a job – and Charlie is never there.' She stops. 'Sorry, my head is splitting – have you any pills?'

'Here.' Angela fishes around in a drawer, finds a packet of Panadol and hands two of them to Lizzie.

'Thanks.' Lizzie fills a glass with water and swallows them.

Angela watches her. 'I wish I knew what was going on in that man's head, and I think you might have it all wrong, but . . . I just don't know, Lizzie. Joe McCarthy has never been one to wear his heart on his sleeve, so it's hard to figure out . . . Mind you, I *do* know that he hasn't been himself these last few weeks, whatever's wrong. He's distracted, he's – I don't know . . .'

'The thing is,' Lizzie says, putting the glass into the sink, 'I've had my fill of hoping and waiting. I did enough of that with Tony.' She forces a tiny smile. 'I think I'll just move on, like you're doing.'

Then she glances up at the clock on the wall. 'And since you're on breakfasts, you'd better high-tail it to bed.'

Angela groans. 'Four and a half hours from now, God help me.'

'Just think of your lie-in on Tuesday.' They've decided to split the breakfasts between them, taking turns, as part of the new arrangement.

'Night, then,' Angela says, heading for the hall door. 'I hope you enjoyed your birthday.'

'I sure did – it was a great night. Thanks, Angela.'

She's just about to open the back door when Angela says, 'Oh, by the way –'

Lizzie turns.

'I've left your birthday present in the door of the caravan. Night.'

'What – ?' But she's gone.

Lizzie walks down the gravel path, breathing in the night air, and stops at the caravan door. There's nothing there. *Angela said she left it on the door, didn't she? What's she on about?*

She shrugs; no doubt she'll find out in the morning. She falls asleep a second or two before her head hits the pillow.

Chapter Twenty-two

'Now, tell me all about it.' Mammy crosses one slippered foot over the other and looks expectantly at Lizzie, who's just settled herself into the sofa. Daddy's chair is still on the other side of the fireplace; every time Lizzie looks at it she feels a stab of sorrow. She doubts that she or Mammy will ever sit in it. Maybe the odd visitor will.

On the face of it, Mammy seems to be coping well with life on her own. She's quieter, more inclined to tears than before, but generally she's managing fairly well – keeping the house as clean as ever, cooking the dinner in the evening the way Lizzie remembers it and meeting a few friends in town like she always has.

She doesn't bake her brown bread any more; Lizzie will supply it now. She brought two loaves with her from Merway and put one and a half in the freezer when she arrived. With only Mammy to eat it, it should last till her next visit. She used Mammy's recipe, amused at the amount of bran that it calls for; no wonder she was always so regular, with the bread and the Bran Flakes.

She wishes she could be sure that Mammy is doing as well as she makes out. Rose is going to come up from Cork for a few days every two or three weeks, and she'll be home often herself, but still . . .

She imagines Mammy sitting alone in front of the fire every evening, in her slippers, with her crossword book and her marshmallows, turning on the telly to watch the programmes that Daddy always watched with her. Does she look at the gardening programme that Daddy never missed? Does she light the fire when she's on her own? Does she bother cooking dinner for herself?

Lizzie wonders, not for the first time, why God has to work in such mysterious ways. What's wrong with a bit of transparency, for crying out loud? Why can't they be able to say, 'Oh, I know what He's going to do now,' and be right? She assumes it'll all be made clear when they meet, and she looks forward to a bloody good explanation.

She looks across at Mammy, sitting with her cross-word book closed on her lap and waiting to hear all about Lizzie's new business arrangement.

'Mammy, it's the best thing I ever did,' she says. 'I really feel I'm where I should be, you know?'

And she realises with a jolt that it's probably the first time that what Mammy wants to hear, and what she wants to tell her, are the same.

She talks about the rota they've worked out for the breakfasts, and the new specials board for the evening meals, and the painting job they're planning for the outside. She tells her about Angela's idea of occasional live music in the evenings. 'We're going to look at a second-hand piano next week, and Angela knows someone who plays the cello; wouldn't that be lovely? And we get on so well; there's never a problem about the work, or who does what. Angela's baking is definitely improving, and she's taught me so much, too . . .' She trails off – is she going over the top a bit, gushing about her wonderful new circumstances, while Mammy is still trying to cope with the huge change in her life?

But Mammy nods, pleased. 'That's great, love – it's so much better than trying to start a business yourself from scratch.'

She takes a marshmallow and chews it slowly. Lizzie opens the magazine on her lap and glances down at it.

After a minute, Mammy says, 'Lizzie, there's something I have to tell you, before you hear it in town tomorrow.'

Lizzie looks up.

Mammy fiddles with her Biro. 'It's Tony O'Gorman. Remember I told you he started seeing Pauline Twomey after the two of you . . . well, after you –'

After I dumped him. 'Yes?'

Mammy presses the top of the Biro up and down, up and down. 'Julia told me yesterday that they've got engaged.'

'Engaged?' Lizzie says blankly. 'But they've only been going out for a few months.'

It took him six years to decide he wanted to marry me. Mind you, they'll probably take forever to walk down the aisle.

'And Lizzie, love, they're getting married at Christmas.'

'Christmas?' *Three months away. Nine months from first date to altar; a slight improvement on seventeen years.*

Maybe Pauline is pregnant.

Mammy is looking at her as if she's an invalid. 'It's for the best, love; you know ye weren't suited.'

Is she really worried that I'm upset? Can she actually imagine that this news would come as a disappointment? Lizzie thinks of Tony – his V-neck jumpers with the crocodiles or alligators or whatever on them, his golf, his bags of Liquorice Allsorts that gave him a black tongue, his drip-dry shirts.

Then she thinks of Joe, and the grass growing out of the Ripe sign and the silly jokes over tea that had her in stitches and the spicy scent of him that drives her mad, and the way he wrapped her up in the church and held on to her. *'Sorry, Lizzie.' For what, for what? What were you sorry for?*

She makes a big effort and smiles brightly. 'That's great news, Mammy; I'm happy for them. Julia must

242

be delighted.' And Mammy's face relaxes as she reaches for another marshmallow.

For a second Lizzie considers telling her about Joe – but what would she say? *There's a man in Merway that I'm mad about, but I don't think he feels the same way, and now I'm trying hard to forget about him, when all I want is for him to love me back half as much as I love him . . .*

Hardly; Mammy isn't quite ready for that yet.

And she can't tell her about Pete, either – Mammy would have them married off before you could say, 'But he's a jobbing American who probably doesn't intend to settle down for another twenty years.' No, she'd better not bring up the subject of Pete.

Even if she's secretly decided that he's really very cute. Very, very cute indeed.

And funny. The night he came to dinner at The Kitchen, Lizzie nearly choked on her wine at least three times. Pete and Angela were the perfect double act; they seemed to spark each other off.

'Hey, I really like this room – got a good karma here,' he said, walking around the kitchen, taking it all in.

Angela gave him her most innocent look. 'Karma? Is that something you put petrol into?'

Pete was well able for her. 'No, honey,' he said, deadpan, 'karmas run on diesel – in the States, anyhow.'

Angela turned to Lizzie, frowning. 'Didn't Johnny Morris have an old yellow karma that took petrol?'

Over the leek-and-ham pie Angela asked Pete how he'd got there. Of course she meant how he had got to Merway that evening, and of course he knew that; but he pretended to consider, a forkful of pie halfway to his mouth. 'Well, it all started when my mom fell in love with my dad . . .' Angela's fork clattered onto her plate.

He raved about the food, especially the gooseberry crumble flan. 'Hey, I haven't had stuff this good since my mom's home cookin' back in the States.'

'Don't tell me – pecan pie? Blueberry muffins? Hash browns?' Angela's American accent was atrocious.

He gave her a withering look. 'My mom makes a mean pizza base, lady. I must ask her to write you with the recipe.'

He wore a dark-green T-shirt under a green-and-beige checked flannel shirt, and a slightly less faded pair of jeans – probably his good ones. On his feet were the boots he should have been wearing in January. There was a nice lemony smell from him – shampoo? aftershave? Not that he shaved too often, by the look of him. His eyes were greenish-brown – was that what hazel was? Lizzie hadn't really noticed them before.

Pete caught her studying him and smiled that lazy smile of his. 'Do I pass?'

She blushed and grinned – 'Sorry' – feeling about seventeen, especially with Angela smirking over at her. She ducked her face into her glass and drank. He'd brought a bottle of Australian wine, darkly woody.

The first time Deirdre put her head round the door – she was waitressing for the night – Angela introduced them.

'Dee, this is Pete, a strange American gentleman that Lizzie picked up somewhere. Say hello and then leave quickly, for your own safety.'

Deirdre smiled shyly at Pete. 'Hi. Take no notice of my mother.' She filled a carafe with water, then took a bread-basket and cut a few slices from the loaves on the table. 'Mam, one lasagne, one pie, and one red and one white wine.'

'Hi, there.' Pete looked at Deirdre in surprise, then back at Angela. 'I'd no idea you had kids.'

'Just the one – and if you think I don't look old enough, you're dead right; I was a child bride. And anyway, Dee is only ten.'

Deirdre just grinned and raised her eyes to heaven. When she left the room Angela told Pete, very matter-of-factly, that she and Deirdre's father had split up. Pete didn't comment, just nodded.

They managed to have an almost uninterrupted meal – there were only a few customers after Pete arrived, and Angela and Lizzie took it in turns to dish up the meals that Deirdre collected and brought out.

'When do *you* get to eat?' Pete asked her at one stage.

'Oh, I don't eat – Mother doesn't allow it.' Deirdre looked back at him with Angela's innocent expression; it was the first time Lizzie had seen a resemblance.

245

'Although if there are any leftovers she might let me finish them in the morning, depending on her mood.' She made a face. 'They're not that nice cold, though – she doesn't allow me to heat them up.'

Pete grinned and leant back in his chair. 'Looks like you're raisin' your very own wise guy there, Angela.'

'Why, thank you, Pete,' said Angela modestly. 'I do my best.' She watched fondly as Deirdre disappeared out the door. 'And, in case you're wondering, she had her usual hearty dinner before any of us.'

Pete told them he'd be working with Donal Harris for another few weeks.

'What do you do there?' Angela forked up a piece of flan and held out her glass for Lizzie to refill.

He shrugged. 'Whatever needs doin': fix a fence, milk the cows, take a trip to the mart, bring in the hay, go to the bog for peat – I mean turf . . .' He put on an Irish accent on 'turf'.

'Were you farming in the States?' Angela asked.

He nodded. 'Some of my family have farms, so I was brought up in that environment. Farming ain't that much different over here.'

'And when you finish up with Donal?'

He shrugged again. 'Who knows?'

Lizzie loved the way he was so easygoing; living like that must be almost stress-free. Although she wondered if she could handle the not-knowing-where-you-were-going-to-sleep-next bit.

The last of the customers left by ten-thirty, so they helped Deirdre to clear the tables and load the dishwasher. Pete insisted on lending a hand. 'Hey, we call this bussin' at home; I bussed at the local steakhouse all through high school.'

'By any chance, Pete,' Angela asked him over a pile of plates, 'is there anything you haven't done?'

He narrowed his eyes and pretended to think. 'Brain surgery, I guess – and I ain't been to the moon yet.'

Angela looked at Lizzie. 'He might come in handy around here. What d'you think?'

'He might.' Lizzie wasn't sure how serious Angela was.

Pete looked from one to the other. 'Guess you'll let me know if you need me, then.'

Angela said nothing, just winked at Lizzie.

They walked out to the front with him when he was leaving. Lizzie looked up and down the road. 'Where did you leave the car?' She assumed he'd borrowed one from Donal Harris.

'Car? I ain't got a car; you know that, Lizzie.'

Lizzie stared at him. 'You didn't get a loan of one?'

He shook his head and stuck out his thumb. 'I used my regular mode of transport to get here.'

They both looked at him in bewilderment. Then Angela said, 'But how are you going to get home?' They couldn't drive him – they'd both been drinking wine all night.

Pete was amused at her incredulous face. 'I'll walk, hon. Can't be more than five or six miles to Harris's, right?'

Angela shrugged. 'Well – yes, I suppose so. In broad daylight it'd be a nice walk, but – now? Nearly midnight?'

He grinned at them. 'What's the matter with you Irish guys? Can't take a little stroll at night?' He looked up. 'Clear and starry – perfect walkin' weather; I'll be home in a little over an hour.'

'Pete, you can't –'

'Stay in the spare room –'

He laughed. 'You guys – I'm fine, honest. I love walkin', specially at night, close to the ocean. It ain't a problem for me, honest.'

And Lizzie imagined walking along a peaceful country road in the silvery light, hearing the sea across the field, breathing in deep the salty smell, feeling the stars so close, all around you. It would be a little spooky on your own, though; she wouldn't fancy hearing a rustle in the silvery bushes. But if she was with someone . . .

Pete's voice drifted back as they watched him stride off down the street. 'Sweet dreams, ladies; thanks for a really cool evening.'

When he was out of sight, Lizzie said, 'Think we'll see him again?' They hadn't made any arrangement, apart from a casual 'drop in any time' suggestion.

'Definitely.' Angela stood looking down the street for another few seconds. 'Next time he feels like a good feed.'

As they walked back towards the restaurant, something nudged at Lizzie's memory. She stopped outside the kitchen door.

'Angela, you said something the other night – the night of my birthday. I'm only after thinking of it now.'

'What was that?'

'You said my real birthday present was on the door of the caravan – but when I went down there was nothing there.'

Angela clapped a hand to her mouth, then linked Lizzie's arm and began to walk her down the gravel path to the caravan. 'God, sorry, Lizzie; I'd forgotten all about that. Come with me and all will be revealed.'

They reached the caravan door. Lizzie looked at it, then at Angela. 'See? Nothing.'

'I didn't say *on* the door, I said *in* it.' Angela reached over and pulled the little key out of the door. She handed it to Lizzie. 'Happy birthday; it's yours.'

Lizzie looked down at the rusty little key in her palm. It took a few seconds. Then she looked slowly back up at Angela.

'You're giving me the caravan?' No, she had to be wrong. This was a joke.

But Angela nodded. 'It's yours, Lizzie. I felt that as a full partner you'd need a place to call your own . . . and I thought this might do, for the moment, anyway.

You'll probably build your own mansion eventually, and you can park this in your back garden as a souvenir.' Angela put her hands in her pockets and smiled.

'I can't take this, Angela.' Lizzie's fingers tightened around the key. 'It's much too big – you can't just hand it over . . .'

'Excuse me,' Angela said, grinning, 'I have to correct you there. I *have* just handed it over, and you *are* going to take it.' She looked down in amusement at Lizzie's tightly shut fist. 'I don't think I'd be able to get it back now, anyway, even if I wanted to.'

Lizzie was afraid she might burst into tears. She took a breath and held out her arms to Angela. '"Thank you" seems such an understatement.'

Angela hugged her back. 'It'll do fine. Happy birthday once more.' Then she stepped away. 'Now go to bed; I'm terrified you'll sleep it out tomorrow and I'll have to do the breakfasts.'

Lizzie shook her head slowly. 'There's no way I'm going to be able to match this for your next birthday, I'm just warning you now.'

Angela laughed and started up the path. 'Oh, I'll think of something – I've plenty of time.' She waved a hand in Lizzie's direction.

Lizzie watched her until she'd gone into the house. Then she took the key and put it in her pocket. She opened the door that was never locked and walked into the caravan. She closed the door behind her and stood leaning against it, smelling the familiar smell, knowing in the dark where everything was. This was good dark, friendly dark.

A one-bedroom caravan had never been on her list of dream homes. Castles, villas, dormer bungalows with thatched roofs, stone cottages covered in ivy – they'd all featured at one time or another. When she was thirteen she would have given anything to live on a houseboat. After *Shirley Valentine* all she'd wanted was a flat-roofed, whitewashed little house with a vivid blue door, on a sunny Greek island.

She used to think horse-drawn caravans were very romantic – but they were just for going off and being romantic in, not for using as your everyday home. What if the horse got sick, or decided he'd had enough of hauling you around? And as for this kind of caravan – well, she'd never once considered living in one of these; not once. These were for family holidays, with Mammy bringing her to the toilet across the tarmac in the middle of the night, and Daddy trying to open the tiny window in her tiny bedroom so she'd have enough air to breathe.

And now she'd just been given one – *Here, Lizzie, have a caravan* – and it was like someone had handed her the keys to Buckingham Palace. She moved through the darkness to the end of the caravan – her caravan – and opened the big window so she could hear the sea.

Then she just sat in the dark.

Chapter Twenty-three

'Are you ready?' Lizzie shouts up from the hall.

'Coming.' Angela's voice floats down the stairs, and a few minutes later she appears. She's wearing a pair of baggy sky-blue trousers that Lizzie hasn't seen before and a pale-blue top, with a cream cardigan thrown over her shoulders. Angela, a lover of chocolate Hobnobs and sticky toffee pudding, and deeply suspicious of anything that might loosely be described as exercise, has been a size 8 since she was seventeen.

Lizzie tries hard to hate her, but can't. 'Hey, great trousers.'

Angela swaggers down the stairs. 'Aren't they? End-of-summer sale; I got a real bargain.'

'Lovely – and the make-up artist has been at work.' After very respectable Junior Cert results, Deirdre is in the first term of transition year. Her beautician course has started, and Angela is a willing guinea pig whenever she's looking for a face to practise on. After a few weeks of deep cleansing and various masks, Angela's normally well-behaved skin looks freshly polished.

'You're not too bad yourself,' she says, looking Lizzie up and down. 'Are they new?'

Lizzie points to her white cropped trousers – 'Five euros' – and flowery top – 'Four fifty. You're not the only one who can spot a bargain.' Every so often she trawls through Seapoint's charity shops, and now and again she comes across a gem.

Angela's mouth drops open. 'My God, I'm going shopping with you in future; mine seem like daylight robbery now.' She heads for the kitchen door. 'Come on, we're already fashionably late. Have you the present?'

Lizzie holds up the package. After much thought, they decided that the one thing Dominic simply couldn't leave Ireland without was a book of modern Irish poetry, sprinkled with paintings from the National Gallery.

At the door Angela turns back and shouts up the stairs, 'Dee, we're off. Don't wait up.' Deirdre's voice floats back down over a Norah Jones CD – for once she seems to be staying indoors on a Sunday night. On their way through the kitchen, Lizzie grabs her maroon shawl from the back of a chair and Angela picks up the bag with the two wine bottles that's sitting on the draining board.

Outside they check the sky. It looks like Dominic is going to be lucky. October is turning out to be the best month of the year – the days are still fairly long, and mostly warm and pleasant, with just the odd shower. Nights are mild with no hint of frost, and windows stay open till late.

Angela sniffs the evening air. 'Perfect barbecue weather.'

As they reach Dominic's little house, they hear music and voices from the back. The light is just beginning to fade.

'Sounds like a few ahead of us,' Angela says. 'Hope we beat Pete to it.'

Dominic's garden, like Angela's, backs onto the beach. Unlike hers, though, his has no boundary wall or fence – the lawn where he always perches his easel simply disappears into the pebbles. Lizzie wonders how he keeps the tourists from picnicking on the grass in the summer.

There are four garden tables on the lawn, with various mix-and-match chairs around them. Each table has a different-coloured glass lantern with a candle. A canvas hammock is slung between two palm trees to the left of the tables; Lizzie can just imagine Pete swinging lazily there on warm afternoons. In a corner of the flagged patio there's a trestle table holding bottles and glasses and salads in bowls, and dotted with more little lanterns in orange and blue and red glass. Something soft and jazzy wafts from an open window. A few rugs are tossed onto the grass just before the beach begins.

There are about a dozen people already there, sitting around the tables or sprawled on the rugs; a few of them spot Lizzie and Angela and wave. The smell of roasting meat drifts across to them from the barbecue; Dominic, on duty with his fork, gestures them over. Angela sniffs hungrily. 'Mmm – food.' She puts the bottles of wine on the table, and they go over to Dominic.

He's turning chicken joints and steaks and sausages, and brushing them with a reddish-brown liquid that makes them sizzle. There are several potato-shaped tinfoil bundles sitting on a hotplate at the side. Angela looks down approvingly. 'Dominic, any time you're stuck for a few bob, come on over and I'll put you to work in my kitchen.'

He laughs. 'It's your marinade that's made the difference – I'm afraid my only skill is brushing it on.' He gestures towards the table. 'Please help yourselves to drinks; the next batch of food is almost ready.'

Angela goes to pour wine and Lizzie looks around. 'Are you expecting many more?'

Dominic considers, checking around the garden. 'Three or four at the most, I'd say. Your young American hasn't arrived yet.' He dips his brush into the bowl again and daubs marinade generously over the meat.

My young American. I'm pretty sure he didn't mean that the way it sounded to me. And he's not mine, anyway – not yet. The jury's still out on that one.

255

Angela arrives back with two glasses of red wine and hands one to Lizzie. 'Now pass me that fork,' she tells Dominic, 'and go and get yourself a drink and chat to people for a while. It's your party.'

He holds on to the fork. 'And you're here to enjoy yourself, not to work – this is your one night off in the week.'

But she insists – 'Look, the truth is I don't think anyone can do it right only myself. Take ten minutes, anyway' – and Dominic gives in and goes to talk to an older couple Lizzie knows to see. She takes her glass of wine and wanders down the garden.

And there he is, sitting at a table with Big Maggie and Brian from the newsagent's. Lizzie waves over at them and keeps walking, down to Rory and Aisling from the laundrette, sprawled on a rug at the bottom of the garden.

After a while Angela joins them with plates of steak and salad; and ten minutes after that Pete arrives with his guitar, and they wave him down to them. They eat with their fingers – Angela forgot the cutlery, and they can't be bothered to go up and get some – and listen to Dusty Springfield and James Taylor and Enya drifting out from the open window, trying to compete with the wash of the waves on the pebbles.

The sky goes from blue to navy, and one by one the stars blink on. Pete brings up the empty plates and arrives back with a bottle of wine, and Angela takes a lantern from an empty table, and Rory and Aisling head home to their teenage babysitter.

When they've gone, Pete pours the wine. 'Hey, good spot, you guys; thanks for fixin' me up here.' He puts the bottle carefully down on the grass and stretches out on the blanket, one arm behind his head, eyes closed.

Angela winks at Lizzie. 'Would you say, now, there's good karma here, Pete?' Her voice sounds pure and innocent.

He doesn't turn his head – doesn't even open his eyes – but a lazy, slow smile spreads across his face. 'Hey, lady, I'm on to you. I ain't gonna rise to your teasin'.'

But after a minute he says, 'Yeah, excellent karma.'

Angela smiles over in his direction, sitting with her arms wrapped around her legs, and then turns and looks out at the blackness of the sea again.

Lizzie glances down at Pete. Funny, the way things work out; who'd have thought, a couple of weeks ago, that he'd be getting ready to move into Dominic's house?

It was Angela's idea. She asked Pete out of the blue one day – he dropped by now and again for coffee – if he was any good at painting.

He nodded. 'Sure – I can paint. You got a job that needs doin'?'

'We were thinking of getting the front of the restaurant done. It could do with a fresh coat; I'm sick of that whitewash. And you're finishing up soon at Harris's, aren't you?'

Pete nodded. 'Week or so.' He looked from Lizzie to Angela. 'You guys wouldn't be kiddin' me, would you?'

'No – this time we're quite serious,' Angela smiled. 'But you'd have to be dirt cheap, and highly skilled.'

'Hey – you'd pay me too?' Pete looked pleasantly surprised. 'Gee – yeah, sure, I'd be interested. But I'd need a place to stay; I'll be homeless when Donal throws me out.'

'Yes, I figured you would,' said Angela, 'and I was going to suggest you stay here – I usually have at least one free room at this time of year – but then I had a much better idea.'

Lizzie wondered a little nervously what was coming; she hoped to God Angela wasn't about to suggest that Pete move into the caravan.

She wasn't. 'I asked Dominic if he'd like a house-sitter while he's away.' Angela looked enquiringly at Lizzie. 'What do you think?'

'Hey, that's a great idea.' It made perfect sense to Lizzie – Dominic's house would be an ideal base for Pete. 'What did he say when you asked him?'

Angela turned to Pete. 'Dominic is a friend of ours who's moving to the States, funnily enough, for a couple of months. He has a lovely little house just down the road, practically on the beach.' She turned back to Lizzie. 'He said that's fine – he'd like the house to be occupied. As long as we can vouch for Pete, that's good enough for him.' She looked sternly back at Pete. 'You'd have to be on your best behaviour, mind. No skinny-dipping at midnight, or wild American parties – unless we're invited.'

The thought of having to behave didn't seem to bother Pete in the least. 'No problem – that sounds great.' He was probably delighted at the prospect of having somewhere to live for a decent length of time – not to mention somewhere with a front door that worked, and a roof with no holes.

The following day they brought him around to meet Dominic, and the deal was struck. Pete would move in after Dominic left, and maintain the house and generally keep it tidy until he got back.

And now Dominic is all packed up and leaving tomorrow afternoon, and Pete will move in two days after that, when he's finally finished at Donal Harris's. He'll paint the outside of The Kitchen and tidy up the garden – replace the battered fence at the bottom, finally – and do any other jobs they find for him; and then he'll look around Merway for more work.

And he'll be close enough for Lizzie to meet him often, probably every day, even when he finishes working at The Kitchen. She looks down at him again, still lying with his eyes closed. *Wonder what would happen if I leant over and kissed him? Wonder would anyone sitting at a table notice?*

Angela goes off to get a fresh plate of chicken, and comes back with news. 'Hey, Pete, I just told our biggest gossip about you, knowing that she'd spread the word quicker than anyone. Of course she already knew that you were moving in here – but guess what? When I told her about the painting you're going to do, she said she's looking for someone to paint her place. I told her to hang on and see what kind of a job you do for us first, just in case you mess it up.'

'Relax, lady,' Pete says, waving a lazy hand in Angela's direction. 'You're talkin' to a true professional here; see, they're already linin' up to get me.'

Angela snorts and picks up a drumstick. 'I'll reserve judgement till I see your work.'

Lizzie stands up; she's stiff from sitting. 'I'm just going to stretch my legs for a while – see you later.' She wanders down to the water's edge, then turns to walk along beside it.

The night is still dry, but after a few minutes she notices the first hint of a nip in the air – she's sorry she left her shawl sitting on the rug. She considers going back, but then decides to chance it; it's not that chilly. Her head is buzzing pleasantly from the wine. She walks quickly, rubbing her arms every now and again, keeping about a foot away from the little ripples of water that run up the pebbles. She breathes in deeply and smells seaweed. The sky is dotted with stars that get brighter as she leaves the lights behind. The moon is barely there, just a curving sliver.

When she's nearly out of range of the party noise, she stops and looks out to sea, slightly out of breath. Then she realises that someone is crunching along behind her. She turns and sees a dark shape approaching.

'Hello?' They're totally isolated, and suddenly Lizzie wonders if anyone would hear a scream. Her heart quickens.

The shape comes closer – someone tall. Pete? No – the build is wrong; Pete is slimmer.

'Lizzie, it's me.'

Joe stops beside her, close enough to touch – but she can hardly make out his expression in the dark. He must have followed her from Dominic's house.

'I hope I didn't scare you. I've been wanting to have a word, but we never seem to meet any more. Can we walk a bit?'

Lizzie nods, then realises that he probably didn't see it. 'Yes.' She starts walking again, and he falls into step beside her. She wonders what's coming, forces her mind to go blank and just wait.

She hasn't seen him since her birthday, the night in the pub. She still can't bring herself to go into Ripe, which she fully realises is ridiculous. Every day she tells herself, *Tomorrow I'll go in and chat away*; but so far tomorrow hasn't come, and she buys her fruit and veg in the supermarket, or in Seapoint.

Every time she walks down the street, she wonders if she'll meet him. You wouldn't think you could go over a month in a place the size of Merway without seeing everyone at least once. But you can. You can pass a window ten times a day and never glimpse the one face you're dying to see.

'Lizzie, there's something I need to tell you.'

She wishes she could see his face now, but, even with the millions of stars, it's still just a shadowy outline. Where's that full moon when you need it?

Suddenly she's nervous of what's coming. She senses that it's not good.

'It's about Charlie.'

No, she definitely doesn't want to hear whatever he has to say. 'Joe, it's none of my –'

'Hang on.' He stops and faces her, forcing her to stop too, and still she can't see him properly. 'I want you to know – I want to tell you that Charlie . . . he's my son.'

Now she's glad she can't see his face, because it means he can't see hers. She probably looks like a fish who's suddenly been pulled out of the water, all goggle-eyed and open-mouthed.

Charlie – surly, sulky Charlie – is Joe's son. Not his nephew, his son. He's got a son. He's a father. Whichever way she puts it, it still sounds wrong.

She breathes out slowly. 'My God.' She starts to walk again, rapidly, and Joe falls into step with her. Their feet crunch on the pebbles. Lizzie's head is bursting with questions, but she doesn't know where to begin.

After a few seconds, Joe says, 'It's not something I'm proud of – a moment of stupidity in London, years ago – but I'm not ashamed of him, either. It's not something I've deliberately tried to hide.'

But he *has* hidden it. 'Joe, you told everyone he was your nephew –'

He shakes his head – she can barely make out the movement in the faint starlight. 'No, I didn't. When he turned up here, I told whoever asked that he was family from England. Everyone assumed he was my brother Tom's son – Tom's been living there for years – and . . . I just let them go on thinking that.'

There's something hard in his voice that Lizzie hasn't heard before. 'It's nobody's business but mine whose son he is, but I wouldn't lie about him – I never did that.'

You didn't exactly tell the truth, either. Lizzie remembers Angela saying how private Joe was, how hard to figure out. Suddenly she feels that she doesn't know him at all. Can this possibly be the same man who joked and teased and laughed with her in the shop? Who made her read *McCarthy's Bar* – 'The funniest book you'll ever pick up, I promise' – who raced her to finish a crossword, who got up early to climb up a ladder and stick grass behind a sign with masking tape? Who held her as she cried in a church?

They crunch over the pebbles – they've left the barbecue well behind; the only sound is the sea. A stiff breeze is starting up, and Lizzie shivers involuntarily; her flowery top is definitely too light now.

Joe takes off his jacket and puts it around her shoulders. 'Here.'

She's wrapped in his warm spicy scent; she pulls the jacket around her, drinking it in. 'Thanks.'

'You're probably wondering why I'm telling you this now.'

She stops again; she can't concentrate while they're walking. 'Yes, I am.' Thank goodness for the sound of the sea; if it weren't for that, he'd surely hear her heart thudding.

They've walked past the outskirts of Merway, about a quarter of a mile from the backs of the first cottages, and the beach is petering out. Joe gestures towards a low stone wall. 'Here, sit for a minute; I won't keep you long.'

He won't keep her long. Part of her wants to bombard him with questions; another part just wants to stay wrapped up in his jacket, here on this dark beach.

When they're sitting, Joe says, 'I'm telling you because I feel bad about the way things went with you in the shop. I felt terrible, letting you go just like that – especially when Angela told me about your father.'

Lizzie nods in the dark. 'Yes, the timing was bad – but you weren't to know that.' She watches the blackness that is the sea, and holds the edges of his jacket tightly around her.

Then she turns to face him. 'Who raised Charlie?'

'My brother Tom and his wife. They adopted him when he was a baby.'

So technically he is Tom's son – but Joe is his father. The waves wash up and drag the pebbles back.

Joe's face is turned away; he looks out towards the sea. 'I kept in touch, of course – supported him and what-have-you. His mother moved to Australia when he was still a baby, and we lost contact. Then, last year, he . . . decided to come over and get to know me. He always knew he was adopted, and that I was his real father; we never hid that from him.'

The breeze is getting stronger. Joe must be cold in his shirt, but he shows no sign.

'He's a handful – you can see that yourself. Since he arrived here, he's caused me nothing but grief. He spends every cent I give him, makes no effort to find any kind of work. I suggested that he help me out in the shop, when I was asked to supply the carvings, and he made some feeble excuse – said he didn't know how long he'd be staying around, it might be better to get someone local in. So I . . . thought of you.'

She remembers the mornings in the shop, listening to the radio in the back room, knowing he was there. Watching the clock till the tea break.

'The more he used me, the madder I got. Finally I decided I'd had enough – he was milking me dry, making a fool out of me. So I told him he'd have to shape up, or get out. That was when I let you go. I told him if he wanted to stay he'd have to work, even though I knew I was wasting my time – and I was right. He didn't even last a morning before I told him to forget it; he was more of a hindrance than a help. I just didn't know what else to do.'

So it wasn't anything to do with me. Suddenly Lizzie feels a stab of anger. All the time she spent beating herself up about why he'd let her go . . .

Joe's face is close to hers, but she can't read his expression. 'You might have told me at the time, Joe, instead of spinning some yarn about him wanting to work there.' She looks out to sea again, planting her hands on the wall on either side of her. 'You could have told me the truth, Joe; it wouldn't have gone any further. I didn't know what to think when you let me go just like that.'

'I know, I know – I'm sorry . . .' He sighs deeply; she can feel his eyes on her, but she keeps looking out to sea. 'I've made a mess of things; I can see that now. I've treated you badly, and that's the last thing I'd want to do –'

She senses a small movement, and then feels his hand resting lightly on hers. Her heart leaps in her chest.

'Lizzie, I have to confess that . . . when I asked you to come and work for me, my motives . . . weren't the purest.' His fingers stroke the back of her hand, so gently they barely touch it, but she feels the heat that comes from them.

She turns back to him, heart thudding, anger fading. 'They weren't?'

He takes the edges of the jacket that's thrown over her shoulders and gently draws her towards him. 'No.'

His face is almost touching hers. She closes her eyes, reaches for his hands . . .

Then, abruptly, he pulls away. 'Sorry – I can't do this.' He stands up.

Lizzie can't believe it. What just happened there? Is the man trying his utmost to find the best way to humiliate her? The anger rises in her again, stronger now, blazing. She whips his jacket off her shoulders and flings it at him.

'Would you ever go and sort yourself out, Joe McCarthy – and in the meantime, kindly leave me alone.' She whirls away from him, nearly losing her balance on the pebbles, and stalks back the way they came. The anger warms her – she can feel her face blazing.

She doesn't care whether he follows her or not. Her thoughts tumble over one another. How dare he treat her like this, playing havoc with her feelings? He must know that she's – but she shoves that thought away as soon as it pops into her head. She's finished with him, that's what she is; him and his stupid, ignorant lout of a son. She's well rid of him. To think that she wasted so much time . . .

Suddenly, with another lurch of her heart, she sees someone coming down the beach towards her.

'Lizzie?'

Thank goodness; a bit of normality. 'Pete, I was just on my way back; I walked further than I meant to.' Hopefully he'll put her breathlessness down to the fast walking.

Pete holds out her shawl. 'Angela thought you might be cold, so she sent me to find you.'

'Great – thanks. It has turned chilly, hasn't it?' She wraps it around her, then puts her arm through his. 'Come on; we'd better get back, or tongues will be wagging. Have you discovered how gossipy Irish villages are yet?'

She's amazed that she can chatter away to him on the way back, as if nothing has happened. The food was great tonight, wasn't it? She loves eating outdoors – of course, he must be used to that from the States. And where did he say he'd learnt to play the guitar, again, and what kind of songs does he like to play? Oh, she loves Neil Young too, played *Harvest* till she'd worn it out – wasn't 'The Needle and the Damage Done' brilliant? Yes, Eric Clapton as well – but doesn't Pete think 'Layla' is so much better with an acoustic guitar? And has he come across Christy Moore's music at all? Or Van Morrison? And has he ever heard of Paul Brady?

Slowly her thoughts calm down; her breathing returns to normal, and the fire in her face dies away. *That's it – no more of that.* No one follows them back; Joe must have decided to go home by the road.

Back at Dominic's house, Angela is helping to clear the tables and gather up the rugs; and Lizzie probably imagines the searching look she gives her as she and Pete walk up from the beach.

'There you are – just in time for the sing-song; but it'll have to be inside, unless we all want to end up with frostbite.'

And the half-dozen who are left gather around Dominic's fire and Pete plays songs that everyone knows, and Lizzie looks into the fire and pretends to join in.

Chapter Twenty-four

The Kitchen is being transformed.

After hours of deliberating and negotiating and trawling through colour charts and rejecting umpteen of each other's ideas, Lizzie and Angela finally agree on a rich terracotta for the walls and a warm yellowy-cream for the windowsills. When they come to their decision, Angela sits back in relief. 'Thank goodness for that; I have to say it was a lot easier last time round, when I only had myself to please –' She spots Deirdre coming into the room and adds hastily, 'And you, of course, pet.' Deirdre makes a face at her and crosses to the sink.

Lizzie smiles. 'Yes, and look what you ended up with – whitewashed walls, for goodness' sake, and red windowsills; how clichéd is that? All you were missing was the thatched roof and the half-door with the chickens running around.'

She looks at Pete, across from her, for support. The table is littered with colour charts – she can hardly see him.

Wisely, Pete chooses not to get involved. 'Hey, leave me out of this one.' He looks at the clock on the wall – he never wears a watch – and stands up. 'Well, you guys, I'm off to my bed; see you in the morning, Lizzie.'

He's going to Seapoint with her to get the paint. 'I'll be over about ten,' Lizzie says. 'I'm lying in tomorrow.' The B&B is empty tonight, and Lizzie and Angela intend to take full advantage.

After Deirdre has gone back upstairs, Angela looks at Lizzie. 'Seeing as we've no breakfasts to get up for, what would you say to a little vino?'

Lizzie grins. 'I'd say hello, little vino.'

When they're settled with two glasses, Angela holds hers up. 'To romance.'

It's so unexpected that Lizzie bursts out laughing. 'And just which romance would that be?' Since he moved into Dominic's, Pete has been equally friendly to both of them; he's shown absolutely no sign that he's attracted to either of them. And there's no one else on the scene.

'Oh, I don't know,' Angela says vaguely. 'I suppose it's just me putting two and two together and coming up with seventy-nine. Maths were never my strong point. Just because you're going to Seapoint with him in the morning, and just because you've been spending time in the kitchen with him every afternoon – '

Lizzie laughs again. 'He asked me to teach him how to bake, you know that. I'm only doing him a favour. And you said yourself his scones aren't half bad.'

She looks sideways at Angela. 'Anyway, who's to say Pete's interested in *me*? He could just as easily fall for you; he sees you nearly as often.'

It's Angela's turn to laugh. 'Me – a divorcée-to-be, saddled with a teenager? Cop yourself on; any man would run a mile.' She smiles ruefully. 'It'd be nice, though – an old cuddle at night, a bit of how's-your-father . . . I miss that.'

Watching her topping up their glasses, Lizzie wonders if Angela is truly over John. How long does it take to recover from a marriage of so many years? Does she ever think about him?

Maybe a fling with Pete is just what she needs. Maybe it's just what they both need. Lizzie hasn't laid eyes on Joe McCarthy since the night of the barbecue; she's avoided Ripe like the plague, and luckily she hasn't bumped into him anywhere else.

Yes, a fling would certainly be welcome right now. Maybe they could share Pete; he probably wouldn't object.

Three days later, Lizzie watches as Pete puts the finishing touches to the front wall of the restaurant. 'What's that, Jones?' She bends her head towards the giant ball of ginger fur in her arms. 'He missed a bit? Oh, you're right – I see it. D'you think we should tell him?'

Pete manages to wave the paintbrush threateningly at them without turning around or falling off his ladder. 'Careful there, Jones – you might end up a different colour, buddy.'

He hasn't missed any bits. On the contrary, he's making a very good job of the painting – and he's clean, too: there are very few drops on the plastic sheet he's spread on the ground beneath him. He's dressed in what have to be his oldest jeans – more patches than jeans, and so faded they're almost white. His light-grey checked flannel shirt is faded too, and the sleeves are rolled up above his elbows. His feet are in his sandals, even this late in the year, and they're deeply tanned, like his arms.

Altogether he's extremely fanciable, up on that ladder. Lizzie wonders whether she fancies him. She's fond of him – who wouldn't be? he's so easygoing and pleasant – but that's not the same thing.

Maggie Delaney called around earlier and arranged for Pete to come and see her flat as soon as he's finished this job; obviously she liked the look of what he was doing here. Seems like he'll be around a while. Plenty of time for him to grow on her.

'Pete, what I really came to say was that dinner's ready.' He's being fed in The Kitchen while he's doing the painting.

'Great – I'm starvin'.' He gives a final dab at the corner, then comes down from the ladder, covers the paint pot carefully and wraps a plastic bag tightly around the brush. 'I'll head home and clean up, and see you guys in a couple minutes, OK?'

Lizzie looks after him as he ambles down the road holding the paint and the brush. So fanciable . . . Then she puts Jones down and they walk around to the back of the restaurant.

Chapter Twenty-five

'Anyone home?'

Lizzie drops her bag inside the back door and goes through the kitchen into the hall. It's just after half seven; Angela's usually around at this time on a Sunday night, cookery books and menus spread out on the table in front of her, portable TV on in the corner, getting organised for the week ahead with half an eye on *Coronation Street*.

The house seems deserted; the door into the restaurant is locked, there's no sound from upstairs. Deirdre's probably out – they hardly see her these days. Lizzie shrugs and heads back into the kitchen; she'll unpack and freshen up – Angela's bound to be back soon. Maybe she ran out of milk and headed down to the shop.

As she dries off after her shower, Lizzie thinks about the weekend she's just spent with Mammy. She's still lonely for Daddy, of course – they both are – and she's definitely quieter than she was before; but she seems to be coping well enough.

Lizzie called over to Claire next door while Mammy was lying down on Saturday afternoon – something she started to do after Daddy died – and Claire insisted on bringing her in for coffee.

'She's out and about a fair bit, Lizzie; she visits the grave most mornings. She seems in good enough spirits when I meet her. I don't think you need to worry. It's early days yet; it'll take a while for her.'

They went to the grave on Sunday morning. Lizzie had bought two little variegated holly bushes in pots from Big Maggie, and she positioned them on either side of the O'Grady headstone.

'They look nice,' Mammy said. 'He'd have liked those in the garden.' Then she bent her head and started whispering words. Lizzie thought about Daddy leading her as a child around the garden to show her the new plants coming up, teaching her how to say 'dahlia' and 'cyclamen' and 'primrose', marking off a patch for her to plant bulbs in autumn, rubbing a mint leaf between his hands and letting her sniff it. Bringing her by the hand to join the library when she was barely able to read. Teaching her how to brush her teeth. Helping her with her homework . . . How lucky she'd been to have him.

Later Mammy stood under an umbrella waving her off, looking small and old and very alone. Rose was due in two days to stay for a week or so. Driving back to Merway, Lizzie decided to phone home while Rose is there, to see how she thinks Mammy is doing.

She's just finished dressing when the door of the caravan opens.

'Lizzie?' Angela calls. 'Are you there?'

'In here – just coming.' Lizzie opens the bedroom door and nearly collides with her.

'Dee's missing.' Her face is chalk-white; her hands, as they grab Lizzie's wrists tightly, are icy cold.

'What? Angela, hang on – she's probably –'

Angela shakes her head impatiently. 'No, no, no, she's gone, she's been gone all day – I've phoned all her friends, she's not with any of them. I've just come from the McCoys' – I could only get the answering machine, and I thought maybe – but she's not there, she's nowhere, I can't find her . . .' Her words are tumbling over one another; when she stops talking, her lips tremble.

She drops Lizzie's wrists and puts her hands up to her face. 'God, where is she? Where is she, Lizzie?'

'Hang on – have you tried her mobile?' Lizzie says calmly, taking her by the arm. She's surprised that Angela has worked herself into such a state; isn't Deirdre always off out with her pals?

Angela takes her hands down from her face and blinks. 'Her phone is switched off. None of her friends have seen her all day . . . Oh God, Lizzie, what'll I do? What if something's happened her? She's still only fifteen – oh God –' Tears fill her eyes; she puts a hand back to her mouth.

'Angela, I'm sure she's OK.' As if she could possibly be sure of that, having been away all weekend. But Angela is watching her and nodding, desperate for reassurance, tears running down her face.

Lizzie speaks firmly. 'Look, she's sensible, Angela. She wouldn't do anything stupid. She's probably trying to get hold of you right now to tell you she's fine. Maybe her mobile is out of credit – did you think of that? I'm sure there's a simple explanation.'

She racks her brains for something else to say, anything to calm Angela. 'She might have had a date, not told you because she was afraid you wouldn't approve . . .'

But Angela is shaking her head rapidly. 'She wouldn't do that – she's no interest in boys yet. Have you ever seen her with one?'

Suddenly Lizzie thinks of Charlie and Deirdre, outside the chip shop in Seapoint, a few weeks ago. She immediately decides not to mention it – the state Angela's in, she'd definitely hit the roof if his name came up. And there's no way Deirdre would be daft enough to have anything to do with someone like him; he was probably just trying to impress her that day, the creep.

She begins to steer Angela towards the caravan door. 'Look, let's go up to the house and try and figure out . . .' What? She hasn't a clue what the next step should be. But, if nothing else, the house will be warmer – and it's where Deirdre will surely turn up before long, wherever she is.

In the kitchen, Lizzie sits Angela at the table and takes the chair beside her. Thank goodness there are no meals to cook tonight, and no one staying over. 'Now, when did you last see her?'

'This morning,' Angela says, sounding distracted. 'She left here early, about nine – said she was going to spend the day with her pal Judy. She brought a bag with her – I assumed it was the make-up kit . . . And she's done that before – gone to Judy's for the day, I mean – so I thought no more about it . . .'

Suddenly she pushes back her chair and stands. 'She wasn't back by six, so I phoned to see if she wanted a lift home –' She paces the floor, pulling at her hair. '– Judy lives about a mile and a half away . . . No answer from her mobile, so I called Judy's house. She never went there – Judy was there all day, she never saw her . . .'

She's starting to get frantic again. 'Since then I've been phoning, and going, and – what'll I do, Lizzie?' She paces rapidly, hands balled into fists, breathing ragged.

Lizzie has to ask. 'Have you phoned John?' Maybe Deirdre went to him, for some reason. And if she didn't, he should be told that she's missing.

Angela looks at her, blankly at first, then with dawning understanding. 'You think he's taken her.'

There's something new in her voice that makes Lizzie nervous.

'What? No, of course not – I just thought she might have –' But Angela is already in the hall. She grabs the phone and punches numbers. She waits, mouth tight; then – 'It's me. Is Deirdre with you?'

Lizzie watches her face as John speaks. It goes from fear to impatience – 'Obviously I know that; have you seen her since then?' – to anger – 'I wouldn't be asking you if I knew' – and back to fear: 'Not since this morning, about nine – she said she . . .' Her shoulders slump; after a minute she says, 'Right,' in an empty voice and hangs up.

They go back into the kitchen and Angela leans against the worktop. 'He's coming over. He hasn't seen her since Saturday week.' Lizzie remembers John calling to take Deirdre out, for the first time in ages. He didn't come in, like he used to, just sat in the car till she came out to him. But at least he came for her. And she came back from Seapoint with the new boots that she'd wanted for ages.

Angela is biting her nails – Lizzie doesn't remember ever seeing her do that before. She takes her hand gently.

'Have you checked to see if she took anything with her – in that bag, I mean? Let's go upstairs and see.' She may as well keep Angela busy doing something – it's better than sitting and brooding herself into another state.

Angela nods, and they go up to Deirdre's room together.

Lizzie has never been inside it; it's smaller than Angela's but brighter, at the back of the house. It's got the usual teenage things: posters of young people who look vaguely familiar to Lizzie; a dressing-table scattered with make-up and brushes and bits of sponges and cotton-wool balls; clothes hanging over the back of a chair, more thrown in a bundle in a corner, shoes in an untidy pile beside the half-open wardrobe door; a shabby-looking blue furry rabbit sitting on the pillow; some books stacked on the chest of drawers, more on the floor beside the bed.

Lizzie takes Angela's arm and guides her to the wardrobe. 'Look and see if you can tell what's missing – any clothes, or shoes maybe . . .' She glances out the window – it's pitch-dark by now – and feels a stirring of panic herself. 'I'll go and get some paper and we'll make a list.'

Twenty minutes later they're back downstairs, sitting at the kitchen table. Deirdre hasn't taken much – just one change of clothes, a pair of shoes and a few toiletries. Most of her make-up is still there, apart from a lipstick or two.

But her passport is gone.

Angela drinks a little of the brandy Lizzie has insisted on pouring. Her colour hasn't come back, and her eyes look huge and black against the whiteness of her skin. Her hand shakes as she puts the glass down.

'We'll have to call the guards.'

Lizzie nods. It's raining now; they can hear the drops slapping against the window.

Just then, the kitchen door opens and Pete walks in. As soon as she sees him, Lizzie remembers that the three of them had planned to go to Doherty's that evening. The Sunday night out.

'Hey –' Pete's grin fades as he catches sight of Angela's face. She looks at him and dissolves into tears. He's beside her in three steps, lifting her from the chair, rocking her in his arms and stroking her hair. He says softly, into her ear, 'Hey, shh – easy, hon . . . shh . . . it's OK, darlin' . . .'

He looks over her shoulder at Lizzie, and she says quickly, 'Deirdre's missing. I'm just going to phone the police.'

She goes out to the hall, picks up the phone and dials Joe's number – before she changes her mind, or loses her nerve.

He answers after a few rings. 'Hello?'

She grips the receiver tightly. 'Joe, it's Lizzie.' Without giving him a chance to respond, she rushes on: 'Deirdre has disappeared – she's been gone all day. Angela is out of her mind with worry.' She stops, glances over her shoulder at the closed kitchen door, then races on. 'Joe, I saw her with Charlie a few weeks ago in Seapoint. Have you any idea if they were seeing each other?'

There's a second's silence. When he speaks, he sounds shaken. 'No, none at all. But . . .'

He stops. Lizzie closes her eyes, takes in a shuddering breath; what now?

'Charlie has gone too – with yesterday's takings. I only discovered it a while ago. If you saw him with Dee, we have to assume that they might be together now. Have you called the guards?'

'No – I'm just about to.' *Oh, God – Deirdre with that man . . .* She prays for it not to be true.

'Right; I'll talk to them too.' Joe hangs up abruptly, and she hears the buzz of the phone in her ear.

After she's spoken with a garda in Seapoint, she replaces the receiver. Then she forces herself to examine the awful possibility that Deirdre and Charlie might be together.

It makes no sense. Deirdre is so sensible, so level-headed; why would she look twice at someone like Charlie?

Because he meets her in secret, tells her how pretty she is, talks like someone on the telly. Tells the shy little Irish girl that he loves her, that they have to go away so they can be together. The thought comes out of nowhere, makes Lizzie draw her breath in sharply. And starts to make some kind of awful sense.

She remembers Deirdre hurrying up from the beach with flushed cheeks, looking relieved when Lizzie tells her that Angela isn't home – relieved that her mother isn't there to witness what Lizzie chooses not to notice: the look of excitement on her face.

The more she thinks about it, the more sense it makes. It would have amused Charlie that the innocent little Irish colleen was so gullible, so easily satisfied. A few compliments, a few kisses in the moonlight, and she'd be ready to run away with him to God knows where.

Lizzie goes back into the kitchen with a heart full of dread. Pete is still holding Angela, who leans her head against his shoulder and grips his shirt tightly. He strokes her hair and murmurs to her. They could be lovers; Lizzie almost feels in the way.

Angela lifts her head; her eyes are swollen, her face still deathly pale. 'Are they coming?'

'They'll be right out,' Lizzie says. She fills the kettle, trying to convince herself that there's nothing to be gained by mentioning Charlie; Angela will hear it soon enough.

They're halfway through the second cup of tea when the doorbell rings. Lizzie opens the front door; Joe is standing there in the rain with two uniformed gardaí. She clenches her fists as she follows them into the kitchen.

'Mrs Byrne.' The gardaí introduce themselves and take Deirdre's details from Angela, who holds Pete's hand tightly as she answers their questions in a low voice. Joe stands just inside the door, head bent. Lizzie doesn't look in his direction, but she's acutely aware of his presence.

Then the garda who seems to be in charge looks up from his notebook and explains to Angela that Mr

McCarthy has informed them that his son is also missing, and that they're checking out the possibility that the two disappearances might be linked.

Angela looks blankly at him. 'What are you talking about?'

Joe steps forward slightly, and Angela seems to notice him for the first time. She stares at him for a few seconds. 'Son? What son?'

The garda checks his notebook. 'A Mr Charlie McCarthy – he's been staying with Mr McCarthy for the past –'

'That's not his son, that's his nephew, and he's got nothing to do with my daughter – they didn't even know each other,' Angela says, exasperated. 'Tell them, Joe.'

'He is my son, Angela.' His voice is hardly recognisable, so low and defeated.

As he speaks, Lizzie watches Angela's face. It goes from incomprehension to denial, as Joe tells her gently that Deirdre and Charlie were seen together, to horror. And then to rage.

She pulls away from Pete and stands up slowly. 'My God – you knew, didn't you? You knew they were seeing each other.' Her eyes blaze into Joe; he's shaking his head, but she ignores it. 'You knew – and you did nothing to stop it.' Her knuckles are white where they grip the back of the chair.

'Angela, you must believe me –'

'Shut up!' she practically screams. Lizzie flinches; she's never seen her in this state. 'Shut up, Joe McCarthy! Your good-for-nothing *son* –' She spits out the word, ' – that . . . that *scumbag* . . .'

Joe just stands there, stony-faced; in spite of all that has happened, Lizzie's heart goes out to him as Angela rages.

'If that bastard has touched a hair on her head, if he's done *anything* to her, I'll hold you responsible, Joe McCarthy – and I will *never, ever* forgive you for this.'

Joe says nothing as Angela rants on, accusing him of letting them meet in his house – maybe he even introduced them, thinking it might help Charlie to settle down? Maybe that was why he brought him over from England in the first place, to find him a nice innocent Irish girl?

John Byrne arrives in the middle of her tirade and tries to calm her down. 'It's not Joe's fault, love – you can see he's as upset about all this as we are. You can't blame him –'

But Angela is beyond reasoning with; she's pale and shaking, cold and dry-eyed one minute, raging with hot floods of tears the next. She flings John's arm off, spins round and stabs a finger at him.

'You keep out of this! Where were you when she went missing? What do you care what happens her? What do you care about anything except your fancy woman? Coming over here and taking Dee out, pretending you give a damn, spending money on rubbish in Seapoint . . .'

They let her continue – what else can they do? In the end she collapses into Pete's arms, exhausted, and the two gardaí leave with a photo of Deirdre, promising to call the minute they have news. Joe leaves with them, looking haggard.

Lizzie fills the kettle for what seems like the umpteenth time, and the four of them sit around the table like survivors of a nuclear war. John stares down into his coffee cup with a face like thunder, pretending he doesn't notice Pete's arm across Angela's shoulders, her head leaning against his chest.

Lizzie sits miserably at the table, praying for news.

Several cups of tea, four glasses of brandy, a few rounds of ham sandwiches and twelve hours later, the phone rings.

Chapter Twenty-six

'They took a Ryanair flight from Dublin to Birmingham yesterday evening; we had a positive sighting from one of the stewardesses. And your daughter's bank card was used to withdraw two hundred pounds from a cash machine in Birmingham at ten fifty-two last night.' The garda is reading from his notebook; Angela's eyes never leave his face. 'She gave herself up early this morning – just walked into a police station.'

'On her own.' Angela is only repeating what she already knows.

'It seems they had some kind of falling-out,' says the garda. 'From the information she gave us, we were able to intercept Mr McCarthy when he arrived in Euston Station in London.'

Angela's whole face is transformed; even streaked with tear-tracks, blotchy with lack of sleep, it looks

288

beautiful. Since they got the phone call, she's been smiling.

'She's safe,' she says, so low it's almost a whisper.

The garda nods. 'Probably feeling a bit miserable, but otherwise she's fine, and on her way back. They're putting her on a plane to Shannon, and then she'll be driven here. She should be home by late afternoon.' He closes his notebook and stands up. 'Mr McCarthy has been detained for questioning in England.'

'Thank you.' Angela takes the garda's hand and shakes it. 'That's wonderful – thank you so much.'

He nods again, a bashful smile spreading over his face; he can't be more than twenty-five. Lizzie is happy for him, that he's able to bring good news – he'll surely have plenty of terrible visits to make to other homes in the future. 'No problem, Mrs Byrne. I'm just glad your ordeal ended well.' He looks at the four of them standing in the doorway. 'Maybe you should all try and get some sleep before she arrives; it'll be a few hours yet.'

When she's closed the door behind him Angela leans against it, suddenly looking exhausted.

Pete smiles at her. 'You heard the man, honey; you get some shut-eye now, hear? Everything's OK.' He squeezes her hand briefly.

She gives him a tired grin. 'Yeah, I think I'd better lie down before I fall down. Thanks for being here, Pete.' She turns to John, her smile fading. 'Sorry I shouted at you earlier.'

'No problem.' He shrugs. His face looks drawn. 'You were worried. I may as well head off too; tell her I'll phone in the morning – and can I come and see her on Saturday?'

Angela nods. 'Drive carefully.' They're like polite strangers.

After Pete and John leave, Lizzie heads down towards the caravan, telling Angela she'll see her later. They've put a 'Closed' sign on the restaurant door.

Her eyes are gritty; it hurts to blink – but she feels that sleep would be impossible; her head is spinning. Maybe a walk . . .

She finds herself on the beach, scrunching along by the sea as she has so many times before. It's not yet noon, but the day is grey and cold; winter is well on the way. She walks a bit faster and tries to sort out the jumble of thoughts and questions cluttering up her head.

How on earth could Charlie and Deirdre's relationship have gone unnoticed in Merway? How long had it been going on? Where did they meet? No doubt Deirdre will tell Angela everything . . . eventually. How is she feeling now, on her way home? And why didn't she go to London with Charlie? What happened to make them split up in Birmingham? She's probably on a plane right now, maybe the same one that took her and Charlie to England last night. Lizzie glances up at the white sky; it's too cold for the seagulls. She hugs her arms tightly around herself – she should have put on a jacket.

And Joe . . . God knows how he's feeling this morning. She assumes the gardaí have been in touch with him, too, to let him know. What a horrible thing for him to have to deal with – his son facing a criminal conviction . . . Will Charlie be charged with abduction, since Deirdre is underage, even if she went with him willingly?

Lizzie shakes her head – too many questions. She makes her way back to the caravan and lies on the bed fully clothed, sure she won't sleep.

Eight hours later she wakes up to the sound of knocking. She drags herself up and opens the door; Angela is standing on the step with a bottle of wine.

'She's back, she's asleep.' She holds up the bottle. 'I need it, even if you don't.'

Lizzie smiles blearily and moves aside to let her in. When the fire is lit and they're sitting with two full glasses, Angela tells her everything.

'He swept her off her feet. He told her she was the only girl he'd ever loved – can you imagine? – said they'd get married once she was sixteen, he had a friend who'd give him a job in London . . . and the little innocent creature swallowed every word.'

She shakes her head slowly. 'And this was going on for months, Lizzie – since way before the summer. How could I not have seen it coming? How could I have been so blind?'

Lizzie takes a sip; the wine has a full, spicy taste. 'What happened when they got to Birmingham?'

Angela's face hardens. 'He robbed her, that's what happened. They went to the station and he took her wallet to get their tickets, left her minding the bags – and vanished. Can you believe it?'

'Oh, God.' Lizzie thinks of Deirdre, sitting there waiting for him; watching the time go by, becoming more and more anxious, telling herself that he'll be back . . . and slowly realising that he's gone. 'The poor thing.'

Angela nods. 'He left her penniless in a strange city – in a foreign country. Thank God she had enough sense to go to the police.'

'How did they meet?' Lizzie thinks again of the scene outside the chip shop, and wonders guiltily if she should have mentioned it at the time; could all this have been avoided?

'She was at a bus stop in Seapoint, and he drove up in Joe's car and offered her a lift – she knew him to see, knew he was staying with Joe, so she got in. Can you imagine him holding any kind of conversation, that moron?' Angela's face twists again. 'She says she wanted to tell me about him, but he insisted she shouldn't. Of course he did. He knew fine well I'd have put a stop to it.'

She takes a gulp of wine. 'He was taking money from her, Lizzie, telling her he was putting it away for them. She had over a thousand euros saved from what I gave her for working here; it's practically all gone. He even made her take out that two hundred pounds in

Birmingham – told her that the money she'd given him was in a bank account in London, that they couldn't touch it till they got there. Not that I care about the money – but if I had him . . .'

She pours more wine for them both, then looks over at Lizzie. 'Did you know he was Joe's son?'

Lizzie knew she'd ask at some stage. 'He told me, the night of the barbecue – but I didn't feel it was my place to repeat it.'

After a minute, Angela says, 'I suppose it wouldn't have made any difference . . . we'd still have had no idea that they even knew each other . . .' She looks up at Lizzie again. 'I saw Joe following you down to the beach – I wondered what that was all about.'

Lizzie shrugs. The memory of that night is too raw – she can see herself flinging back his jacket, telling him to leave her alone . . . She looks down into her glass. 'I'd rather not go into it – we had a bit of a falling-out.'

'Oh, Lizzie; I thought you were down in the dumps lately.'

They're both quiet for a while. Then Angela says, 'I said some terrible things to him last night. D'you think he'll ever forgive me?'

'Of course he will. You were out of your mind with worry; anyone could see that. He knew you didn't mean a word of it.'

Angela still looks worried. 'I hope you're right . . . It's just that I went down to the shop earlier, to apologise to him, and it was closed.'

Lizzie looks up quickly. 'Was it?'

Angela nods. 'I suppose he needed to take a bit of time out . . . I'll go down again tomorrow.'

She pauses, then starts to speak again, more quickly. 'Lizzie, I'd like to take Dee away for a break somewhere – maybe up around Connemara; she loves it there. I think she needs to go someplace where no one knows her for a while. D'you think you and Trish Daly could manage the restaurant for a few days? You could close the B&B till we got back, and you'd only have the evening meals to do.'

'Of course – that's no problem. When were you thinking of going?'

Angela considers. 'Tomorrow's Tuesday . . . If I got myself sorted, we could go on Wednesday maybe, till the weekend.' She twirls the stem of her glass. 'Pete might be good to have on standby, if you need extra help; I'll call around to him at some stage tomorrow and ask him, if you like.'

As she says his name, a slight blush creeps into her cheeks. Lizzie decides to ignore it – they've had more than enough intrigue and drama for one day. Besides, she's not altogether sure she's comfortable with the notion of Pete and Angela disappearing off into the sunset. What about *her*?

When Angela eventually leaves, Lizzie changes into her pyjamas and goes back to bed, because it's what you do when night comes. After an hour of counting sheep, she reaches up and cranks the window open an inch; maybe the sound of the sea will soothe her. The cold, salty air drifts in – at least it's stopped raining – and she pulls the duvet up around her ears. At her feet, Jones gives a soft mew. She can just make out the faint rattle of the water on the pebbles. She breathes in deeply, letting her thoughts drift.

I suppose we'll be open for business again tomorrow evening – just as if nothing has happened. I'll head into Seapoint to do the shopping in the morning . . . I'll need to get together with Trish, too; I could call to her on my way home . . . Wonder what Pete thinks of us all now, after the high drama – probably wishes he was back in the States . . . I hope Mammy remembers to bring back those library books – she's been getting very absent-minded lately. I'd be happier if she had an electric cooker; that gas could be dangerous . . .

And, inevitably, her thoughts veer towards Joe. *It was good of him not to say that I was the one who'd seen Charlie and Deirdre together . . . considerate, even in the middle of that mess . . . Wonder how he's feeling now . . . I wish I hadn't shouted at him . . .*

When she closes her eyes, she sees Angela draping an arm around his shoulders in Doherty's one night and saying, 'Lizzie, did you ever see such a hunk in your life?' and Joe grinning up at her and threatening to have her arrested for harassment. She thinks of the little wooden fuchsia on a silver chain that he gave Angela for her birthday, and how she threw her arms around him and kissed his cheek. She sees him in the back room of the shop, head bent over a piece of wood, sensing her there and looking up and smiling at her.

She remembers his face last night as he stood and listened to Angela pouring all her fear out on him. And today the shop was closed.

Eventually, towards dawn, sleep returns.

Chapter Twenty-seven

Two days later, Angela and Deirdre head off in Angela's old Opel. Deirdre is pale and subdued, avoiding Lizzie's eye as she walks out to the car with her canvas bag. Lizzie pretends not to see her – Deirdre spent most of the previous day in her room, obviously not wanting to meet anyone.

Angela appears in the doorway with two much bigger bags. 'Give us a hand, Lizzie.'

The weight of one bag takes Lizzie by surprise. 'Hey, I thought you were only going for a few days – this feels like you've packed for six months.'

Angela winks at her. 'Well, we thought if we liked the look of the place we just might stay there altogether – didn't we, love?'

Deirdre smiles faintly, still not looking at Lizzie. They load the bags into the boot, and Angela gets into the car and rolls down the window.

'Now, you've everything you need, haven't you?' Lizzie nods. 'Remember to say it to Trish about using the lettuce in the fridge first – she's a terror for not checking what's there. And you have my mobile number – and Nuala and Ríodhna will be around in the –'

Lizzie flaps a hand at her. 'Look, would you ever get going? I'm tired of reminding you that I'm a full partner now, and any disasters will affect me just as much as you. To tell the truth, it'll be great to have the place to myself – I'm planning all sorts of changes.' She bends down and grins in the window, conscious of Deirdre staring straight ahead in the passenger seat. 'I always thought you could fit a few more tables in the restaurant – and a bit of Indian food would be nice for the next few nights.'

Angela gives Lizzie a dangerous look. 'You move one thing in that restaurant, change one ingredient of my menu –'

But Deirdre ignores them; she's not interested in being humoured. Lizzie gives up – it's probably too soon for her to laugh at anything – and moves away from the car. 'OK, OK, I'll do as I'm told. Have a lovely time, and give me a ring when you get a chance, to let me know how ye're getting on.'

She waves them off and walks around to the back of the restaurant. She's quite excited about being in charge for the first time – and Trish is well used to how things are run. They shouldn't have any problems.

She wonders briefly if she should have mentioned to Angela that Pete is coming around tonight. But Angela herself suggested that Lizzie use him as a backup; and that's all she's doing, really. Trish will go home around nine, and Lizzie and Pete will finish up, and then sit down and have dinner. And maybe some wine. She's not trying to seduce him, for God's sake. She's just decided that she needs a bit of distraction.

Especially as Ripe is still closed – or it was when Angela called around yesterday afternoon.

'Maybe he's gone to England – you know, to be with . . . ' Angela couldn't bring herself to say Charlie's name.

Lizzie nodded, and tried to shove away the feeling of dread. Is Joe gone for good? Has he decided to leave the place where his son has done such damage, and make a start somewhere else? For the rest of the day she can't get him out of her head.

So she needs some distraction. She heads into the kitchen to get organised for the day.

Pete arrives in the evening; when everyone has gone home, he and Lizzie have a late dinner and drink a bottle of wine and talk for a long time. And when they finish talking, Pete hugs her tightly and kisses her cheek and goes back to Dominic's house, and Lizzie heads down to the caravan and goes to bed.

Early the next morning, before any shops in Merway are open, there's a knock at her door.

He looks terrible; pale and unshaven and desolate.

She leans against the door-frame and looks at him.

Chapter Twenty-eight

It's as if someone has lifted a veil, or rubbed away a patch on a misty mirror. Lizzie looks at him standing there on the caravan steps and knows, as clearly as she knows her own name, that she will love him till the day she dies. Whatever he does.

'Come in.' She steps back to let him through.

Joe steps past her into the caravan, shrugs off his jacket and slumps into the nearest seat. He rests his elbows on the table and rubs a hand over his chin; she hears the rasp of his stubble. The skin under his eyes looks blue-white.

She pulls the cord tighter around her dressing-gown and puts the kettle on, then takes out cups and sugar and milk and spoons. He doesn't say a word, just watches her with weary eyes. When the tea is made, she puts the pot on the table and sits opposite him.

'Lizzie, I have to talk to you.'

Lizzie says nothing, just holds on to the empty cup in front of her and wonders if she'd manage to pour tea without spilling it.

'I just got back from England.'

When he says nothing more, she finds her voice. 'What happened?' She's surprised at how normal she sounds.

He plants his hands on the table and looks at them. 'He's being remanded in custody; they wouldn't agree to bail. And he may be extradited; no one's sure yet.'

He looks back up at her. 'Lizzie, he was responsible for the break-ins here – the cinema and the newsagent's; they identified his fingerprints . . . Not only did he take what he could from me, he stole from my friends – and then Dee . . .'

Lizzie reaches over and pours his tea. Then she puts down the pot and covers one of his hands with hers.

As soon as her hand touches his, he slowly laces his fingers through hers and pulls her hand to his chest. It's as if he needs something to hold on to. She feels the heat of him through his shirt, feels his heart thumping.

'Lizzie . . .' He presses her hand against his chest. Her name, when he murmurs it, sounds different. He lifts his eyes again and looks at her. Such intensely blue eyes. She waits, afraid to speak.

He takes a deep breath. 'Lizzie, I know I've messed up . . .' He holds tightly to her hand. 'I've been a total idiot.' The ghost of a smile flashes over his face.

Her eyes travel from his face to her hand, trapped under his, pressed into him. 'You have.' If her heart goes any faster it'll take off.

Joe nods, still looking at her. Then he takes her hand away from his chest and cradles it between both of his on the table. 'You know I'm mad about you, don't you?'

Lizzie can't talk; all she can do is look dumbly at him and pray that she doesn't break into hysterical laughter. His palms are warm; her hand is on fire. Joe's eyes never leave her face as he talks. 'When you worked in the shop, you were like . . . a breath of fresh air coming in in the mornings. I forgot to worry about him while you were around . . .' One of his thumbs strokes the inside of her wrist softly, back and forth, back and forth; something behind her knees responds.

'But – and I know how daft this must sound, believe me – I felt I couldn't make any move towards you while he was here, acting the way he was. I needed to sort that out before I . . . started to get involved with anyone.' Another bashful smile flies across his face, his eyes crinkling slightly.

Before I started to get involved. Every word he says is music. Lizzie realises that she's holding her breath, and lets it out slowly. Damn and blast that table between them; only for it, she'd be all over him. On second thoughts, maybe it's just as well that it's there.

For the moment, anyway.

The heat in her hand is travelling up her arm; she feels her neck begin to get hot. She wills him to get to the point before it gets all red and blotchy.

302

Joe takes a hand away from hers to rub his face again. He looks exhausted; she wonders when was the last time he got any sleep.

'And now . . .' He drops his eyes; she holds her breath again. 'Well, with everything that's happened in the last few days . . .'

He pauses again; and suddenly Lizzie decides that she can't wait any longer.

'Joe McCarthy – are you or are you not asking me out?' God, what is it about him that turns her into such a brazen hussy?

He looks at her in amazement. 'No, Lizzie, of course I'm not asking you out.'

No, you're not asking me out? Have I made some massive, gigantic mistake here? She looks at him blankly, heart plummeting.

Then he lifts her hand to his mouth and presses his lips against her palm. 'Lizzie O'Grady, do you think for one minute I'd be happy with just a date?'

He watches her face as it softens and clears, and he sees the smile begin. 'I knew the minute I laid eyes on you, that first day you came into Ripe and admired the sign and asked me where the woodcarver's shop was – I knew that day that if anything ever happened between us . . .' He kisses her palm again, so softly, eyes never leaving her face. '. . . it would be quite . . . momentous.'

Her whole body is melting. His voice is curling around her, wrapping her up. 'That ridiculous April

Fool was worth it just to see your face . . . When you said you'd take the job, I couldn't believe my luck . . . Every time you walked into that back room and put on the kettle, I wanted to grab hold of you . . . When you picked up the pieces I was working on, I watched your hands . . . I couldn't get your face out of my head; I could hear you laughing when you weren't there . . . You have no idea what your smile does to me . . .'

And as he speaks she comes around and sits beside him and curls up in his arms and slides her hand between his shirt buttons and feels his chest tighten as she touches it, and shudders at his mouth on the back of her neck. And then she opens his shirt and tastes his skin and hears him say, 'Darling Lizzie . . .'

And later, much later, Jones leaves his spot at the bottom of the duvet and pads out of the bedroom, looking for someplace quieter to sleep . . .

And in Dominic's house Pete dreams of Angela . . .

And in Connemara Deirdre sleeps peacefully, and Angela lies awake in the other bed and watches her . . .

And Mammy sits at the kitchen table in Kilmorris and drinks tea and watches the dawn breaking . . .

And the sea laps up on the pebbles at Merway like it always has, as if nothing at all had happened.

Chapter Twenty-nine

'Lizzie, would you ever hold still? I can't stick these feckin' flowers in your hair if you keep turning your head.' Angela flaps a white rosebud in exasperation.

'Sorry – I'm just admiring Deirdre's handiwork; she's brilliant.' Lizzie flutters her eyelashes – her longer, darker, curlier eyelashes – and puts a hand up to stroke her smooth, freckle-free cheek. Angela instantly slaps it away – 'Get off; stop pawing it' – and rapidly clips another rosebud into the side of Lizzie's hair.

Then she stands back and puts her head to one side. 'Right, I think that'll do. Stand up till I see you properly.'

But Lizzie stays sitting, watching her in the mirror. 'Angela – did you ever think you'd see the day? Really, now?'

Angela grins back at her. 'Listen, girl, didn't I always tell you I'd fix you up in Merway? You should have listened to Auntie Angela.'

Lizzie laughs. 'Hey, you didn't have anything to do with it; I got him all by myself.'

'No way.' Angela shakes her head firmly. 'I had a quiet little word with him, told him what a good catch you were – a wife who'd bake for her husband all day long – not to mention the novenas I sent up to Saint Jude on your behalf.'

Wife. Husband. The words sound unreal, as if they belong to another language – one that Lizzie has never learnt to speak fluently. But today she's becoming a wife – and getting a husband.

She turns and looks out the window. The wind rattles the glass, the rain lashes against the panes.

Perfect. Everything's perfect.

'But seriously, Lizzie . . . are you really sure you know what you're doing? I mean' – Angela puts up a hand as Lizzie starts to speak – 'some people might say you're rushing into it; it's not as if you've known him a long time, really.'

Lizzie looks at her in the mirror – is she pulling her leg? 'I know him well over a year.'

Angela sighs. 'Yes, dear, but remember your last relationship. How many years was it again?' She's as good as Joe with the poker face.

Lizzie swivels in her chair and gives her a dig in the ribs. 'Drink your champagne and shut up.'

'All right, dear.' Angela blinks innocently back at her before picking up her champagne glass from the dressing-table and draining it. 'Yum.'

'Here's to lucky escapes, and short engagements,' Lizzie says. She tips back her glass and swallows the cold, delicious bubbles; then she stands up.

Angela divides the last of the champagne between their glasses, then puts out a hand and tweaks at Lizzie's dress. 'Aren't you glad I made you buy it?'

It's white, with giant splashes of mauve and turquoise flowers, and it falls gently from the deep V of the neckline to just above her ankles. It's not too fitted, not too full, with sheer sleeves that hug her arms and end just below her elbows. She feels like a bride in it.

Around her neck she wears Granny's single pearl, on a thin gold chain, that Mammy wore on her wedding day. She has little white kitten-heeled shoes on her feet, and five tiny white rosebuds from Big Maggie in her hair.

There's a rap on the bedroom door. 'Lizzie, are you ready?' Mammy puts her head around the door; she's unfamiliar in her pale-peach suit and little pillbox hat, and lipstick, which she rarely wears.

'Mrs O'Grady, you look absolutely gorgeous,' Angela says, hugging Mammy. 'And what do you think of the bride?'

'I think she's beautiful.' Mammy smiles as her eyes fill with tears, and Lizzie pulls a tissue from the box on the dressing-table and hands it to her. Mammy's been tearful all morning, since she handed over Granny's pearl at breakfast.

She's not the only one who keeps remembering Daddy; Lizzie would have loved him to walk her up the aisle – or, in this case, up the passage between the chairs in the sitting room.

When Lizzie found the courage to tell Mammy they wanted to get married in the house, Mammy looked at her in disbelief.

'What – you don't want a church wedding?' Her expression wasn't encouraging.

Lizzie hastened to explain that of course she wanted Father Lehane to marry them – it wasn't the religious ceremony she was avoiding. 'But it would be so much more . . . meaningful, here where I grew up – and where . . .' She spoke carefully, not wanting to upset Mammy any more. '. . . I feel Daddy is still here, in a way . . . And we could suit ourselves about the day, and the time – provided Father Lehane is free, of course – and maybe do a little sherry reception beforehand?' That might sway her – Mammy loved her Bristol Cream.

And she finally agreed, if a little doubtfully. Julia O'Gorman was sent an invitation – Tony and his new wife were not, of course – and so were Claire and Peter from next door, and Aunt Rose and a few other uncles and aunts, and one cousin who lived three streets away, and of course a group from Merway, who all booked into the Kilmorris House Hotel for the night.

Lizzie made the cake – a rich, rum-soaked fruitcake, just one tier – and she and Angela spent yesterday morning walloping pots in the kitchen, stopping only to call Mammy in for ham-and-cream-cheese rolls at lunchtime. Then Angela shooed them both out of the kitchen for the afternoon, and they spent it cleaning the rest of the house and borrowing chairs and glasses from the neighbours. Then they all went out for dinner to a new steak restaurant – Mammy's choice. Lizzie was just happy that she hadn't chosen O'Gorman's.

Now the fridge is full of food, the dining-room table is covered with borrowed bowls and plates and dishes and platters, Angela and Lizzie are finishing off a bottle of champagne in the bedroom, and eighteen people full of Bristol Cream are down in the sitting room waiting for Lizzie to come and get married.

Mammy has disappeared again, after being assured that they'll be right down, when there's another tap on the door. Angela goes over and opens it.

'Lizzie, it's time.' She fusses for a minute with Lizzie's hair, then hands her the little bouquet of lilac and white freesias. 'Right – knock 'em dead.'

Lizzie takes a last sip of champagne and goes out to Pete on the landing.

He's dressed in a shirt that looks blue-white against his tan, and chinos that she hasn't seen before. He's shaved and cut his hair for the occasion; but Lizzie knows, by the look she gave it when she saw it, that Mammy still considers it too long.

He looks at Lizzie and whistles. 'Hey, you look great.' Then he puts out his arm. 'Ready?'

She nods – 'Ready' – and takes his arm.

Angela comes out of the bedroom. 'Hey, what about me?'

Pete puts his other arm around her shoulders and kisses her. 'You look beautiful too, honey.' Angela smiles, and steps back to let them walk downstairs ahead of her.

At the door into the sitting room they pause. Deirdre presses a button on the CD player; 'Here Comes the Bride' begins to play, and everyone turns and looks at Lizzie and smiles. She and Pete walk slowly towards the other side of the room, and the scent of the flowers Maggie Delaney brought mixes with perfumes and sherry, and Julia O'Gorman puts an arm around Mammy, and Aunt Rose takes a photo.

And there, standing between Father Lehane and Mammy's china cabinet, Joe McCarthy is waiting for her.

Chapter Thirty

'Blast.' The handful of confetti that Angela has thrown is scooped up by the wind and carried high into the sky. Pete takes the box from her – 'Hey, do it right, lady' – and empties what's left of it over the heads of Joe and Lizzie McCarthy, as they stand brazenly kissing on the side of the road in Kilmorris for everyone to see.

They draw apart, laughing and shaking the tiny coloured horseshoes and crescent moons and hearts from their hair, but Joe keeps an arm around Lizzie's waist. Angela looks at him and thinks, *He can't bear to let her go*, and prays that it'll always be like that.

She drapes an arm over Joe's shoulder like she always used to – how could she ever have thought he wouldn't forgive her? – and wags a finger across him at Lizzie.

'You do realise, don't you, that you're making off with the only eligible bachelor that Merway had to offer?'

The smile that's been on Lizzie's face for the last hour widens. 'I don't see why that should bother you,' she says, looking significantly at Pete, who's just said something to make Mammy and Rose laugh; such a charmer.

Angela follows her gaze and watches him fondly for a minute. 'Yeah, I'm not complaining.' Then she turns back to Joe and Lizzie. 'Now remember, you two – no disappearing off into the sunset forever. You have two weeks, then it's back to work.'

Lizzie salutes with the hand that's not pressed against Joe's side. 'Yes, ma'am.'

They're going to Greece, because Joe remembered her saying she'd always wanted to see it. They've found a travel company that sends people to some of the tiny islands, and they've got a house on the tiniest they could find. Lizzie imagines them sitting on a white-washed balcony, surrounded by bougainvillea and jasmine, eating fat olives and feta cheese and sipping ouzo and watching the sun staining the sky red as it sinks slowly over the sea. And she knows that, even if it isn't a bit like that, she'll still love every minute.

When they come back, Lizzie McCarthy will move out of the caravan and into Joe McCarthy's house. She'll work in Ripe in the mornings, while Joe carves, and in the afternoons she'll go to The Kitchen to bake for a couple of hours, and every second evening she'll go back later to help serve the meals and clear up.

And when school finishes for the summer, in three more weeks, Deirdre and Angela and Pete will hook Lizzie's caravan to the back of Angela's car and head off to explore the west coast for a fortnight.

And in August Deirdre will get a new half-brother or sister.

Angela told Lizzie a few weeks ago. 'I got the shock of my life when John told me, but actually, it's the best thing that could have happened. It lets us all move on. And Dee's really excited.'

Connemara sorted a lot out for Angela and Deirdre. 'We talked like we hadn't in a long time,' Angela told Lizzie. 'I realised how much I'd missed. I'd been assuming she was coping fine with the separation – which she wasn't, of course. She was hurt and confused and looking for reassurance – and then that man came along, just when she was vulnerable.'

When Deirdre and Angela arrived home from Connemara, Pete was waiting.

'He's so sweet, Lizzie – a real tonic; just what I need. It's probably not a forever thing – I don't know that I believe much in that any more – but while it lasts, I'm going to enjoy it.'

Six months later they're still enjoying it. When Dominic got back from the States, Pete moved his things into The Kitchen – by then he was well established as the local handyman – and he's showing no signs of wanting to move on. If the way he looks at Angela is anything to go by, Lizzie thinks that, in the grand scheme of things, they stand a pretty good chance of survival.

And in eight years, less with good behaviour, Charlie will be released from jail. And there's time enough to worry about what will happen then.

'Back in a sec.' Lizzie plants a kiss on her new husband's cheek, unwinds his arm from around her waist and goes through the house, past the dining-room table littered with leftovers – Jones and Dumbledore will have a feast when Angela goes home tomorrow – and down to the bottom of the garden.

She stands among Daddy's roses – not open yet – and sees him bent over them, lifting the leaves, touching the buds gently. She puts out a hand and feels the tight parcels of velvety petals as they think about starting to unfurl.

Life going on. Her life going on.

After a minute, she turns and walks back up the garden.